PENGUIN BOOKS

COME THE EXECUTIONER

M. S. Power was born in Dublin and educated in Ireland and France. He has worked as a TV producer in the United States but now lives in Scotland. His first novel, *Hunt for the Autumn Clowns*, was published to critical acclaim in 1983. The three novels *The Killing of Yesterday's Children*, *Lonely the Man Without Heroes* and *A Darkness in the Eye* were published in 1984, 1986 and 1987 respectively. This trilogy was filmed by the BBC and shown under the title *Children of the North*. *Bridie and the Silver Lady* followed in 1988, *The Crucifixion of Septimus Roach* in 1989 and *Crucible of Fools*, also published by Penguin, in 1990.

M. S. POWER

COME THE EXECUTIONER

PENGUIN BOOKS

PENGUIN BOOKS

Published by the Penguin Group
Penguin Books Ltd, 27 Wrights Lane, London W8 5TZ, England
Penguin Books USA Inc., 375 Hudson Street, New York, New York 10014, USA
Penguin Books Australia Ltd, Ringwood, Victoria, Australia
Penguin Books Canada Ltd, 10 Alcorn Avenue, Toronto, Ontario, Canada M4V 3B2
Penguin Books (NZ) Ltd, 182–190 Wairau Road, Auckland 10, New Zealand

Penguin Books Ltd, Registered Offices: Harmondsworth, Middlesex, England

First published by Hamish Hamilton 1991
Published in Penguin Books 1992
1 3 5 7 9 10 8 6 4 2

Acknowledgement is made for permission to quote from the following songs:
Breathe (in the Air) (Waters/Gilmour/Wright) © 1973 PINK FLOYD MUSIC PUBLISHERS LIMITED
Brain Damage (Waters) © 1973 PINK FLOYD MUSIC PUBLISHERS LIMITED
The Tide is Turning (After Live Aid) (Waters) © 1987 PINK FLOYD MUSIC PUBLISHERS LIMITED

Printed in England by Clays Ltd, St Ives plc

For all the Dowlings: John and Joan,
Siobhan and Aoife, and, of course, Betty

'. . . and so, young men are taught to kill and told that it is a noble and honourable exercise. They take it upon themselves to dispense a wicked verdict and absolve themselves by calling it justice. Alas, the folly of this is only made clear to them when, in turn, the executioner inevitably comes to call on them, and their pleas for pity are ignored and their young lives are wiped away by others seeking the insane power that the infliction of death seems to imbue.'

From *The Visits and Visitations of Arthur Apple*

ONE

Whoever they were, they were very professional about it, keeping calm and being meticulous about details. Larski knew they were men who took considerable pride in their work, and the fact that their work was murder didn't enter into it. They would have done any job with equal fastidiousness.

Altogether there were three of them in the car: the driver – a small, wiry man who had an itch and scratched his neck a lot – and Larski in the back wedged against the door by one other. His hands were tied in front of him, the leather thongs biting into his skin and making the veins in his forearms throb. His eyes were slightly bloodshot, and the pockets under them were black with fatigue. There was several days' growth to his beard. His jacket and trousers were creased as though he'd been in them day and night for quite some time, and the collar of his shirt was torn. The laces had been removed from his shoes. He wore no socks.

This was no high-speed drive through the back streets of Belfast, ending with his body being dumped on waste ground. The car moved slowly, not so slowly as to attract attention, but slowly enough, and the killing that would take place would have been properly calculated. It would, thank God, be quick and ritualistic, his body left in a place strategically chosen. Each time the driver braked, Larski felt his stomach heave. Yet, when the car did finally come to its destination and stopped, he felt nothing. No fear, certainly. Only a little sadness perhaps, and not for himself, which was curious.

The man beside Larski opened the door and stepped out, gesturing for Larski to follow. The driver joined them. He lit a cigarette and inhaled deeply.

In single file they walked away from the car, stopping when they came to a wooden gate leading into a field. The man behind Larski told him, almost politely, to lie down. When he did, awkwardly, the man shot him expertly in the back of the head. Then both men returned to the car. The driver reversed, turned, and drove carefully back the way they had come.

'I hate it when they're quiet and obliging like that,' the man who had shot Larski commented. His accent, surprisingly, was very English.

Michael and Edwina Larski waited for the phone to ring. But it was the doorbell that shrilled, making Edwina jump.

'Mrs Larski?'

Edwina nodded.

'I'm Major Temple. I'm frightfully sorry – eh, is Mr Larski at home perhaps?'

'Tell me,' Edwina said. 'My husband isn't well. Tell me and I'll tell him.'

'I'm most frightfully sorry. Your son – Peter – it's been confirmed, I'm afraid.'

'Thank you for coming,' Edwina said, and shut the door.

All night Edwina worried that she had been impolite to the Major, shutting the door in his face so abruptly. Beside her she could feel her husband shake as he wept. She longed to comfort him, but she could think of nothing to say. Anyway, it was probably better that he got his grief out of his system in his own way. Bottling it up would surely bring on another heart attack.

Towards dawn, exhausted, Edwina dozed. When she woke, her husband was dead beside her.

'Goddamn it,' Robert Larski swore, groping for the phone beside his bed. Didn't these Americans ever sleep? 'Yeah?'

'Robert?'

'Hey – Mum! How are you? This is a surprise.'

'Robert, I –' Edwina Larski choked.

Robert swung his feet out of bed and reached for a cigarette. 'Mum, what's the matter?'

'Can you come home, dear?'

'What's happened?' Robert tossed the unlit cigarette back on to the table.

'It's Peter . . . and your father . . . they . . .'

'Mum? Mum?'

'They're both dead, Robert.'

'Oh, Jesus.'

'Can you come home? I'm sorry, dear, it's just that –'

'Of course I'll come home, Mum. I'll get the first flight possible. Just wait for me, Mum. I'll be with you as soon as I can.'

A couple of hours before Edwina Larski telephoned her son in New York, two men sat either side of a log fire in a large, ornately furnished room. One was in uniform, the other in a dark blue, double-breasted suit. Both were about fifty.

'The trouble with England,' the man in civilian clothes said, 'is the weather. So bloody unreliable.'

Brigadier Carlisle looked at his companion as though he could think of a great many more things, more important things, that were the trouble with England. But he just nodded and waited.

The civilian rose and went to the window, peering out on to the parkland. 'Just look at it. Bucketing down. Never seems to stop, does it?' He returned to his chair, and sat down again with a little shiver, folding his hands primly on his lap. 'So,' he said finally, studying his nails. 'The matter is closed?'

'Let us hope so, sir,' the Brigadier said.

Sir raised his eyebrows theatrically. '*Hope* so? A little more definite than that, *I* hope.'

'Well, Larski is dead,' the Brigadier told him.

'So?'

The Brigadier shrugged.

'You're not expecting repercussions?'

'There are always repercussions, sir.'

Sir became testy. 'Yes. Yes. I know there are. But nothing you can't cope with surely?'

'No.'

'Good. Good. Or is it?'

The Brigadier stared into the fire.

Sir repeated his question. 'Or is it?'

'Yes.'

'That's better. Now – parents been informed?'

Brigadier Carlisle nodded. 'Temple has done that already.'

'Excellent.'

'He had a brother.'

Something about the way the Brigadier made the casual announcement made Sir uneasy. 'Meaning?'

The Brigadier shrugged again. 'He had a brother. A reporter. What they call an investigative reporter, I believe.'

'I see.'

'Damn good one too, I'm told. In New York.'

'New York?' Sir sounded slightly relieved.

'Not for long, I shouldn't think.'

'Oh? Can he find out anything?'

'Who knows? If he digs deep enough . . .' Again the Brigadier hid behind a shrug.

Sir's attitude changed. His benign face hardened. His eyes narrowed. His voice had a brittle edge to it. 'If this brother should start to dig you'll simply have to bury him, won't you?'

'It might not be that simple, sir.'

Sir waved a hand expansively. 'My dear Jeremy, *everything* is simple when you have the wherewithal.'

'Perhaps.'

'There's no perhaps about it. It's one of the great true facts of life. It's called democracy – those that have make all the rules, and those that don't have behave themselves. It's how we run the country, dammit.'

'We'll see.'

'We'll do more than see, Jeremy. Or you will. It would be most unfortunate – for all of us – if, shall we say, the have-nots learned that the haves had been . . . er . . . naughty.'

'Naughty?'

'Just a word.'

'Of course.'

'Anyway, I must be off. Keep me informed, like a good chap, will you?'

'I will.'

'And if you need any – help? – don't hesitate to ask.'

'I won't.'

Alone, Brigadier Carlisle poured himself a Scotch, and swallowed it neat. Then he picked up the telephone and dialled.

'Yes?'

'Carlisle, sir.'

'Yes?'

'He's just left.'

'And?'

'*He* seems satisfied.'

'Does that mean you're not?'

Brigadier Carlisle hesitated for a moment. 'No,' he said finally. 'I'm satisfied also.'

'Good. Well done,' the voice said, and the line went dead.

As soon as he had finished speaking to his mother, Robert Larski made another call to England.

'Uncle Frank? Robert here.'

'Ah, Robert.'

'Mum just phoned.'

'So you know?'

'Only what happened. None of the details.'

'I see.'

'What *did* happen?'

'Your father had another heart attack.'

'And Peter?'

'All we've been told is that he's been killed in Belfast. What they call a "routine" killing, would you believe?'

'Look. I'm coming over as soon as I can get a flight. If I get word to you about the time of my arrival, will *you* meet me?'

'Of course I will.'

'Thanks. How's Mum taking it?'

'Her usual way. The way she's always taken bad news. Stoically is the word, I think.'

'Keep an eye on her for me, will you?'

'You know I will.'

'Yes. Thanks.'

'Robert . . .'

'Yes?'

'Nothing. Nothing. We'll talk when we meet.'

'OK. Where's Peter now?'

'I don't honestly know. Nobody's saying anything. They tell us they'll let us know in time. When it's appropriate, they said. Whatever that means.'

'Oh.'

'By the way, I was going to try and arrange to have them both buried on the same day. Is that all right?'

'Yes. Quite right. Thanks, Uncle Frank.'

'It might mean a delay – until the army release Peter's body.'

'I see. How does Mum feel about it?'

'She says she'll agree to whatever you say.'

'In that case we'll wait. Better for Mum to have it all over in one day, isn't it?'

'That's what I thought.'

'OK. I'll see you some time tomorrow.'

'Fine. Take care, Robert.'

'I will. And you, Uncle Frank – you take care too.'

TWO

'They flew Peter's body into Brize Norton early this morning,' Uncle Frank said. Apart from an almost perfunctory welcome it was the first thing he had said, and they were now on the motorway, heading for the Larski home in Grendon Underwood, Buckinghamshire.

Robert Larski nodded. He suddenly felt desperately weary. Not jet-lagged or tired from lack of sleep. Just abysmally weary and drained. It was drizzling, and the wipers swinging back and forth were almost hypnotic. He shut his eyes.

'They refused to let us see the body,' Uncle Frank went on. 'Your mother wanted to, but they wouldn't let her.'

'Why?'

Uncle Frank hesitated, and changed lanes before answering. 'They told me he'd been mutilated.'

'Oh shit!'

'It's what they do now apparently.'

'I'm sorry?'

'The IRA. They mutilate their victims.'

'Hey – wait a minute. I thought he was shot on patrol?'

Uncle Frank gave Robert a quick glance from the corner of his eye. 'So did we. I don't think I was *meant* to be told any different.'

'Who told you?'

Uncle Frank shrugged. 'No idea. A voice at the end of the phone. Someone trying to be kind. Nobody in authority has been in touch since a major called Temple told your mother that Peter was dead.'

'Well, I'll bloody soon make them get in touch.'
'I thought you might.'

'Hi, Mum.' Robert Larski put both arms about his mother and cuddled her tightly.
'Oh, Robert. Robert.'
'Shush, Mum.'
'It's so awful.'
'I know. I know. I'm here now. I'll take care of everything.'
'They won't even let me see Peter.'
'I know. I'll sort something out. It's just the army being stupid.'
'You think so? That's all?'
'Sure that's all. You know what they're like. All paperwork and no brains.'
'I'm trying so hard not to –'
'You're doing fine, Mum. Tell you what – how about a cup of tea? They can't make tea in New York, you know.'
Edwina smiled thinly. 'Of course. I'm sorry, dear. I should have thought.'
'I won't stay, Edwina, if you don't mind,' Uncle Frank said.
'Won't you?'
'I'd better get home.'
'Oh. Of course. How selfish of me.' She turned to Robert. 'Frank has been so kind. Doing everything for me. Arranging things.'
'I know,' Robert said. 'Thanks again, Uncle Frank.'
'I'll look in tomorrow. Meantime, if either of you need me . . .'
Alone for the moment, Robert slumped into a chair. On a table beside the chair was a silver-framed photograph of his dead brother, looking smart and proud in his uniform of captain of the Scots Guards. Robert stared at it. Odd, he thought, even if you hadn't known you could somehow tell from the picture that he was dead.

Robert Larski waited until his mother had gone to bed,

giving her a good half-hour to settle down before he made the phone call.

'Jimmy? Bob Larski here.'

'Bob! I've been trying to call you all day.'

'I'm home. Here in England.'

'Jesus, Bob, I'm sorry. It only came in on the wire this morning. Jesus, I'm sorry.'

'Thanks, Jimmy. Listen, I need a favour.'

'Name it.'

'I need you to get on to some of your army contacts, and start asking a few questions. Stir things up a bit. Make it sound as if you know more than you actually do. You see, there's something – shit, I don't know, something wrong somewhere. About Peter. All we've been told is that he was shot, but they won't let us see the body because *now* someone's let slip that he was mutilated –'

'Oh, Christ!'

'Put it about that I'm home and not satisfied. That I'm going to raise hell unless some explanations are given.'

'Leave it to me. I don't promise I'll get anywhere though. The army doesn't exactly love journalists and certainly not you. But I'll do my best.'

'Thanks, Jimmy.'

'My pleasure. How long are you staying?'

'No idea.'

'Can I come to the funeral? I mean, is it just family?'

'I'd like you to come, Jimmy. Thanks.'

'I'll be in touch.'

'Right. By the way, be careful not to actually *say* anything. Just make it sound as though – oh, hell, you know what I mean.'

'Should do by now. Bound to have learned something in twenty years, eh, Robert?'

'See you.'

'See you.'

Brigadier Carlisle was furious. His body, quite literally, shook with anger. His small, chubby face reddened and his jowls quivered. He rounded on Major Temple. 'Well, *who* released that Larski had been mutilated if you didn't?' he demanded.

'I don't know, sir.'

'You don't know. You're *supposed* to know, dammit.'

'Does it make a difference, sir? After all, he *was* mut –'

Brigadier Carlisle turned away sharply. 'I'm quite aware of that,' he snapped. 'It pointed the finger at those we wanted blamed.' He went to his desk, picked up a paper-knife, and started tapping it on the blotter. When he spoke again his voice was considerably less aggressive. 'And of course it makes a difference, Temple. We do our best not to inflict unnecessary pain on the family in these unfortunate cases. It would have been quite sufficient for *them* to be told simply that he was shot, and leave it at that.'

'Yes, sir.'

The Brigadier sat down, and ran his fingers through his hair. 'He has a brother, I understand?'

'Captain Larski? Yes, sir. A younger brother. In America, I believe.'

'A reporter?'

'Freelance. Yes, sir.'

'He's come home, naturally.'

'I didn't know that, sir.'

'I'm telling you, Major.'

'Yes, sir.'

'You better get in touch with him. Calm things down. Make sure he understands we're being entirely open and frank about the whole incident.'

'Very good, sir.'

'But tell him nothing. You understand?'

'Yes, sir.'

'Good. And have the body released as soon as possible. The sooner we can rid ourselves of this matter the better I'll like it, and there's nothing like a burial to terminate things.'

'Yes, sir. Sir . . . it will be difficult to tell him *nothing*.'

'What I meant, Temple, was tell him nothing he doesn't already know.'

'Oh. Right, sir.'

'Just pacify him before we find ourselves spread all over the front page of some damn newspaper.'

'Yes, sir.'

'And let me know when the funeral is. I'll have to attend.'

'Yes, sir.'

'I assume full military honours have been arranged for the captain?'

'Yes, sir.'

'Well, that's something at least.'

'Major Temple – the man who called to tell us about Peter's death – he's been asking for you, Robert,' Edwina Larski said. 'Been on the phone twice.'

'Oh?'

'He asked me to get you to ring him when you got in. The number's by the phone.'

'I'll do it later, Mum.'

'As you please, dear.'

'Mum . . . was Peter in touch with you all the time he was in Belfast?'

Edwina frowned. 'Yes. I think so. As much as he ever kept in touch. He wasn't a great one for letters, you know. Why, dear?'

'Just wondered.'

'Is something wrong?'

'No . . . oh, no.'

'Something *is* wrong, isn't it? You never could lie very well.'

'Nothing's wrong, Mum. Honest. I just need to know a bit more about how Peter actually died.'

'How strange.'

'What is?'

'That's just about the last thing your father said – that he'd want some explanations about Peter's death.'

'Did he say why?'

Edwina gave a small smile. 'You know your father never explained things to me.'

'But he was worried?'

Edwina thought for a moment. 'No. Not worried. Angry, I think.'

'When I told him what the Major had said, he grunted and replied, "I'm not satisfied with *that*."'

'Poor old Dad.'

'Yes. He was so proud of you both. You in particular, Robert.' Edwina sighed. For the first time since the tragedy she felt herself on the point of breaking down. She wanted to cry tears of rage. But Edwina Larski had never cried in front of her children. 'I'll get us something to eat,' she said stiffly.

'Fine. Thanks, Mum.'

Robert heard the eggs being cracked on the edge of a bowl, and then being whipped with a fork. He went to the phone, staring at it for several seconds before dialling. 'Major Temple,' he requested. Then, 'Yes. Tell him Robert Larski is returning his call. Larski. L-A-R-S-K-I. Larski.'

While he waited he shook a cigarette from its pack and gripped it between his lips. He didn't attempt to light it.

'Mr Larski,' Major Temple said. 'Thank you for ringing back.'

'Yes,' was all Robert said.

'I wondered if we might meet?'

'Why?'

'There are one or two things I would like to discuss with you – preferably not on the phone.'

'When?'

'As soon as possible. I'm actually in Bicester at the moment. This evening if you can manage it.'

'All right. What time?'

'Eight? Eight-thirty? How would that suit?'

'Eight-thirty. Where?'

'Oh dear – let me see . . .'

'You know the Trout in Wolvercote?'

'That's in Oxford, isn't it?'

'Yes.'

'I'll find it certainly.'

'I'll meet you there at eight-thirty then.'

'Fine. Thank you, Mr Larski.'

Robert hung up.

Edwina was putting his omelette on the table when he came into the kitchen. She glanced at him, but didn't ask what the Major had wanted. She never asked questions. She had never quizzed her husband about anything, and had, from sheer habit, refrained from quizzing her sons. If Edwina Larski had one regret, it was that she had never had a daughter, someone in whom she could confide, someone with whom she could share those little secrets that she had to keep bottled up inside herself through the years.

'He wants to meet me,' Robert volunteered.

'I see.'

'I'm meeting him later this evening.'

'I see, dear.'

'I'll try and get Peter released as soon as possible, Mum.'

'Thank you, dear.'

'Hmm. This omelette is good.'

'Good.'

Being a Tuesday there weren't many people in the Trout. Robert recognized Major Temple instantly despite the fact that he was in civilian clothes. You could always tell. The shoes too brightly polished, the trousers too well pressed, the hair too slick. He was sitting at a table outside, staring at a pair of swans on the river.

'Major Temple?'

The Major rose and held out his hand. 'Ah, Mr Larski. Kind of you to come. What will you have?'

Robert shook Temple's hand. 'A lager. A half.'

Temple finished his own drink and, taking his empty glass with him, marched smartly into the pub. He returned with a half-pint of lager and another Scotch for himself. When he was seated, and Robert had taken his first sip, Temple said, 'A dreadful business this. I'm most frightfully sorry.'

'Thank you.'

'It's so difficult to know what to do for the best under such circumstances.'

'I'm sorry?'

'How much to tell the family, how to break the news. That sort of thing.'

'I'm sure.'

'One would like to tell the truth but that's not always possible, you know. One has to be considerate, to avoid inflicting unnecessary pain.'

'I'm sure,' Robert said again. Then, 'You said there were a couple of things you wanted to discuss.'

Major Temple nodded slowly. 'Yes. There are.' He swirled the ice in his glass. 'I understand your mother is . . . eh . . . aggrieved at not being allowed to see your brother's body?'

'*Do* you?'

Major Temple looked a bit ruffled by that. He placed his glass carefully back on the table, and took to turning his signet ring round and round on his finger. 'Very natural, of course. But we felt it better – kinder. Still feel so, really.'

Robert nodded. 'Can I ask you something?'

'Of course.' Major Temple leaned forward, indicating he was only too pleased to oblige in any way he could.

'Why weren't we told right away that Peter's body had been mutilated?'

The Major sought help from the swans that were making their way down river, dipping their heads in the water. 'That was my doing,' he confessed. 'There was nothing sinister in it, I assure you. Had I been allowed to speak to your father I would certainly have told him. But when I called, your mother insisted that I tell her. I didn't think it, well, proper, to . . . to upset her further.'

'It was never mentioned in any of the press releases.'

'Well, no.'

'Just that Peter had been shot on patrol.'

'Well, yes.'

'Well, why?' Robert asked, loading *his* 'well' with sarcasm.

'Ah, that would be the responsibility of our press department. Nothing to do with me.'

'I see.'

'They do tend to play things down rather. Better all round. Don't want to give the terrorists too much publicity.'

'Terrorists?'

'IRA.'

'So it was the IRA who killed Peter?'

The Major looked surprised. 'Of course.'

'They've claimed responsibility?'

'Well, no.'

'I understood they always did that.'

The Major became uncomfortable again. 'Sometimes. Not always,' he said.

'And not this time?'

'No. But it had all their hallmarks.'

'Oh?'

'You sound doubtful, Mr Larski.'

'Oh, no.' Robert shrugged. 'No. I just like to have everything tidy. Part of my training, I suppose. No loose ends. Everything proved and ratified before going to press.'

'Ah, yes. Of course. Anything else?'

'Pardon?'

'Anything else you wanted to ask?'

'When can we have Peter's body?'

'We've completed all the paperwork now. We would like to accord him full military honours – if you agree.'

'When?'

'As soon as you give us the date of the funeral.'

THREE

Jimmy Fermin travelled up to Bicester from London the afternoon before the funerals. He checked into the Littleworth Hotel, but spent the evening with Robert Larski at his home. Fermin was a small, muscular man in his early fifties, jolly by nature, and the sombreness of grief was alien to him. He cried easily.

'Jesus, I'm glad you came, Jimmy,' Robert told him.

'Hope I can be of some help.'

'You are, just being here.'

'Good.'

It was almost midnight. The two men were in the sitting-room. On a table between them was a bottle of wine, one of the two Robert had opened with the meal Edwina had cooked.

'Your Mum's taking it really well.'

'Mum takes everything well on the surface. I don't think it's sunk in yet.'

'And you?'

'Me?' Robert shook his head. 'It's weird, Jimmy. I haven't honestly been able to feel any sorrow. Just anger. You know when we worked together on that racism article? How we were shunted from department to department and how everyone sounded so bloody plausible? And yet we both knew we were being given the great run-around?'

Jimmy Fermin gave a snorting laugh. 'Sure I remember.'

'Well, it's the same thing now. I can't prove a damn

thing but there's something – shit, I don't know. The answers are all too pat.'

'You know something, Bob? When you first rang me and said you were worried about the information on Peter's death I thought you might be just going off half-cock. Just because he was your brother.'

'And now?'

Jimmy Fermin reached for his glass, and stared into it. 'Has Gemma been in touch with you?'

Robert frowned. 'Gemma? Gemma Larkin? No, why should she?'

'She asked me if she should come to the funeral. She said she *wanted* to come but was worried about intruding.'

'That was thoughtful. No, she hasn't been in touch.'

Fermin gave a small smile. 'She quite fancies you, I think.'

'I thought it was you she liked.'

Fermin guffawed. 'My job, Bob. That's what she'd like. My job. And she'll probably get it.' He cleared his throat. 'She's been doing a bit of digging. Coming from Belfast, she has her contacts over there.'

'That's true.'

'I think you're going to need her. She can find out things we can't.'

Robert nodded.

'Like the fact that Peter was in civilian clothes when they found him.'

Robert had been on the point of drinking some wine when Jimmy spoke. He froze, the wineglass suspended halfway to his mouth. When his hand started shaking, he placed the glass on the table. 'Say that again.'

'When they found Peter's body he wasn't in uniform.'

'You're sure?'

'Gemma is.'

'That doesn't make sense.'

'Not if you accept what the army's been saying. No.'

Robert reached for his glass and emptied it in one gulp. The wine tasted suddenly acid, and he shuddered.

'Gemma . . .' Jimmy began.

Robert shook his head. 'Hang on. Hang on a tick. The army tells us that Peter was out on a routine patrol, became separated, and was later found shot and mutilated.' He folded his hands, making a steeple out of his forefingers. 'If Gemma's information is correct, he can't have been on patrol.'

'No.'

'So what *was* he doing?'

'You tell me.'

'And why would the army give us this cock-and-bull story? Christ, Jimmy, they must have *known* we'd find out sooner or later.'

Jimmy Fermin just raised his eyebrows.

'Jesus, Jimmy, my instincts were right, you know. This whole business stinks.'

'Maybe.'

'What d'you mean maybe? Why the hell are they giving us the run-around, telling us lies?'

'They're not. They're just not telling you everything.'

'Same bloody thing.'

'As you say, but –'

Robert interrupted. 'It's never been mentioned *anywhere*, has it, that Peter was in civvies?'

'Not to my knowledge. Certainly not in any of the official releases we've had.'

'You don't know where Gemma got her information, I suppose?'

'No. Didn't ask. She probably wouldn't have told me anyway. She might tell you.'

'She could be mistaken.'

'Gemma doesn't make *that* sort of mistake.'

'No. No, she doesn't. Could you ask her to double-check it?'

'Why don't you – ask her, I mean?'

They buried Robert's father first, simply and without fuss or pomp. Captain Peter Larski's funeral was a different matter. A Scots Guards piper played a lament. An army captain read the lesson. A bugler played the Last Post.

Standing at the graveside beside his mother, Robert spotted Major Temple having quiet words with another officer, an officer with plenty of brass although Robert couldn't be certain of his rank. It was, however, this officer who came to express his condolences after the ceremony, shaking his head and muttering, 'Tragic, tragic,' almost convincingly, after introducing himself as Brigadier Carlisle. He held Robert's hand for a long time. 'If there is anything more we can do,' he said. 'Anything. For you or Mrs Larski, don't hesitate to ask.'

'You could give me a minute of your time,' Robert told him.

The Brigadier looked taken aback, but recovered quickly. 'Of course. Now, you mean?'

Robert nodded. 'Now.'

They left the other mourners and walked between the gravestones. Major Temple, who had been eyeing them all the while, looked as if he was about to follow, but changed his mind.

'So young,' was the first thing the Brigadier said.

'Yes,' Robert agreed. 'You don't mind me dragging you off like this, I hope?'

'Of course not, dear fellow. Of course not.'

'There're just a few things I'd like to clear up. To make my mother feel happier, you understand.'

'Naturally. Anything I can do to ease the pain. I do understand how difficult it is when there's no . . . I'm afraid we, the army that is, isn't very good at the personal touch.'

Robert paused. He thought about lighting a cigarette, but somehow a cigarette in a graveyard seemed blasphemous. Instead he pulled a handkerchief from his pocket and wiped his forehead. 'It's all a bit confusing,' he told the Brigadier, trying to sound confused.

'Of course it is,' the Brigadier said sympathetically.

'Peter was on patrol when he was shot, wasn't he?'

'That's right. Unfortunately he became separated – God knows how, but these things do happen under fire – and was shot. By snipers, I understand.'

'But he was definitely on patrol?'

The Brigadier stiffened slightly. 'I just said so,' he replied in the manner of a man unaccustomed to being questioned.

'Oh, I don't disbelieve you, Brigadier. Sorry. Just getting things clear, that's all.'

The Brigadier relaxed. 'Yes. Of course.'

'And nobody's claimed responsibility yet?'

'No. They don't always.'

'So Major Temple told me. Clearly the IRA though?'

'I don't think there's any doubt about that. The – I'm sorry – the mutilation –'

'Yes. That was odd, wasn't it?'

'Odd?'

'Odd that snipers should come out into the open just to mutilate their target.'

The Brigadier said nothing.

'Odd, too, that they did it to Peter. I mean, that's usually reserved for informers, isn't it?'

The Brigadier fidgeted, tugging at his collar. 'I wouldn't know.'

'Yes. It is. I *do* know.'

The Brigadier moved forward a few paces, leaving Robert standing where he was. Then he turned and came back. He didn't say anything for a few moments, just looked Robert squarely in the face as if waiting for him to level some accusation. Robert obliged.

'Just one thing you could do for me, Brigadier. For my mother really. It's silly – a bit morbid, *I* think – but she'd like the clothes Peter was wearing.'

The Brigadier scowled, then brightened. 'I'm afraid all uniforms remain army property,' he said.

'Oh. Of course. Peter was in uniform.'

'I – of course he was. He was on patrol.'

'Yes. I forgot. Ah, well. Anyway, I expect his personal possessions will be sent to us eventually.'

'Certainly.'

'*All* his non-military clothes and things?'

'Of course,' the Brigadier affirmed with what could have been a tiny wince.

'Thank you, Brigadier.'

'Saw you having quite a chat with that Brigadier,' Jimmy Fermin mentioned.

They were in the garden. Relatives and close friends had come back to the house for a drink, but they had nearly all gone by now. Only Uncle Frank and his wife were indoors with Edwina, helping her to tidy up. Robert nodded. 'Know him?'

'Of him. A bit shadowy. Linked to Intelligence but not *of* Intelligence if you get my drift.'

'A shit shoveller?'

'Something like that. With gloves, of course. Find out anything?'

Robert shook his head. 'Nope. I don't think I handled it too well. Tried to be subtle. I think now I should have just come out and asked him why Peter was in civvies.'

'He'd simply deny that.'

'Probably.'

'So what now?' Jimmy Fermin asked, bending and plucking a sprig of catmint and rubbing it between his hands.

Robert shrugged. 'I just don't know.'

'When do you go back – to the States, I mean?'

'Huh, I don't know that either. There's no rush. Why?'

'Do you really *want* to pursue this?'

'Yes. And no. I'm scared as to what I might find out. About Peter.'

Jimmy tossed away the catmint. 'Why not come down to London for a while. You could stay with me.'

'I might just do that.'

'You'd be welcome, you know.'

'I know. Thanks, Jimmy.'

'And speaking of London, I'd better make a move.'

'Driving back tonight?'

Jimmy nodded. Then, '*Do* try and come down for a while.'

'We'll see.'

'So he could start digging,' Brigadier Carlisle was saying gloomily.

'We wouldn't be at all pleased if that was allowed to happen.'

'I'm aware of that, sir.'

'So you must simply see to it that it doesn't happen.'

'I'll do my best.'

'Please see to it that your best is good enough, Jeremy.'

The Brigadier blinked, but said nothing.

'For someone who's only been back in England a few days this Robert Larski seems very adept at finding things out, does he not?'

'Too damn adept.'

'I'm confident that you can arrange he uncovers nothing more. We're *all* counting on you, Jeremy.'

'As I said, I'll do my best.'

'And as I said, let's hope – and perhaps pray – that your best is good enough,' the Minister said, rising, and checking his appearance in the mirror over the mantelpiece. 'And now I must away. Margaret is entertaining, and I have to be there. God knows why.' The Minister gave a wicked chuckle. 'She can't stand the sight of me, if the truth were known.'

Alone, the Minister's parting phrase loomed into the Brigadier's mind. If the truth were known. Christ God Almighty! If the truth *were* known! He went to the door, stuck his head out, and asked, 'Is Major Temple still around, Curry?'

'No, sir,' Curry said smartly, jumping to attention behind his desk. 'I saw him leave about twenty minutes ago.'

The Brigadier closed the door again and leaned his back against it, frowning. 'Damn,' he said to himself. 'Damn, damn, damn.'

'Everything all right, Mum?'

'Yes, dear. Thank you. It's been just as hard for you as it has for me. Are *you* all right?'

Robert nodded. 'Fine. A nightcap?'

'A sherry, perhaps.'

Robert poured the drinks, a sherry for his mother, a vodka and bitter lemon for himself.

'It was a nice ceremony, didn't you think?'

'Yes.'

'That Last Post always sends shivers up and down my spine. It gives me goose-pimples even when I hear it played for someone I don't know.'

'Yes.'

'Thank you, dear,' Edwina said, taking her drink, watching her son as he sat down in the chair opposite. Now, for the first time, it dawned on her that if he returned to America she would be quite, quite alone. 'When do you plan to go back to the States, or haven't you decided?'

'I haven't decided yet, Mum.'

'Robert . . . I don't want you to feel you have to stay here because of me, you know. I'm perfectly all right. I'll manage beautifully.'

'I know that, Mum.'

'You must get on with your life now. You're so young, and your whole life is ahead of you.'

Robert smiled wryly. 'Yes, Mum.'

Edwina gave a small laugh. 'I'm not lecturing you.'

Robert laughed too. 'I know you're not.'

'Your father had a good life. And Peter always wanted to be a soldier. That was all he ever wanted. He knew there was always a risk something awful would happen.'

'Yes.'

Robert struggled out of his chair, and walked to the window. The family cat, a wily, tortoise-shell creature of unpredictable affection, was stalking a bird. He watched the animal creep its way across the lawn and pounce. The bird, a thrush, flew into the hedge, screaming with laughter. 'Mum,' Robert said, without looking round. 'If I tell you something, will you promise me you won't get all worried and upset?'

'I can't *promise* you that, Robert, until I hear what it is you have to tell me. But I'll *try* not to get all worried and upset, as you put it.'

'I think there's more to Peter's death than we're being told.'

His mother nodded calmly, and took a sip of her sherry

before replying. 'I guessed as much, dear. You might have left home some time ago but I still know when something's bothering you. And when I told you Major Temple had been phoning you, your face was like thunder.'

Robert came across the room and sat on the arm of his mother's chair. He put his arm about her shoulder and kissed her lightly on the top of her head. 'If I looked into it, and if I found . . . if I found out something that wasn't in Peter's favour, would you be very upset?'

'Yes, Robert. I'd be very upset. But I think you should look into it all the same. You'll have to live with this ghastly business far longer than I will, and it would upset me a great deal more if I thought you had to spend the rest of your life wondering what had really happened.'

'Thanks, Mum.'

Edwina patted Robert's hand. 'You've already made up your mind anyway, haven't you?'

Robert nodded and smiled. 'Yes. I'm going to go down to London for a while. I'll stay with Jimmy.'

'Yes. That would be sensible. Now – I want you to promise me something. I want you to promise me that no matter what you find you'll tell me. No matter what, mind.'

'You're sure you want to know?'

'I'm sure.'

'You've got a deal.'

FOUR

'So, where the hell do we start?'

Robert Larski lobbed the question across the desk to Jimmy Fermin who volleyed it back. 'We?' he asked, raising his eyebrows.

'Yes. We. You and me.'

'Oh, so I'm in this too, am I?'

'Bet your life you are.'

'That's what worries me.'

'Ha.'

'How old are you now, Bob? Twenty-four? Twenty-five?'

'Thanks. Twenty-nine.'

'Well, I'm over fifty. Getting far too old for all the razzmatazz. Prefer the quiet life now. Give me a good savoury political scandal with fornicating ministers, or dolly birds having it off with a bishop. Something I can titilate my readers with without my having to expend too much energy.'

'You don't half lie.'

They were in Fermin's office. It was a tiny room, one he'd occupied for over twenty years, one he had flatly refused to vacate despite the lure of more salubrious surroundings as befitted his seniority. The walls were covered with photographs, some faded, and with framed headlines from the magazine dating back a quarter of a century. There were hundreds of books stacked about the room: the bookcase in the corner had long since collapsed and never been repaired, its shelves sloping down under the weight of folders, files and sheaves of paper held together by slowly shredding elastic bands.

'I mean it.'

'Seriously?' Robert asked, now concerned.

Fermin grimaced. 'In a way. You know I'll help you in any way I can – if I can do it from here, mind you.' He slapped the arm of his chair. 'Just don't expect me to do any of the leg-work, or stay up past my bedtime.'

'Thanks, Jimmy. So, where do we start?'

'Take Gemma to lunch. See how it goes. *She's* the one who can really help you. Not me.' Jimmy put his feet up on the desk, twirling a pencil in his fingers. 'Anyway, you owe her a lunch at least for the information she's already got us.'

'I suppose I do.'

'Hello, Robert.'

'Hello, Gemma.'

'How are you?'

'OK.'

'You know how sorry I am.'

'Yes. I know. Thanks.'

The waiter came and hovered, order-pad at the ready. They ordered two salmon salads and two glasses of house white.

'You're looking well. The States must agree with you.'

Robert nodded. 'I like it there for the time being.'

'When do you go back?'

'I've not made any plans about that yet.'

'Oh.'

'I'm staying with Jimmy.'

'I know. He told me.'

Their food came, and they ate in silence for a while. It was a trendy little place, a mock bistro, filled with young executives and career women who talked in loud shrill voices. 'Well, cheers,' Robert said, raising his glass.

'Cheers.'

Throughout the rest of the meal they chatted, mostly about his work in America and hers in London. Finally, the waiter took their plates and glasses away, and brought coffee. As he stirred sugar into his, Robert said, 'Jimmy told me you'd found out that Peter wasn't in uniform when he was found.'

Gemma nodded.

'Are you positive about that?'

Gemma nodded again. 'Very positive,' she said. 'You don't grow up in Belfast without learning to check all information carefully.'

'I suppose not.'

'And you learn who you can trust and who you can't.'

'Jimmy says I'm going to need you to help me.'

Gemma smiled. 'He might be right.'

'Will you?'

'If I can – and provided you trust me. You'll have to keep me up to date with everything *you* find out.'

'Yes, I'll do that.'

'And you'll have to be careful.'

'Oh, I'll be careful all right.'

'I mean it, Robert.' She glanced at her watch. 'I'd better get a move on.' She flashed him a smile. 'I'm late now as it is.'

Robert paid the bill and walked with her to the pavement, waiting as she hailed a taxi. 'Gemma – thanks for offering to help.'

'That's OK. I'm thinking of the story.'

'No you're not.'

'Yes I am – partly anyway.' She dived into the taxi, waved, and was gone.

'Well, tell me, how did it go?' Jimmy Fermin asked.

'Fine.'

'She'll help?'

'If she can.'

'Good.' He smiled wickedly. 'Nice girl, isn't she?'

'I'd never have thought of you as being a Cupid, Jimmy.'

Fermin laughed ruefully. 'I'm the world's best at arranging other people's love lives. Never could do shit about my own, though.'

'How come you never married, Jimmy? Christ knows you've had enough beauties in tow from time to time since I've known you.'

Jimmy Fermin heaved himself out of his chair, walked across the room to the television and switched it on. He turned down the sound and looked at the clock on the mantelpiece. Then he went back to his chair again, taking with him the remote control 'gizzmo', as he called it. The ashtray on the arm of his chair was filled with cigarette butts. On the floor close by were one full and two empty cans of lager. He sat down heavily. 'You want the truth or what I tell everyone, including myself?'

Robert grinned. 'Either.'

'Well, what I *say* is that I never had the time to find the right girl. The truth, however – you know something? I don't honestly know what the truth is. I just buggered up every promising relationship by not turning up on time, or not at all, chasing some story, making a name for myself, as I thought. And not caring either. That was the main trouble. Simply not caring.'

'Well, you've made a name for yourself all right.'

'Have I shit, Bob.'

'Sure you have.'

'Have I shit,' Fermin said again, and opened the third can of lager.

The ten o'clock news started. 'Mind if I watch this, Bob?' Fermin asked, turning up the volume without waiting for an answer.

The two male newscasters seemed particularly chummy that evening, smiling at each other as they swapped headlines. It was amazing, Jimmy thought, how news could be slanted with just the tone of voice, and these two buckoes were past masters at that. The verbal fracas in the House of Commons between the Labour Leader and the Prime Minister was reported in tones of stern reproval. Starvation in Africa merited sympathetic gravity tempered with little inclinations of the head that said to the viewer, See how lucky *you* are! The crisis of the homeless in Britain was reported with some speed, and with a touch of disbelief, suggesting that the statistics were probably grossly exaggerated. And there was something cynical in the voice that said another successful meeting had taken place between the Chief Constable of the RUC and Chief Inspector Harwood as, indeed, there was in the film clip that showed those two men sitting opposite each other, smiling tightly.

Fermin suddenly guffawed. 'Poor bloody Harwood,' he said aloud, meaning only to think it.

'Why do you say that?' Robert asked.

'Hmm? Oh. Harwood? Somebody must really be gunning for him.'

Robert Larski waited.

'He's doomed, and he knows it. You can see it in his face. Poor bastard. How they have the hypocrisy to say that anyone from the mainland can hope to investigate RUC irregularities is beyond me. They must really think we're morons.'

Now a spokesman was being interviewed, clearly governmental since he used those phrases beloved by politicians. No stone would be left unturned, he assured everyone, until 'that small core of wicked, misguided men had been eradicated from the force'. And, no, indeed no, he could see no reason why the actions of a few in passing secret information to either the UDR or the UFF should undermine the confidence, the very real and genuine confidence, the people of the province had in the RUC. And, with a scoffing, nervous laugh, of course it would not affect the Anglo-Irish agreement.

'Dear Jesus,' Fermin sighed.

'I can assure everyone,' the spokesman went on, warming to his subject, 'that nothing is going to be swept under the carpet. Chief Inspector Harwood is recognized as being a thorough, dedicated police officer who has been given total co-operation by the RUC, who, I would like to point out, are as keen as we are, maybe even keener, to have their good name vindicated.'

'Ha!' Jimmy Fermin snorted, using the remote control to switch off the television as the newscaster shifted to giving information about some heatwave taking place in

Florida, and pictures appeared of a rabbit cooling itself in a tub of water. 'Total co-operation by the RUC,' he repeated, mimicking the newscaster's voice. 'With this going on it's going to make it doubly hard for you to find out anything about Peter's death. Especially if there was something untoward.' Fermin finished his lager and crushed the can between his fingers, then, aiming at the waste-paper basket, he tossed the can and scored.

'I didn't expect it to be easy.'

'Easy? Jesus, Bob. You don't know the half of it.'

'That's why I'll need your help.'

'Well, you've got that, for what it's worth.'

'Thanks.'

Fermin stood up, and stretched. 'Well, I'm for bed. Maybe I'll be more optimistic in the morning.'

'I've never known you to be optimistic, Jimmy.'

'Doesn't pay. Doesn't pay.'

Robert yawned suddenly.

'Sorry,' Fermin said. 'Lousy host. You must be all in.'

'Knackered!'

'Let's get some sleep. A new day will bring new thoughts, and who knows where they might lead us.'

Robert snorted. 'Up shit creek, probably.'

Jimmy Fermin snorted too. 'Yes. Probably.'

'See you in the morning.'

'Please God. Sleep well, Bob.'

'And you.'

The guest room was in the front of the terraced house, overlooking the road. Despite his fatigue, Robert spent quite a while gazing out of the window at the people and the traffic passing below him. He watched a woman hurrying along, carrying a plastic shopping bag. Cars slowed down as they reached her, their drivers craning their necks, then picked up speed again and drove off as the woman ignored them.

There was an all-night café on the corner, doing a roaring trade, or filled with people anyway. Mostly youngsters sitting over cups of tea or coffee, possibly homeless, seeking companionship in their misery and a bit of warmth. A police car moved slowly down the road but didn't stop.

Robert drew the curtains shut, undressed and hopped into bed. He had unpacked earlier. On the table beside the bed he had placed the silver-framed photograph of his brother. He'd felt a bit guilty taking it, but his mother had insisted. He stared at the picture. You couldn't even see Peter's eyes the way the cap was jammed down over them, Scots Guards style.

On an impulse he grabbed the photograph and took it into bed with him. He held it very close, his arms folded protectively over it.

FIVE

The table was nicely set. It was covered with a linen cloth trimmed with lace, and there was a small silver bowl of roses in the centre. The plates and cups were of thin, fine china, plain white but for a narrow rim of gold. There was a salver of scones and two sorts of cake, jam sponge and fruit. It was set for six, and could have been for a Women's Institute tea party.

A small, plump woman came in and placed a teapot at the head of the table, covering it with a crocheted cosy in the shape of a thatched cottage. She stood back, looking at the table, sucking the tip of one finger. She turned and smiled as her husband entered the room.

The Commander-in-Chief of the Provisional IRA returned his wife's smile and kissed her tenderly on the cheek. 'That's just grand, dear,' he told her. 'Just grand.'

'I'll leave you to it, then. If you want more tea, just call.'

'Thank you, dear. I'll do that.'

'Will I tell them to come in?'

'If you would. Thank you.'

The Commander seated himself at the head of the table, at the other end from the teapot. He was a tall, thin man, with a beard. He wore spectacles that gave him a curiously benign air, that of a schoolmaster but a kindly one. Indeed, he sometimes thought of himself as being just that, a schoolmaster, a headmaster whose senior staff were now about to join him for Sunday tea. He heard them talking in subdued voices as they made their way across the hall, and he adopted an appropriate pose, folding his hands in front of him and cocking his head a little to one side.

He didn't rise when the five men came in. He nodded to them curtly, and waved a hand, indicating that they should sit wherever they wished. However, as they were about to sit, he said, 'Brian, perhaps you would sit by the teapot and play mother,' and he smiled at his little whimsy.

Brian Delaney sat where he was told and played mother, pouring the tea with great care. He was an enormous man, well over six feet, and as broad as they come. He was given to sweating a lot and was sweating now. The tea poured, he stuck a finger inside his collar to ease the tightness, mentally rebuking his wife for starching it.

The Commander offered a scone to Douglas Makin on his right, and then to Tomas Brophy, who sat on his left. It was interesting that these two had chosen to sit so close to the Commander, since there was an unspoken rivalry between them, each feeling himself entitled to be considered the Commander's heir presumptive. Not that either expected the Commander to relinquish his authority in the near future. But one never knew. In Northern Ireland the unexpected could always befall those in power. And pretty damn quickly at that. So it paid to be ready.

The other two men at the table were older than the rest. One, James Fox, was a solicitor with a slight tick in his left eye. The other, Declan Finch, was an extortionist, although he referred to himself as a fund-raiser, and was proud of the fact that one of his victims had made the remark that Finch only had to look at him with his cold, grey eyes to send the fear of God into him.

They all ate sparingly, one scone apiece, one slice of cake apiece, and none of them partook of a second cup of tea. They spoke very little. Indeed, the only comment that caused some discussion was Fox's when he praised the home-made jam. Finished, they folded their napkins neatly and placed them on the table in front of them, following the Commander's example. Then they sat back in their chairs, waiting.

'I apologize for bringing you out on a Sunday,' the Commander began, and looked irritated at the small ripple of forgiveness that came from his guests. 'However, there is a good reason. Two reasons, in fact.' He pulled a pipe from his pocket and started to pack tobacco into it, slowly, putting a little at a time into the bowl as if layering it. But he made no attempt to light the pipe. When it was filled to his satisfaction he placed it on the table, putting a box of matches beside it, lining them up carefully. 'Firstly, and most importantly, there is the matter of the British Captain, Larski. Tomas here assures me that after what he calls exhaustive inquiries he can be certain that none of our members was responsible for his death. I am right, I think, Tomas?'

Tomas Brophy nodded. True, he nodded slowly, but this in no way reflected a lack of certainty. As Head of IRA Intelligence he deemed it proper to take his time about things, to be absolutely sure before committing himself to any affirmation, knowing that if anything rebounded he would be held responsible, and therefore answerable. 'Yes,' he agreed finally. 'Everyone's been thoroughly quizzed, and I'm satisfied it wasn't any of us that shot him.'

'Likewise,' the Commander went on, 'we can assume it wasn't any Loyalist faction that shot the Captain. I trust I *can* be sure that our security is tight enough that no Loyalists could have left the body where it was left without us knowing?' He stared hard at Brian Delaney.

Beads of sweat stood out on Delaney's forehead. He whipped a handkerchief from his breast pocket and wiped them away in a violent scrubbing motion.

'I *can* be sure, Brian?' the Commander repeated, his voice kindly enough, but with a cold film over his eyes.

'Absolutely sure,' Delaney assured him. 'No Loyalist got within a mile of the place that night, or any other night for that matter.'

'So,' the Commander said, spreading the palms of his hands upwards. 'So who, then, killed this Larski, and is trying to make it look like we did?' He leaned forward and put his elbows on the table, cupping his chin in his hands, moving his head slightly every few moments so that he gave each man the benefit of a short stare. '*No* suggestions?' he asked finally.

'Brits?' Declan Finch was foolhardy enough to hazard.

'Thank you, Declan,' the Commander said, smiling too generously, his voice withering. Declan Finch recoiled as though struck, blushing like a child. The Commander appeared to relent. 'I can only assume you're right, Declan,' he said.

'Can't have been,' Brian Delaney put in quickly.

'No?' the Commander asked.

'We'd have known by now.'

'Would we?' The Commander sounded doubtful.

'Yes,' Delaney insisted.

'There were no British in the area that night?'

Delaney hesitated. 'Just the usual patrols.'

'Just the usual patrols,' the Commander repeated, mostly to himself.

James Fox gave a short, muted cough. 'There is one other possibility,' he said. Everyone turned to look at him. As a solicitor his pronouncements carried weight. 'It could have been a special Brit squad who were *let* in.'

That didn't go down too well, yet no one refuted it. It was, they all knew, a possibility. Just as they could, from time to time, find someone to help them, so too the Brits could, rather more rarely it was true, persuade one of theirs to be of assistance.

'That had crossed my mind,' the Commander said at last. He turned his full attention to Brophy. 'Tomas,' he said quietly, 'I want to know precisely who was responsible. And I want to know soon. I don't want to hear it was the Brits or the Chinese or the Zulus. I want names, Tomas. Surnames and Christian names. The names of their wives and children if they have any. I want to know everything there is to know about them. And when I have that information, *I* will decide what is to be done about it. I do *not* want those responsible . . .' – he hesitated, choosing his words carefully – 'interfered with in any way.' He glanced down the table to Brian Delaney. 'Understood, I hope?'

All five men nodded, their heads strangely in unison as if the same string were controlling them all.

The Commander relaxed visibly. He reached for his

pipe, struck a match and lit the tobacco, closing his eyes briefly as he sucked the first mouthful of smoke into his lungs. He extinguished the match with a single sharp puff of smoke-laden breath. 'Now to the second matter,' he said. 'You will recall at our last meeting it was agreed that certain information should be . . . should be received . . . by the gentleman who is holidaying here . . . Harwood?' Again the Commander smiled at his way with words, and his staff smiled also. 'James – you've drawn up the proposed release, I believe. I'd appreciate approval.'

James Fox took a briefcase from his chair and produced a folder. From this he took several sheets of paper and passed them around the table. One was offered to the Commander, but he declined. He contented himself with sucking his pipe, now smokeless, and by watching the others read. 'No objections, I trust?' he asked when they had finished. There were none.

'It is agreed, then, that this should reach Harwood?' Again the men nodded, Brian Delaney saying, 'Sure.'

'Excellent,' the Commander said, then took to smiling again. 'It is only right, is it not, that we do our bit to assist the good Chief Inspector with his investigation?' He allowed his staff to enjoy his witticism before rising. 'Well, thank you again, gentlemen, for coming,' he said, adding, 'James, would you stay a minute? One or two legal matters I need your advice on.'

As if by magic the Commander's plump little wife appeared at the dining-room door and ushered the four men out. 'More tea?' she mouthed silently to her husband. The Commander shook his head. He walked across the room to the door and leaned his back against it. Only when he heard the front door close and the sound of the car wheels on the gravel die away, did he relax and return to his chair.

'That was naughty,' James Fox said.

'Very.'

'And risky. What if one of them *had* objected?'

'I'm sure that between us we could have persuaded him to see the wisdom of our action, James.'

The solicitor smiled thinly.

'Anyway, what they don't know won't hurt them. The fact that you've already given the information to Harwood merely saves time.'

James Fox nodded.

'What I wanted to ask you, James – not that I doubt you in any way, mind – are you quite, quite certain that it was Captain Larski you saw in the corridor? I mean, there's no doubt in your mind whatever?'

'Absolutely none.'

'And it was your impression that he was being detained?'

'I *think* so . . .'

'Indulge me, James. Tell me again, will you?'

James Fox leaned back in his chair and closed his eyes. A small frown settled on his brow. Clearly he was trying to visualize the scene again.

'I'd just been visiting a client –'

'That was in Castlereagh?' the Commander interrupted.

'Yes. Castlereagh. I was leaving. Walking down the corridor between the interview rooms. Three men walked towards me. An RUC officer, someone in civilian clothes, and, bringing up the rear, a military policeman. That's what made me look at the man in the middle – the MP.'

'And the one in the middle was Larski?'

'I'd swear to it.'

The Commander smiled. 'I won't ask you to do that, James. Just as long as you're certain.'

'I am.'

'Right. Now what was it that made you feel he was actually under arrest, James?'

Fox grimaced. 'I could tell,' he said, opening his eyes and looking a bit sheepish. 'I've dealt with enough detainees to know one when I see one. They have a very special look about them, you know.'

'But you admit you *could* be mistaken?'

'Could be. But I honestly don't think so.'

'Interestinger and interestinger,' the Commander said.

There was silence for a few moments, the Commander

thinking, his eyes fixed on Fox's face. Finally, it was Fox who spoke. 'I take it the others' – he waved his hand at the empty places at the table – 'don't know anything about *your* meeting with Larski?'

The Commander gave his companion a look that expressed clearly what he thought of the question.

'No. I don't suppose they do,' the solicitor said with a mischievous grin.

'I think *someone* does, though, James. I think someone has found out, and it's that which worries me.'

Across the city, in TAC HQ, two men were reading. They were in a small room, furnished with only one bunk, a chest, a table, one chair. Yet there was something about it that made it seem unmilitary. Or perhaps it was the men who created that effect.

Captain Legg lay on the bunk, his eyes glued to a paperback, holding the book in front of him with one hand, the other hand tucked under his head. He was naked to the waist. His dog-tags lay in the centre of his chest; a small gold crucifix on a gold chain had slipped to one side. He had a look of contentment about him. A man at peace with the world, one would have been forgiven for thinking. One would have been mistaken.

Corporal Bayliss sat on the chair. He was thumbing through one of the Sunday tabloids, but he kept turning back to an article on page two, reading it assiduously as if trying to learn it by heart. He was a bigger man than the Captain, and more handsome. It was curious that he was in the Captain's quarters at all. Curious, too, that there was such a familiarity between them. Neither seemed ill at ease in the other's company: there seemed to be an unspoken bond between them; the sort of bond children might make while playing the dangerous game of blood-brothers.

The Corporal glanced across at the Captain. 'They buried Larski yesterday,' he said in a flat voice.

'Oh,' the Captain answered, neither putting down his book nor looking up.

'Full military honours.'

'Good.'

'Doesn't seem right.'

'What doesn't?'

'You know.'

The Captain lowered his book at last, and raised his head. 'If I did, I wouldn't ask.'

'Having us top him and then giving him all the honours.'

'What did you expect?'

'Just doesn't seem right.'

'You worry too much. That's your problem.'

'I'm not worried. Just fucking cheesed off.'

'You'll get over it.'

'I don't like being made to kill one of our own.'

'You think I do?'

'No.'

'Well, then, forget it. It was just another shitty job. Think of him as a Paddy-lover and you'll feel better.'

'It's the not knowing why.'

'Ours not to reason,' the Captain said and turned on his side. 'You better piss off now or they'll start thinking we're poofs.'

'Fuck them.'

About a mile away, in the office set aside for his use, Chief Inspector Anthony Harwood stared at the pile of paperwork on his desk, a look of bemused dismay on his face. He was in shirt-sleeves, and tieless. The ashtray on his desk was overflowing, most of the cigarettes seeming to have burned themselves out rather than been stubbed. A cup, half-filled with cold coffee, was pushed to one side. His hands were clasped behind his head, his eyes red with weariness. He had shoved his spectacles on to the top of his head. He swung back and forth on the back legs of his chair, frowning.

He had spent most of the day reading the reports he had collected during the past week, and they got him nowhere. Everything was so pat. Each statement corroborated the next with a precision too exact to be coincidental or truthful. The details were precisely the same, no variations whatsoever as one might have logically expected. Each report stated categorically that, yes, a clear warning had been given (the word 'clear' used in every one of them). That, yes, what looked like guns had been seen. That, no, they couldn't explain why no guns had been found.

He let his chair fall forward heavily on to all four feet. His glasses toppled neatly on to the bridge of his nose, settling in a well-worn groove. He took a key-ring from his pocket, selected a key, and opened the top drawer of his desk. From the drawer he took a small sheet of paper. He unfolded it, and read again the message he had read a hundred times already. NEED TO SEE YOU. SUMMON ME. It was signed, P. Larski (Capt). And he had summoned Larski, careful to make it appear a routine demand, but Larski had been murdered the night before he was due to come.

Harwood put the note in his inside pocket, yawned and stretched. Then he swallowed the cold coffee, grimacing. He put the statements into folders, and the folders into his briefcase. He did that every evening. Took everything away with him. He knew the office was bugged, and he presumed it would get a thorough searching every night. He stood up, rolled down his sleeves, and put on his jacket. He glanced at the window and towards the row of filing cabinets where he knew the bugs had been placed, and smiled contentedly. Neither he nor any member of his team ever uttered anything of import in that room, and it pleased Harwood to think of the poor sods straining away to make something significant out of the innocuous things they did say.

He switched off the lights and left the office, locking the door carefully behind him. That action made him smile again. Once, on purpose, he had left the door unlocked. It had been locked when he came in the next morning. Careless.

SIX

Robert Larski left the tube station at Brixton and hurried past the beggars who squatted about the pavement, hands outstretched, bits of cardboard propped beside them proclaiming that they were homeless and penniless, cold and starving. It was raining again. He turned up the collar of his coat and walked briskly towards Atlantic Road. It wasn't like London, he thought. More like some sleazy Caribbean city. Except for the climate. There were West Indians everywhere, affably selling dope, eating fast food from take-aways that sent the smell of hamburgers and onions and curries and even more exotic foods out on to the steaming, damp pavements, or just talking, gathered in small, protective groups, usually with some music playing.

He was grateful when he reached the Atlantic pub, and pushed his way in. This, too, seemed to belong to another part of the world. The huge mural that ran the length of the bar was of a sun-drenched beach where palm trees swayed. The band, on an improvised stage, was made up of four bearded men who beat steel drums. The air was laden with the heady odour of hash.

Robert made his way to the bar and ordered a pint of lager. Purposely he made no attempt to look about him, keeping his eyes fixed on the bottles that lined the shelves behind the bar. When his beer arrived, he drank deeply and gave a half-hearted belch.

'Nothing changes, does it?'

Robert turned and looked at the tall, skinny, emaciated man who stood beside him. 'Hello, Jerry. No, nothing changes.'

Jerry gave an odd little jerk of his head. 'Let's go over there,' he suggested, indicating the far corner of the bar where the few white customers had settled. 'Quieter. Easier to talk.'

Robert followed him, holding his beer aloft, twisting his way through the crowd. 'You got my message then?'

Jerry nodded. 'Must have done. I'm here, aren't I?'

Robert smiled thinly. 'Yes. Thanks.'

Jerry shrugged.

'I need your help.'

'I guessed that. It's the only time anyone ever asks for me – when they need my help,' Jerry told him, sounding melancholy, sounding as if his dearest wish were that someone would ask to see him without wanting help.

'What is it this time?'

'I need to meet someone.'

'Who?'

'I don't know.'

'Great.'

'Jerry . . . look . . . my brother, Peter, was murdered in Belfast.'

Jerry screwed up his pinched face. 'He was in the army, wasn't he?'

'Yes.'

'I thought so. I remember.' He gave no sign of regret. He was busy getting the facts settled in his mind. 'Murdered, you say?'

'Shot.'

Jerry gave a tired smile. 'You have to expect that.'

'I know. He knew. It's not that which worries me. It's – there's something wrong about the story we've been given.'

Jerry sipped his vodka and lemon. For a while he said nothing. His expression didn't change. He nodded slightly in the manner of a man who expected official information to be untrue.

'I want to find out the truth,' Robert told him.

'The truth?' Jerry smiled widely at that. 'The truth, no less.'

'Yes.'

'In Belfast, you say?'

Robert nodded.

'Nasty. Very nasty. And difficult. Very difficult. Not like here, you know. Now here I know everyone. All the villains. All the good guys too for that matter. Over there – well, that's a very different kettle of fish.' He gave a wicked wink. 'No good guys over there at all, I hear,' he said. 'And way outside my territory.'

Robert waited.

'I suppose, though, I *could* find someone who – very expensive, alas. Amazing how reluctant people are to talk about Belfast and what goes on there. You'd go over?'

'If needs be.'

'Oh, needs will be all right.' Jerry finished his drink. 'I'll have a think on it.' He eyed his empty glass mournfully.

'Another?' Robert asked.

Jerry declined. 'Only allowed three of a night. Doctor's orders. That was number two. Might need the other later, so I'll wait.' He put the glass on the ledge above his head. 'So, what is it you want exactly?'

'To meet someone who can get me started. Someone who might know something about what went on, about what was going on prior to Peter's death.'

Jerry gave a huge sigh. He took off his cap and scratched his head. He clamped his lips together. 'And if I find that someone for you?'

'I'd be very grateful.'

'How grateful?'

'Very.'

Jerry narrowed his eyes and took to nodding. 'Well, it so happens there is someone who might suit, but his payment would be . . . different.'

'Meaning?'

Jerry gave a short burst of laughter and sniffed the hash-filled air extravagantly. 'You understand?'

'I understand.'

'Can you manage that?'

'Can you help me manage it?'

Jerry guffawed and spread his hands expansively. 'You're asking me to rob Paul to pay Paul.'

'Something like that.'

'Yeah, I can help you.'

'Then I'll manage.'

'Leave it with me for a few days. A week, say. You still with the magazine, are you?'

'No. Well, yes. But not here. I've been in New York. You can get in touch with me at the magazine, though.'

'New York, no less? Moving up in the world, aren't we?' Jerry looked genuinely impressed. 'Right,' he said. 'You'll be hearing from me. But don't forget: it'll be expensive.'

'I won't forget.'

'New York, you say?'

'Yes. Why?'

'No reason. No reason.' He smiled mischievously.

At the same time that Robert Larski left the Atlantic pub, James Fox entered what the Commander called his study. It was a small room, sparsely furnished. A long deal kitchen table served as a desk. There were two comfortable armchairs, one either side of the imitation-coal fire. The floorboards had been sanded and varnished. One wall had several prints on it, caricatures of army officers, officers of the British Raj looking like buffoons. On the rug before the fire an old, moulting red setter was curled. It lifted its head and gave a single, economical flip of its tail as Fox came in.

'Ah, James,' the Commander said. He had been reading, and now he carefully marked the page with a postcard and closed the book, placing it on the floor beside him. 'Please,' he said, indicating the other armchair.

James Fox took off his raincoat and folded it. He draped it over the back of the chair before sitting down. He held his briefcase on his knee, waiting while the Commander got his pipe going.

'I've had word from Harwood,' the Commander said finally, clouding any expression he might have betrayed in a billow of pipe smoke. When Fox made no reply, he added, 'He wants to meet.'

'Oh.' Fox sounded dubious.

'You don't like the idea?'

'I . . . I'd be careful.'

'Of course. Careful, of course. On the other hand, you must admit, such a meeting could have serious advantages.'

'Yes. Fine. Provided the advantages are in our favour.'

'Quite. He seemed, however, to be a reasonable man – Harwood, I mean, although –'

'Although?' Fox prompted as the Commander hesitated.

'Although he did say something that struck me as a bit strange.'

Fox waited. Although he would never voice them, he had reservations about the Commander, considering him to be . . . well, if not gullible, too trusting, tending to take people at face value until they proved devious, and by then it had sometimes proved too late. James Fox was a very clinical man, and expected others to be likewise, or seek his opinion at the very least.

'He said – I don't recall the exact words, but something to the effect that it might be prudent if the information stayed between us for the time being, between him and us.'

'Did he say why?' Fox asked, instantly suspicious.

'No.' The Commander shook his head. 'No. He said it was something for us to discuss. Mind you, he did make it clear he had some good reason for suggesting it.'

'I wonder what *that* could be.'

'Your guess is as good as mine.'

On the road outside a terrier yapped and the red setter raised its head and growled. The Commander looked at his dog and smiled. 'Ferocious of a sudden, are we?'

'When are you meeting?' Fox asked.

'We didn't fix a date. I wanted to talk to you first, James,' the Commander said, and his eyes glinted as he noted Fox's pleasure. He was aware that the solicitor didn't think much of him, aware, too, that he had ambitions beyond the legality of things. He would never attain them, though. Too cold, that was his trouble. Too lacking in humanity. Would have no truck with natural frailty or foibles. Still, it kept him keen as long as he thought he had a chance, and that was no bad thing. 'After all, you might have been opposed to such a meeting.'

'Am I to be there?'

The Commander shook his head. 'No. Just the two of us. Harwood and me. But you approve?'

'In principle, yes.'

'Good. I'll have it set up as soon as possible then.'

'You look knackered,' Jimmy Fermin said.

'I am,' Robert Larski answered. 'Totally. Nothing tires you more than running round in circles.'

'That what you've been doing?'

'Seems like it. I saw Jerry Horton. Remember him?'

Fermin nodded.

'I thought he might be able to help.'

'And?'

Robert Larski smiled tightly. 'I just don't know.'

'That's a good start.'

'I know. He *did* say he *might* know someone who could help.'

'How?'

'With introductions.'

'Oh. Useful.'

'Vital.'

Robert lit a cigarette and tossed the packet on to the coffee table in front of him. He inhaled deeply, and let the smoke drift out through his nostrils.

'You'll have to watch your step, Robert. Jerry's all right as far as he goes, but his friends can be decidedly dodgy, to put it mildly.'

'Whoever he has in mind certainly seems to be. Wants payment in pot.'

'One of those.'

'One of those.'

Fermin chuckled. 'Amazing how useless good honest cash has become. God be with the days when a tenner'd buy you all the information you wanted.'

'Inflation.'

'Something like that. Greed too, though. Greed for the power the old drugs give them. You be careful.'

'I will.'

'I mean it.'

'I know you do, and I will.'

'Just thought I'd mention it.'

Jimmy Fermin stood up and patted his stomach with the palms of both hands. 'Well, I'm for bed,' he said, and then added, 'Unless you fancy a wander up the road for a beer first?'

'Why not.'

Brigadier Carlisle poured himself a generous whisky. He had offered Major Temple a drink, but he had refused – graciously, but it was a clear refusal none the less. That had irked the Brigadier. He disliked drinking alone, disliked even more what he had regarded as the somewhat supercilious look the Major had given him. He settled himself in his chair and held his drink in his hand for quite some time before taking a first, tentative sip. That done, he felt better. He took another drink, and then ran a finger along his thin moustache before putting his glass on the table beside him and folding his hands on his lap. He stared into the fire, making the Major wait. It was a trick of his. Make them sweat. Keep them wondering what was going on. That gave him the advantage. When he finally spoke, he kept his eyes on the flames. 'I can tell you I'm not at all happy with the way things are progressing, Major. Not at all happy. I'm under severe pressure to have this entire episode finished with, and what happens? Some moron tells the relatives that Larski's body was mutilated, and on top of that his brother hints that he knows Larski was in civvies when he was shot. Now, how the hell did he find *that* out?'

Prudently, Major Temple remained silent. He had been told to sit, so he sat, but on the edge of his chair ready to bounce to his feet at a moment's notice.

'I didn't hear you,' the Brigadier snapped.

'I don't know, sir.'

'You don't know. Goddamn it, man, is there anything you do know?'

The Major squirmed. In truth, there wasn't a lot he knew, even more that he didn't want to know. His father and his grandfather had been military men, and he had been brought up to believe in those obtuse virtues of honesty, and bravery, and honour. He detested what he thought to himself as the wickedness of the Larski affair, yet his inborn sense of duty made him ready to connive. 'We're having him watched,' he said now, quietly, defensively.

'Watched? Who?'

'The brother. Robert. Robert Larski.'

The Brigadier humphed. 'Watched! Watching him is not going to do any good if he can go about rummaging out information that is no concern of his.'

Even the Brigadier recognized the stupidity of that statement as soon as he had uttered it. He grabbed his glass and finished his drink. He chose a different tack. 'Do we know who carried out the . . . eh, operation?'

'I'm sorry, sir?'

'The names, man. Do we know the names of the men who actually dealt with . . .' The Brigadier stopped before mentioning Larski's name.

'Ye-es,' the Major said hesitantly.

'Well, do we or don't we?'

'Not personally. I mean *I* don't know the names, but I presume they're known.'

'You presume they're known. Well, don't presume any such thing, Major. I want to know them. At all costs we have to prevent that bloody reporter chap from getting to them.'

'Yes, sir.'

'At all costs,' the Brigadier said.

'Yes, sir.'

SEVEN

A week later, true to his word, Jerry Horton contacted Robert Larski. He gave a cryptic enough message: simply that Robert was to go to Picadilly Circus and wait outside the Body Shop at the bottom of Shaftesbury Avenue. He was to be there at nine that evening.

'He's been watching too many videos,' Jimmy Fermin commented.

And now, standing outside the Body Shop, staring vacantly at the potions daintily arranged on straw in pretty wicker baskets for the Christmas trade, Robert felt a slow, monotonous anger building up within him. And when a young man came and stood beside him, and smiled when Robert looked at him, he gave vent to that anger and hissed, 'Piss off.' Instantly he regretted it. He saw the young man, scruffy and dirty and scared, wince as though struck. 'I'm sorry,' Robert said, and searched in his pocket for some change. But the boy was gone. 'Shit!' Robert said to himself. 'Shit, shit, shit.' He thought about going after the boy, made a stride or two, but the boy saw him and ran, terrified, the sole of one shoe flapping.

'Don't look at me. Just follow,' the voice said.

From the corner of his eye Robert could make out someone in a track suit. As he moved off, sauntering, Robert followed. They made their way up Shaftesbury Avenue, and turned left into Dean Street. Here the man quickened his pace. He dived round the corner by the Golden Lion and hurried towards Frith Street. There he jumped into a car and called to Robert to get in quick.

Robert barely had time to close the door when the car moved off. The driver shifted the rear-view mirror a little and said, 'OK.'

'You know you were followed?' the man asked.

'Me?'

'No. Your mother. Of course you.'

'By who?'

'Hear that, Pete,' the man asked the driver. 'Chummy here wants to know who's following him.' The driver cackled. 'How should I know who's on your tail?'

'You sure?'

'Sure I'm sure. It's my business to be sure. Medium built, fortyish, jeans, T-shirt, blue V-sweater, grey zip-up jacket.'

'I didn't know,' Robert confessed, bewildered.

'Well, you do now.'

The man rolled himself a cigarette, sprinkling a small quantity of cannabis on the tobacco before licking the paper and sealing it deftly. He inhaled, and closed his eyes for a while. Then he smiled and offered the cigarette to Robert.

'No thanks.'

'Don't know what you're missing.'

'Probably not.'

The car left the West End. The driver knew what he was doing, moving in and out of the traffic with great expertise. As they approached Balham, Robert asked, 'Are you *sure* I was followed?'

The man opened his eyes wide, giving his face a hugely innocent air, and nodded.

The driver swung into Ritherdon Road and stopped outside one of the terraced houses.

'Right,' the man said. 'Let's go.'

'You want me to pick you up?' the driver asked.

'Naw,' the man said. 'He can get the tube back.'

The man waited for the car to drive off. Then he said, 'This way,' and started to walk up the road.

'Careful, aren't you?'

The man grinned. 'Pays to be. It's what *I'm* paid for anyway.'

'I see.'

'You might try it too.'

'So it seems.'

Halfway up the road the man turned into a gateway and jumped the three steps that led to the front door. He knocked, rang the bell once, and knocked again. The door opened a fraction. 'The merchandise,' the man said, and the door swung wide.

'Merchandise?' Robert asked.

'Sounds good, eh?' The man stood aside and let Robert enter. 'See you around,' he said. 'Watch how you go.'

'A dirty night, isn't it?' the woman said as she closed the door. 'If you'd just wait in there, Douglas will be down in a minute.'

Robert gazed about the room. It was not what he had expected; what he *had* expected was something seedy, dark and decrepit. It was far removed from that. The room could, indeed, have featured in one of those glossy magazines that told the readers how they should be living, how they could live if only they showed a little imagination and spent a great deal of money. The sofas, one either side of the coal fire, and the chairs were covered in expensive fabric, and embroidered cushions were strategically scattered upon them. A Peruvian horse, riderless, stood in the centre of the mantelpiece, flanked by two pottery figures, warriors, possibly Chinese. There were two oil-paintings in ornate gilt frames, both by Deirdre Bannerman. An arrangement of dried flowers stood tall on an Adam table. There was an air of proud comfort about the room; whoever owned it was doing well, and liked to display his well-being with quiet good taste. Robert was bending down, studying a figurine, when Douglas entered. 'Chelsea,' he said. 'Not at all a bad piece. Quite rare. It should be a pair, but, alas . . .' He shrugged, and held out his hand. 'Douglas Parr,' he said.

Robert shook his hand. 'Robert Larski,' he said, trying to size up the man who beamed at him. Like the room, Douglas Parr was a far cry from the image Robert had built up in his mind. He was about thirty, slim and elegant. His dismay must have shown.

'You look surprised,' Douglas said.

'Yes. You're not . . . well, you're not what I expected,' he confessed.

Douglas laughed. His teeth, Robert noted, were exceptionally small, not much bigger than baby-teeth, but very white and straight. 'I've been told that before. A drink?'

'Thanks.'

'Lager, I believe?'

'Yes. How –'

'Jerry Horton told me. I like to know everything about my guests. Saves a lot of questions, and I do hate questions, don't you?' He opened a can of lager and poured it into a tall, slim glass. 'How's that?' he asked, passing the glass. His nails were manicured and polished. He wore no rings.

'Fine. Thanks.'

'A little gin for me, I think. Mother's ruin,' he said, and smiled at his little joke. He poured the gin and added some tonic. He took a sip, added more tonic and sat on one of the sofas, crossing his legs. 'Yes,' he went on, 'Jerry told me all about you. Terrible business – your brother, I mean. I am sorry.'

Robert nodded.

'I can understand your *wanting* to find out exactly what happened. That's why I've agreed to furnish you with what little information I have.'

Robert smiled. 'Nothing to do with the payment, of course.'

Douglas Parr looked genuinely offended. 'Actually no, nothing whatever to do with the payment, Mr Larski,' he said coldly. 'Nothing whatever. Jerry is an old friend of mine. We go back a long way. A very long way. He tells me you have helped him. He respects you. He asked me to help you. I try to oblige my friends.'

'I'm sorry.'

'Accepted,' Douglas told him, and beamed again. 'Well now, to business. There is a man who can certainly assist you. However, you won't be able to approach him directly. He's – well, let's just say he's involved in the politics of Northern Ireland. The illegitimate politics, that is. He has to be careful. Very careful, but he owes favours.' Douglas paused, as if allowing his information to sink in. Satisfied, he went on. 'So, the first thing you have to do is meet a man called Clancy. Sam Clancy. He lives in Dublin. I'll tell you where exactly later. He's the one who can arrange for you to meet Delaney.' Douglas put down his drink and, kneeling, poked at the fire. When he sat back again, it became clear he had used the action to give himself time to think. 'I just wonder, Robert – I may call you Robert? – I just wonder if you really know what you could be getting yourself into. I say this because I know Jerry is concerned.'

'I think I do.'

'Yes, I know you *think* you do, but – well, once you start the wheels in motion you won't be able to stop them. Word will get round that you're nosing about, and these people don't really like outsiders nosing about. And they show their displeasure with some finality, you know.'

Robert nodded. 'I know.'

Douglas Parr shrugged. 'As long as you *do* know, and take reasonable precautions.'

Robert smiled. 'I'll try.'

'Trying won't be good enough.'

Somewhere in the house the phone rang. Douglas Parr frowned and cocked his head. The woman who had answered the door came in, smiled, and said, 'It's for you, dear.'

'Excuse me a moment,' Douglas said. 'Please, do help yourself while I'm out.'

Robert emptied the remains of the lager can into his glass. Clancy and Delaney. They sounded like country-and-western singers. Indeed, the very innocuousness of the names gave the men an added hint of danger. Mind you, that was always the way, wasn't it? The quiet, mild men, the ones with the most benign look, were always the dangerous ones. Perhaps it was because they had the brains and assurance to reason their villainy, make it all seem logical and right.

'Sorry about that,' Douglas said. 'More business. Different to ours but business none the less.' He picked up his drink and glanced sideways at Robert's glass. Noting it had been refilled, he smiled and sighed, 'Ah, good.' He sat down again, frowning. 'I was going to say something to you,' he said. 'Gone, I'm afraid. Maybe it'll come to me before you leave.'

'Clancy's address,' Robert said.

'No, that wasn't – oh, I see. Yes. I must give you that, mustn't I?' he said, grinning. He took a small diary from his pocket, checked something on one of the back pages and scribbled. He tore the page from the diary and passed it to Robert. 'You don't have to be too wary of him. He does what he's told.'

'Thanks. Thanks a lot.'

'I hope it helps.'

Robert finished his drink and stood up. 'About payment –'

Douglas held up his hand. 'All taken care of.'

'–?'

'All taken care of,' Douglas repeated. 'Jerry *arranged* something for me. If anything's owing, you owe him, not me.'

'I see.'

'His reason was that he didn't want him – you – handling any stuff. His words.'

'I see.'

Robert put his empty glass on the tray beside the drinks. 'I'd better make a move.'

'Yes. Yes.'

Douglas walked him to the door. 'By the way,' he said. 'I lied when I said that phone call was more business. You know Archie? The chap who brought you here? It was him. He tells me you're being followed.'

'He told me that too. I didn't see anyone.'

'You were hardly supposed to, were you? If you don't mind I'd like to put someone, one of mine, on to you. Just to protect myself, you understand. Just to find out *who* it is that is so interested in you.'

'OK by me.'

'Good. When we do find out, I'll have Jerry let you know.'

'Fine. And thanks again.'

'If you're careful and come out of this unscathed, that'll be thanks enough.'

'So, you've made a good start,' Jimmy Firmin said.

'Well, a start anyway.'

'When do you plan to go to Dublin?'

'Day after tomorrow. I want to nip up and see Mum first.'

'You going to tell her you're going?'

'I don't know. I promised I'd tell her everything, but she'll worry. Maybe I will, I don't know.'

'I think you should.'

'I know I *should*, but . . . I'll see when I get there.'

Across the city, in a small office, a man sat behind a desk and glared at two others who stood before him. Clearly he had received information that displeased him. His face was slightly flushed, and he had narrowed his eyes. He tapped a pencil against his teeth. Then he threw the pencil on to the desk. It skittered across and fell to the floor. One of the men bent to retrieve it.

'Leave it,' the seated man said. He stood up and went to the window, staring out across the rooftops. When he spoke again his voice was clipped, and he didn't turn round. 'So all you can tell me is that you *think* he followed someone in a track suit into Soho, and that he definitely turned up a couple of hours later at that journalist's house?'

One of the men muttered, 'Yes, sir.'

'That's really marvellous. Jesus Christ, I ask you to do a simple job and you mess it up like some bloody amateurs.'

'Sorry, sir.'

'Sorry? Sorry? You bloody will be sorry, you can count on that. Meantime tell me how I'm going to explain this fiasco to Temple, will you? I can't say sorry sir to him.' He swung away from the window. 'Oh, bugger off, the pair of you.'

'You want us to follow him again tomorrow?'

'Yes I want you to follow him tomorrow. I want you to follow him every goddamn place he goes. If he goes for a crap I want you in the next cubicle. If he eats I want to know *what* he eats. If he meets anyone – anyone – I want a complete description, not just what sodding clothes he has on.'

'Yes, sir.'

'Go on then. Get out.'

Alone, the man reached for the phone and dialled a number. 'Major Temple,' he said, and waited.

EIGHT

The flight to Dublin had been delayed twenty minutes. No explanation was given; it was just delayed. But now, over the sea, Robert Larski suddenly realized just how tired he was. Yesterday had been hectic, the drive to Buckinghamshire and back again particularly so, since roadworks had caused long traffic jams. Robert smiled at the pretty hostess, who smiled back. It struck him they weren't as pretty as they used to be. Older too. And plumper. More matronly. Perhaps that was what passengers wanted: a motherly creature to be there in case of accidents, not some flighty wisp of a thing who cared more for her beauty than for efficiency. He was being unfair, he knew.

'It's so unfair,' his mother had said.

'Somewhere along the way there's been a right cock-up, and they're trying to cover their tracks. They always do, you know that.'

'What do they think we'd do if we found out something, for heaven's sake?'

'It's not what we'd do. It's what the papers would do. Heads would roll, as they like to say, and whoever's responsible for whatever it was is making damn sure it isn't his head that rolls.'

'You will be careful, darling, won't you?'

'Of course I will, Mum.'

'You're all I have left now.'

'Nothing's going to happen to me. I'll be fine,' Robert told her, hoping that what he said would be proved true.

'Here, give me a hug.'

Robert hugged his mother, swaying with her, his head buried in her neck. 'I'll phone you as often as I can. I promise.'

'No. No, Robert. Don't do that. If there were a day or two when you couldn't phone, I'd worry myself sick. I can wait until you get home.'

'Not any later,' Douglas Parr said into the phone, a clear warning in his voice, and hung up. He was about to leave for dinner. He checked his appearance in the mirror over the hall table. He patted his hair. He smiled at himself, was still smiling when the phone rang again. Instantly the smile vanished. 'Yes?'

'It's me. Archie.'

Douglas Parr relaxed. 'Oh, you, Archie. I thought – never mind. What is it?'

'Our friend has left.'

'You mean Robert?'

'That's the one. From Heathrow. To Dublin.'

'Ah.'

'And as to the other – no joy yet, I'm afraid. They could be a bit special, if you get my drift,' Archie said, coyly accentuating the 'special'.

'But you're not sure?'

'Uh-huh. Not yet I'm not. Give me another day or two.'

'Yes. But find out. I really want the information on this, Archie.'

'OK. Thy will be done on earth.'

After he had hung up, Douglas kept his hand on the phone. Special Branch maybe. But why? He picked up the phone and dialled, tutting to himself as the connection was made. Then he brightened. 'Jerry? Douglas. Listen. You know Robert has gone to Dublin?'

A sigh came down the line. 'Of course.'

'So you've arranged things over there?'

Another sigh. 'Of course.'

'Adequately, I hope.'

A third sigh. 'Of course.'

'Good. Now something else. Archie just rang. He thinks it might be someone special following him.'

For a moment there was silence. 'Thinks?'

'For the moment, but you know Archie: usually when he thinks something it usually is.'

'What would they want?'

'You tell me.'

'And how will that affect us?'

'Will it?'

'That's what I'm asking you.'

'I don't know.'

'Should we call a halt?'

'Not yet. Not for a day or two anyway. Archie says he should know by then for certain.'

'OK. Let's leave it at that. I'll see what I can find out.'

'Good. I'll speak to you later.'

'Cheers.'

Douglas Parr took a final look at himself in the mirror and left the house, frowning.

Brigadier Carlisle was frowning too, deeply. He was jerky and fidgety, which was unlike him. He didn't sit but paced about the room, his hands clasped behind his back, a small nerve in his jaw twitching. Major Temple watched him. 'Maybe he's just gone over for a holiday,' he suggested, and wished instantly that he hadn't.

'Oh, don't be so bloody absurd, Temple,' the Brigadier snapped. 'A holiday!' he mimicked.

Major Temple reddened. He had the inexorable feeling that the Brigadier's fears were justified. He believed, now, that the Larski affair was soon to be exposed. He believed, too, that a scapegoat would have to be found, and he suspected that scapegoat would be himself. Well, he thought, he wasn't about to allow that to happen. Not without a fight anyway. Although how he would explain it all to his father was anyone's guess. It would kill the old man, that was certain. In his mind's eye he saw the General striding towards him, arms outstretched ready to embrace him, and heard him say how proud he was of his son. That had meant a great deal to the Major. It was the first and only time his father had praised him. And perhaps it was these thoughts that made him say, 'It's not too late to call him in and tell him everything ourselves.'

The Brigadier looked as if he had been struck. He stopped his pacing, and stared at the Major, his fingers clawing at each other behind his back. It was as though honesty were something quite foreign to him, and like all things alien it terrified him. 'Are you mad?' he demanded. 'Have you taken total leave of your senses? Call Larski in and tell him everything? My God, Temple, don't you realize what you're saying?'

'There's the chance he would understand.'

The Brigadier opened his mouth as if to speak, but shut it again quickly in the manner of someone not trusting himself to speak.

'It would be better if he learned from us than if he finds out for himself.'

Clearly the Brigadier had had enough. He came to the fire and sat down. He leaned forward. 'He must not find out for himself,' he said quietly. There was a coldness in his voice that made the Major wince. 'No matter what it takes, no matter what we have to do, Larski must find out nothing. Nothing. Do I make myself clear?'

The Major nodded. 'Yes, sir.'

The Brigadier leaned back.

In the hall outside a clock boomed. A door slammed. Footsteps sounded, passing the Brigadier's room and receding. When the Brigadier spoke again, his voice was almost paternal. 'John, John,' he said, 'I can understand how you feel. You're too young to know anything about war, and this, believe me, is a war, although the politicians like to deny it. And war is not honourable. It is dirty, a dirty filthy business. It simply comes down to this: either they win or we do, and it's our job to make sure we do. That's all there is to it. It doesn't matter a whit what we do so long as we win.'

The Brigadier paused and eyed the Major, trying to ascertain if his message had got through. For the moment there was no way of telling. The Major's face told him nothing. 'You understand?' the Brigadier asked.

Major Temple nodded. Yes, he understood. Perfectly. He wanted to grab the Brigadier by the shoulders and shake him until he rattled. He wanted to shout that the only reason there was a conflict was so that an arrogant, wilful Prime Minister could save face, not be seen to do U-turns, stay in power. Instead, he sighed quietly. 'Yes, sir,' he said. 'I understand.'

The Brigadier looked pleased. 'I knew you would.' His attitude changed. He became military again, the great manipulator. 'Right. Now. The most important thing is that Larski doesn't manage to come into contact with any of the men actually involved in the operation. He must be kept under the closest possible observation. If, by chance, he should show any indication that he has obtained the identity of those men, he must be stopped, immediately, from contacting them.'

The Major nodded.

'And the men must be kept under scrutiny also. Told nothing, mind. Just kept under scrutiny. Clear?'

'Yes, sir.'

'I can trust you to deal with that?'

The Major nodded again.

The Brigadier smiled. 'Excellent,' he said. 'I feel better now that we've cleared the air.' He stood up and seemed to have called an end to the meeting. But he didn't dismiss the Major. He went instead to his desk and took a folder from the drawer. From this he took several sheets of paper. There were passport-sized photographs stapled to each. 'By the way,' the Brigadier said, keeping his voice friendly and casual. 'This woman.' He selected one of the sheets and scrutinized it. 'This Gemma Larkin.' He tapped the photograph. 'What's her involvement?'

'None as far as we know.'

'Another newspaper person, I see.'

'Yes.'

The Brigadier sucked in his breath.

'Just because she works for the press doesn't automatically make her –'

'No. Of course not,' the Brigadier interrupted. He put the folder back in the drawer. 'Still' – he locked the drawer – 'it might be no harm to keep an eye on her. And that chap Larski's been staying with. Fermin . . . I know that name from somewhere . . .'

'It could be difficult watching *everyone* Larski knows,' the Major said.

His sarcasm was lost on the Brigadier. 'Oh, I don't mean full-time surveillance. Just a watchful eye. That's all.'

'His mother too?'

Again the Brigadier was oblivious to any jibe. He considered the suggestion for a moment, pursing his lips. 'Oh, I think not,' he said seriously. 'Not for the moment.'

The dark, metallic-blue, unmarked Sierra left the city of Belfast behind and headed for Clones. Chief Inspector Anthony Harwood, dressed in a dark grey suit, sat alone in the back. His eyes were closed. A member of his team, Detective Inspector Fraser, drove, and drove expertly. He too wore a suit, his navy blue. Under normal circumstances Harwood would have sat beside his driver, but they had decided between them that on this occasion it would be more appropriate for him to settle himself in authoritative isolation. That was what was needed: a proper air of authority in case they were stopped by patrols. It wasn't military patrols that concerned them: the unfortunate squaddies were so instilled with an unquestioning respect for authority that the sight of the Chief Inspector being chauffeured, and the quick, testy flashing of his identification, would be enough to petrify them into signalling him on. It was the RUC patrols that could be a problem. They knew who he was only too well. He was, after all, in their eyes, another enemy, sent to pry into their tactics. Harwood had no doubt that they would instantly contact their superiors, who, without a shadow of a doubt, would suspect him of being up to no good, would prevent him from proceeding, couching such prevention in terms of it being unsafe for him to venture further, of course making it clear that it was nothing but care for his safety that made them reach their decision. In the event they weren't stopped. Certainly they passed one military patrol, but they were waved on, perhaps because Fraser slowed the car allowing the soldiers to have a decent look inside, perhaps because the soldiers were cold and tired and fed up, and wanted to get back to barracks without any hassle.

'Five miles to go, boss,' Fraser said.

'Hmm?' Harwood raised his head. 'Oh. Good.'

'Nervous?'

'Aren't you?'

Fraser grinned. 'Very.'

'I don't suppose he can eat us.'

Fraser looked in the rear-view mirror, and raised his eyebrows, smiling.

'He can, you know.'

'Thanks. Anyway, it's not really him I'm worried about. Has it ever crossed your mind what sort of hell would break loose if this meeting, even an inkling of it, got out?'

'Many times. You'd be out on your neck, that's for sure.'

'I'll probably be out on my neck anyway. Seriously, though, can you imagine the repercussions?'

'What's the word they use – collusion, isn't it? That's what they'd have you for – colluding with the enemy.'

'That'd be for starters.'

'You want to turn back? We still can, you know.'

'Hell no. I'll keep plodding on, trying to find the truth, until they stop me.'

'Good, 'cause it's too late now. Look behind you.'

Chief Inspector Harwood craned his neck and peered out of the back window. A car had swung in behind them.

'Oh boy,' Fraser said.

Harwood turned round. Another car, its hazard lights blinking, was in front of them.

'Our escort,' Fraser said.

'I *hope* that's what it is,' Harwood answered, but he didn't sound overly concerned.

The car in front slowed, then pulled to the side of the road and stopped. Fraser stopped behind it. The third car slid to a stop behind them, sandwiching them in. A man stepped out of the first car, and came towards them. There was nothing furtive about his manner. He was quite young, in his early twenties, and was sure of himself. He walked quickly, though not hurrying, and he swung his arms. As he drew level, Fraser lowered his window. The man peered in. His breath smelt of onions. He ignored Fraser and addressed himself to Harwood. 'Mr Harwood?' he asked.

'Yes.'

'Would you come with me?' He opened the back door, holding it while the Chief Inspector stepped out. 'You follow,' the man said to Fraser. He escorted Harwood to the front car and again held the door as he got in. Then he slid in beside him, slamming the door. 'A precaution,' he explained pleasantly. 'Our car is known. Yours isn't. We wouldn't want anything to happen to you, would we? Not yet anyway.' He smiled at his little joke.

The cars drove slowly into Clones, keeping close together. It was absurd, he knew, but Harwood felt he was being driven through a film set. Some sort of modern-day Western perhaps. The streets were deserted, as if the baddies were on the point of galloping into town. Yet not quite deserted, he now saw. The Sheriff must have sworn in deputies, and these, some alone, some in pairs, stood on corners and nodded recognition and clearance as the cars drove by.

'Here we are,' the man said, as the car pulled up outside a small grocer's shop. He got out, and yet again held the door for Harwood. From nowhere half a dozen men appeared, and shielded them. They kept their hands in their pockets and their eyes darted about, scanning the road and the rooftops.

'In here,' the man said, opening a door next to the grocer's. 'Up the stairs, turn right, and you're there.'

The Commander of the Provisonal IRA was waiting. He still had his overcoat on. His hat was on the only table in the room. For some time the two men stared at each other, each waiting for the other to speak. It was the Commander who broke the ice. He waved a hand at the room, and said, 'Not too comfortable, I admit. But safe.'

Harwood nodded.

'Shall we?' the Commander asked, now indicating the two, straight-backed, kitchen chairs.

They sat down, one either side of the table. The Commander pushed his hat to one side. Then he got to his feet again, crossed the room and switched on a single-bar electric fire. 'No point in freezing,' he commented, retaking his seat. 'You don't mind?' he asked, producing his pipe.

Harwood shook his head.

'Good. Good. Funny thing, I can't seem to think properly without this. Don't even need to light it. Just the feel of it in my teeth helps.' He blew through the stem of his pipe, and then set about filling it. 'No problems *en route*?' he asked.

'No.'

'Good. Good. Well now.' He settled back in his chair, making it clear he had said as much as he intended to for the moment.

'I was surprised when I got your statement,' Harwood said.

The Commander smiled. 'You mean you were suspicious when you got it.'

Harwood returned the smile. 'Surprised and suspicious.'

The Commander made a small gesture with his hands, signifying he was accustomed to suspicion. 'As, indeed, was I of you when we spoke. However, now, for the time being, could we put aside our suspicions?'

'We can try.'

'That's all we can ever do: try.'

'Can I believe what you wrote?'

'You can. I mean there's nothing exactly earth-shattering in it, is there? Just facts, facts which won't really affect us if they're believed or not.'

'You say Captain Larski had gone over to you. I –'

The Commander held up one hand. 'No. I did not say that. I said that Larski was sent to infiltrate our membership – which he did, I regret to say. And that when we discovered our laxity, we *persuaded* him to do one or two things for us. He certainly never came over to us, as you say.'

'Did you know he asked to see me? Asked me to summon him?'

'Yes. We suggested it,' the Commander said blandly.

'Why would you suggest such a thing?'

The Commander smiled. 'Ah, the suspicions, Mr Harwood. Because if he had told what he knew – to the press, say – who would have believed him? If we had said he told us, who would have believed us? No, he had to tell you, convince you what he said was the truth, and let you make it public. You're quite unique in that respect, you know. You *will* be believed – always presuming you're allowed to speak,' he concluded with a wry smile.

'All I want is the truth.'

'Is that all? Ah, well. I wish you luck. In this province, you know, the truth isn't always the truth. That's the problem.'

'You *do* say he was in Armagh when the terrorists were shot?'

The Commander gave him a baleful look. 'When those young men were murdered, yes. He gave the order to shoot. Was ordered to give the order to shoot.'

'And he told you he knew, that everyone there knew the men had no guns before they opened fire?'

'He was about to tell you the same, Mr Harwood.'

'That would have suited you, wouldn't it?'

'Undoubtedly.'

'Was that one of the things you *persuaded* him to do?'

The Commander gave a short, coughing laugh. 'You know, it was something we had considered. Getting him to say some such thing. But that was before Armagh. After that he was ready to tell the truth of his own volition.'

'Just like that?'

'No. Not just like that.' For a second the Commander's face clouded with anger. Then he relaxed again and lit his pipe. 'He was, sadly for him, a good, decent young man. There are some left, you know. He felt it was his duty – and duty was very important to Captain Larski – to report to you. Others felt that would not be a good idea.'

'And you had nothing to do with it – his murder, I mean?'

'Nothing. Why should we? He was far more useful to us alive. Dead he was just another statistic. Another killing to be blamed on us.' The Commander shrugged. 'We can live with that, of course. But, as I say, we certainly didn't want him dead.'

'I almost believe you.'

'Please yourself, Mr Harwood. You said you wanted the truth. I've given it to you.'

'You also said that sometimes the truth wasn't the truth.'

'This time it is. Now let me ask you something.' The Commander clamped a matchbox on the bowl of his pipe and puffed. 'When we spoke, why did you stress the point that you thought it would be better if this information stayed between us?' he asked, waving away some of the smoke that had gathered between them.

Chief Inspector Harwood hesitated before replying. He knew that what he was about to say could be playing directly into the hands of the affable man opposite. He knew, too, that by telling him anything he was, in fact, forming an alliance – something he felt sure he would live to regret. Yet something told him it was the only way he was going to get at the truth, and he didn't really care what he did so long as he achieved that. 'I'll need your word that this remains very much our information,' he said.

'You'll take my word?'

'I don't have much option.'

The Commander nodded. 'You have it.'

Harwood cleared his throat. 'Before I was sent here I was working on something else. It doesn't matter what it was, suffice to say I had occasion to question a man called Douglas Parr. He's a dealer. Drugs. A big dealer. Probably one of the biggest we have still operating. The reason he's still operating is because, in your words, I persuaded him to help me. He's very well connected. Even over here. Certainly in Dublin. A very *useful* man.' He paused as the Commander smiled, enjoying the terminology. 'When Larski's body was found I knew – I sensed – something was wrong. It was just that bit too convenient. When I got your message, I was convinced. I did believe you, you see. It fitted.'

The Commander nodded slowly.

'When I was last in England, a few weeks ago, I contacted Parr. I'd no specific reason. Sometimes in conversation he lets something drop. To keep me sweet, he says. What he let drop this time was interesting. It seems Larski's brother, a reporter, isn't happy with what he's been told about the Captain's death. He's ferreting. He's in Dublin now. Parr gave him the name of a man to contact. It struck me that it might suit me, and you, if we let Larski have his head for a while.'

The Commander made no comment. He sucked on his pipe, blinking from time to time. Finally he took the pipe from his mouth and placed it on the tin ashtray beside him. 'You don't know, I suppose, who he's to contact in Dublin?'

'Parr didn't say. I didn't ask.'

'No. No. I can see why you wouldn't. Not to worry. You think he's capable of – what did you say? – ferreting out the truth?'

'Parr seems to think so. He's got someone's feathers ruffled. It appears the Special Branch have become interested in him. Well, Parr said he believes it's the Special Branch. Whoever it is has been following him.'

'I see. You think he's heading up North?'

'Very little doubt about that.'

'He might, then, ruffle our feathers?'

'He might.'

'Yours too, I mean.'

'I know.'

'That could be messy.'

Harwood shrugged. 'It could. On the other hand . . .' He let the statement taper into silence.

The Commander nodded. 'Dispensable. I imagine your friends in the RUC know about him?'

'Bound to.'

'And you won't be able to help him, will you?'

'No.'

'But you think we might?' The Commander gave a mischievous smile.

'It had crossed my mind.'

'He might not want anything to do with the likes of us.'

'That's possible. But it wouldn't stop you keeping a kindly eye on him, would it?'

'A kindly eye. I like that, Mr Harwood. A kindly eye. No, it wouldn't stop us keeping a kindly eye on him.'

'On the other hand he might not care where he gets his information as long as he does get it.'

The Commander nodded. 'You know, of course, there could be a price to pay for this?'

'There's always a price.'

'This one could be heavy. Heavier for you than for me.'

'I'll take my chance. As it is I'm getting nowhere fast.'

'Did you expect to get anywhere?'

'Maybe I'm stupid, but I did.'

The Commander shook his head. 'You poor Brits. You never learn, do you?'

'We try.'

'Oh you certainly try. Well, some of you do. You know, sometimes, not often, mind, but sometimes, I feel sorry for you. You haven't a hope in hell of ever understanding us. The frightening thing is that so many of your politicians believe, really believe, they *do* understand what's going on here. But they're clueless.' The Commander sighed, and put his pipe in his pocket. 'Right, Mr Harwood. Let's leave it at that, shall we?' He stood up and held out his hand. 'You see? Here, alone, we can shake hands and be civilized. Make agreements. You might pass the message to Westminster.'

'I'm sure they'd listen.'

'None so deaf as those that won't, eh?'

'Something like that.'

'We'll be in touch,' the Commander said.

'Yes. Yes, we will,' Harwood agreed.

'How did it go?' Fraser asked.

The two escorting cars had just left them. It was raining, and the wipers flicked monotonously across the windscreen.

'Better than I expected.'

'What's he like?'

'Like?'

'To talk to. Often wondered.'

Harwood laughed. 'You won't believe it, but he's really very charming. You know something? If I had to say what he was like, I'd call him old-fashioned. That's daft, isn't it?'

'You said it, boss.'

'Old-fashioned and charming,' Harwood repeated to himself, shaking his head in disbelief.

'And you agreed?'

'We did a deal.'

'Oh boy!'

'Precisely. Oh bloody boy.'

'Well, they can only hang us once.'

'Who told you that?'

'My Mum.'

'I thought so.'

The lights of Belfast glimmered before them now. 'Frank?' Harwood said quietly.

'Hmm?'

'He said something that might affect you too.'

'What was that?'

'That there could be a heavy price to pay.'

'We knew that already.'

'I'm serious.'

'So am I. Look, you go down, I'll go down with you. We'll all go down together singing, OK?'

'OK. Singing and with a bang.'

'One hell of a bang,' Fraser said, and accelerated, sending the car speeding through the empty streets.

NINE

The bar in Wynnes Hotel was filled to overflowing. Robert Larski had intended going in for a drink, but changed his mind. He wanted somewhere quiet, a bit less raucous anyway. He had slept most of the afternoon, and after a shower and a change of clothes he felt better, but not, he told himself, so well that he could face the jostling and hullabaloo of an overcrowded bar. He left the hotel and started to walk up O'Connell Street.

He had been to Dublin before, a few times, to see England play Ireland at rugby in Lansdowne Road; once, in fact, with Peter. He'd always had a soft spot for the city, and he was saddened now to see the changes. Not the structural changes so much (indeed, behind him, as he turned briefly and stared, D'Olier street in the rain still reminded him strangely of Budapest), but the changes for the worse that both prosperity and poverty seem inevitably to bring. Expensive cars swooshed by on the street, while on his right, huddled in doorways, beggars, mostly alarmingly young, called to him for a few shillings, mister. God, there were so many of them. He felt guilty as he walked past them, trying to put other pedestrians between himself and their pleas. Outside Clery's six young men stood in a circle shouting at each other. They hopped ceaselessly from foot to foot in the manner of tennis-players awaiting a serve. As he approached, they broke their circle, reforming it around him. For a moment he was truly frightened. He stood there, staring at them, and it passed through his mind how extraordinary it was that no one else seemed to be aware of his predicament. But the youths seemed to be ignoring him, shouting across him, their shouts slurred, their eyes glazed and almost yellow. And there appeared to be nothing malicious in their action, and as he moved again, two of them stood aside and let him go. It was almost as though they hadn't seen him. He crossed the street, dodging the traffic, cursing quietly as the spray from a Mercedes splashed him. Outside the GPO, in the shelter, a group of young people looked as if they were settling down for the night, spreading blankets and sleeping-bags on the ground. What was remarkable was that they were so cheerful, like kids on some grotesque outing. They laughed a lot and called encouragement to each other, ignoring those who walked by. They had a resigned aspect to their faces: this was all that life had to offer, so they determined to make the best of it. Robert's foot hit something. He looked down and saw the syringe; he toed it into the gutter. Further up, beyond Henry Street, an ageing prostitute accosted him, promising him a time like he'd never had, and cheap since he was such a lovely young man. Embarrassed, he shook his head and pushed past her, and heard her call him a fucking queer. He recrossed the street, and went into the Gresham Hotel.

Opposite, a man slowed down and pretended to study the posters outside the Carlton Cinema. He turned and crossed the road, keeping both hands in his raincoat pockets. Before entering the Gresham he paused and looked about him, carefully. He checked his watch. It was nine o'clock exactly.

The newscasters read the nine o'clock news on the BBC. Brigadier Carlisle watched it. He hadn't intended to, but he had been summoned to Whitehall, and when he arrived, the man who had summoned him suggested they watch.

'Never know what we might learn,' he said, and the Brigadier smiled appropriately.

The two newscasters smiled happily at each other as they tossed the items between them. Nothing deleted those smiles, not famine, nor flood, nor political mayhem in

India. It struck the Brigadier that it was almost as if the newsreaders were congratulating themselves that all these upheavals were taking place in lands governed by people devoid of good, solid, British common sense. And he might have had a point, for the moment they touched on Northern Ireland, they started to clip their vowels and talk in the manner of testy schoolteachers. Someone needed a spanking. True, Chief Inspector Harwood was 'progressing' with his investigation. He said so himself now: 'We are making steady progress,' he said to camera, a statement which the Chief Constable of the RUC, standing to the left and a little behind Harwood, seemed to doubt. Possibly he knew something Harwood didn't, but he wasn't about to let on, keeping his face impassive, and glancing about him as if he were both disinterested and without a care in the world. He did, for a split second, jerk his head to the front and stare somewhat menacingly at the reporter who had the temerity to ask of Harwood if he was getting 'the co-operation you need from the RUC'. But he relaxed, albeit with a slightly puzzled expression on his jowly face, when the Chief Inspector replied he was getting the co-operation he had expected.

'Ha!'

The Brigadier glanced at his companion to establish if he was expected to say something. Apparently not. Apparently, too, he had seen as much of the news as he was going to. The Minister flicked the television off by remote control. 'I quite enjoyed that . . . "as much co-operation as I expected",' he said. 'Good that,' he added, and allowed himself a watery smile.

'Very good,' the Brigadier murmured. He was uncomfortable. He disliked these meetings, particularly, as now, when he wasn't certain what the Minister wanted to discuss. He disliked politicians too, and this one more than most. 'Is he?' he heard himself ask, meaning only to think it.

'Is who what?'

'Is Harwood getting co-operation?'

The Minister adopted an air of ludicrous innocence. 'But of course. Some. Enough anyway. Wouldn't want to make things too easy for him, would we?'

'I hope we're not underestimating him.'

Instantly the Minister's expression changed. He seemed to take the Brigadier's statement as something approaching a personal insult. He brushed invisible dust from his coat-sleeve, and sniffed. 'That, Jeremy, is something *we're* not in the habit of doing.'

'I didn't mean –'

The Minister didn't care what the Brigadier did or did not mean. 'We are well aware of the Chief Inspector's qualities, and, indeed, of his reputation. Dogged is what it says on his file. Dogged. A good word that, don't you think, dogged? It means persevering, and we have no doubt that he intends to persevere. That is why he was chosen for the investigation. We had to be seen to choose someone . . . someone . . . well, someone dogged, unimpeachable.'

'And what if he –'

The Minister gave a small clucking noise of irritation. With anyone else he might well have snapped, Don't interrupt me. With the Brigadier he deemed his cluck sufficient reproval. 'Having done that,' he continued, 'it only remained to make sure that we had . . .' He paused, searching for suitable terminology, found it, and continued, 'Contingency plans in case . . .' He spread his hands, leaving the Brigadier to surmise in what event the contingency plans would be used. 'Anyway,' he went on after a while, recovering his cheerfulness, 'it's not *really* something *we* have to worry about too much. Those chaps in Belfast are well able to look after their own interests. The Chief Constable assures me he has everything well under control. If he should lose control . . . well, then we might step in. It's not the most arduous thing in the world to have Harwood recalled on one pretext or another.'

For a while they sat in silence. Then the Minister stood up and gave his waistcoat a little tug. 'Well, let's go and get something to eat.'

The Brigadier looked surprised.

'You seem surprised,' the Minister said.

'Well, yes –'

'It's why I asked you here. I thought we might dine together at my club. Didn't my secretary say?'

'No. Maybe he did. Possibly mine got it wrong.'

'Well, shall we?'

'Thank you, sir. Yes.'

Jimmy Fermin watched the news also; or, rather, he kept one eye on it. He too smiled at the Chief Inspector's answer, a wry smile that showed his cynicism, just as he had wryly smiled when Gemma Larkin had telephoned to confess she was desperately worried about Robert and he had told her, 'He'll be fine. He's a big boy, you know.'

But now, alone in his office, Jimmy Fermin confessed to himself that he too was desperately worried about Robert. Not that he could have done or said anything to stop him. Once Robert made up his mind, that, as they said, was that, and Jimmy knew him well enough to know that had any suggestion been made that he let sleeping dogs lie he would have dug his heels in, and become more determined than ever to do what he believed should be done.

He went to a cabinet and took out a half-bottle of Grouse. He unscrewed the cap and raised the bottle. 'Cheers, mate,' he said. 'Happy hunting.' He took a long slow swig and put the bottle away again.

The Commander of the Provisional IRA and James Fox tuned in to the broadcast. They had eaten a late supper together, in the study, from trays on their laps. To the Commander's surprise and chagrin, Fox had been none too happy when he was told of how well the meeting with Harwood had gone. He had looked gloomy and despondent and shaken his head a lot, forcing the Commander to ask, 'Why so unhappy, James?'

'I don't like it, that's all.'

'Any particular reason?' the Commander asked reasonably.

'It just seems to have gone *too* well. You know what they're like.'

'Tell me.' The Commander was becoming irritable.

'Always, every damn time they seem to be reasonable it turns out they've got something up their sleeve.'

'You keep saying "they", James.'

'They're all the same.'

The Commander shook his head and popped a piece of tomato into his mouth. When he had swallowed, he said, 'Yet you get so angry when someone says that we're all the same.'

'I just don't believe any mainland Chief Inspector is so goddamn keen on finding the truth that he's going to collaborate with us.'

'It's hardly a collaboration, James. We both seek the same thing. We both want to know who killed Larski. We both think we know why, it's the who that puzzles us. Let's just say that to solve the puzzle we are prepared to swap information. No more than that. And I do wish you wouldn't lump him in with your sweeping "they". He struck me as being an honourable man, and God knows, there's little enough of that around here.'

'Well, it's your decision.'

The Commander darted a quick look at the solicitor. 'Distancing yourself, James? Just in case, eh?'

'No. Of course not. You know I go along with anything you decide. I just want you to understand that in this instance I don't agree with you. But I'll support you.'

'Thank you, James ... ah, speaking of the Chief Inspector –'

'... all the co-operation I expected,' Harwood was saying on the television.

'Nicely put,' the Commander commented.

'The Chief Constable didn't think so,' Fox pointed out. 'Looks ready to explode.'

The Commander chuckled. 'It must be galling for the poor man,' he said, but with little sympathy in his tone. 'He really must wonder how often he has to wriggle out of his stupidities.'

'He'll do it, the bastard.'

'Of course he will. Harwood knows he will too. I think that's why I took to him: he knows he's on a hiding to nothing, but he's damn well going to make things as difficult as possible while he can.'

'Maybe for us also.'

'Then we'll have to wriggle a little too, won't we?'

The Commander picked up his spoon, and eyed the trifle with delight. He liked trifle, not as much as he liked bread-and-butter pudding, but well enough. Especially the way his wife made it, not skimping on the sherry. In a moment of frivolousness he had been known to remark that the only capital offence should be the making of sherryless trifle, and bread-and-butter pudding with too few sultanas.

'And what about Larski – the brother, I mean?' Fox now asked, clearly irked that he had been forced to concede defeat thus far.

'What about him?'

'What undertakings did you give?'

The Commander savoured his pudding. 'Only that we would, within reason, keep an eye on him. Guide him in the right direction where possible. No harm in that, is there? Or do you find him sinister too, one of "them"?'

James Fox used the last piece of his bread roll to mop up the mayonnaise. 'I'm only concerned that while he's playing detective he might stir up more than would be good for us.'

'If that seems likely, we will simply have to stop him.'

'That might not be so easy.'

The Commander gave Fox a cold stare. 'There is always one way,' he said.

'And you'd agree to that?' Fox sounded jittery.

The Commander thought about that for a while, scraping his pudding dish clean. Then he nodded. 'If it was the only solution. Yes, I'd agree to that.'

'Another Larski killed. The shit would really hit the fan.'

The Commander winced at the vulgarity. He wasn't by any means a prude, but he regarded vulgarity in his presence as akin to insubordination, as a distinct lack of respect, and that he would not tolerate, not even from his solicitor. Generously he refrained from rebuking him. 'Someone made the Captain's death look like our doing; perhaps when we find out who *did* murder him we could make the brother's death look like their handiwork. Only if it becomes necessary, of course.'

Fox liked that. He put his tray on the floor beside him, and when he straightened he was smiling.

'*That* pleases you, James?'

Fox nodded.

'I'm so glad something does,' the Commander said, but had Fox bothered to look he would have noted an anger in the Commander's eyes. It was a look that appeared rarely, and when it did it boded badly for someone.

Major Temple, relaxing at home, had seen the news, and it crossed his mind that sometime in the not too far distant future there could be another item reported, one that could, quite literally, ruin him. To distract himself from that possibility he absurdly wondered if the newscasters could be having an affair. Maybe groping each other under the desk, or playing footsie, planning a secret assignation for when the sound was muted at the end and they had tidied their papers and switched off their computers. Unfortunately it didn't work. It was all bound to come out. Something so horrific *had* to come out. Why bloody Carlisle supposed it wouldn't was simply crazy. And they were getting deeper and deeper into the mire. Soon it would be impossible to salvage any vestige of a career – if, indeed, it wasn't too late already.

'Lord, but you're miserable tonight,' his wife told him.

He gave a wan smile. 'Tired. Just tired.'

She waggled a finger at him. 'Don't you try and fool me, John Temple. I know when something's worrying you.'

'It's nothing. Just work.'

'Oh. Just work?'

'Hmm.'

'Well, you'd better go up and say goodnight to the children. You know Laura won't sleep until she's had her kiss.'

That was another thing. What about the children?

'Are they all right?' Claire Temple asked when he returned.

'Fine. George was asleep.'

'That boy. I've never known anyone sleep like him. Must be lovely to have such a clear conscience.'

The Major winced. He moved across the room and switched off the television just as Mr Fish was getting into his stride.

'Oh . . . I wanted to . . .' Claire began.

'Sorry, dear. I –'

'No. It doesn't matter. It was nothing. Much better to switch it off. We watch too much of the rubbish as it is.'

'You're sure?'

'I'm sure.'

The Major returned to his chair, and hid behind a newspaper. The *Telegraph*. He didn't read. He listened to the needles click as Claire knitted. It reminded him of his mother. There was something strangely *secure* in the sound. 'Claire?'

'Yes, dear?'

'How would you feel if I left the army?'

The clicking stopped. 'Gracious!' Claire gave a short laugh. 'I'd never even considered that.' She looked across at her husband. 'Put the paper down a minute.' Temple lowered the paper, and she studied his face. 'You're really thinking about quitting, aren't you?'

'It's . . . it's a possibility. How would you feel?'

'I don't know,' Claire said. Then she smiled. 'The same as I do now, I expect.'

The Major stared at her.

'It would hardly be the end of the world, would it?'

'You wouldn't mind?'

'It's whatever you want, John. You *are* considering it, aren't you?'

'Yes. Yes, I am.'

When Robert Larski left the Gresham Hotel, it was almost eleven o'clock. It had stopped raining, but there was the promise of more in the wind that blew down the street. He had enjoyed his dinner. Expensive, too damned expensive, but good. He had treated himself to a bottle of wine and drunk most of it, thinking of it morbidly as the condemned man's last meal. God alone knew what tomorrow would bring. Standing on the steps, it dawned on him for the first time that it could, indeed, bring death. He shivered, turned up his collar and started off back towards Wynnes. It was as though nothing had changed in the last two hours. Across the street the old prostitute still hopefully paraded. The youths who had encircled him were still there, but quieter now, leaning against the store window, looking anxiously down the street as though expecting someone.

The bar was less crowded. He decided on a brandy. Nothing quite like a brandy to warm the bones. And a double would warm the bones twice as effectively. Grinning, he ordered a double brandy. The barman gave him a funny look, perhaps suspecting him of being drunk, but he gave him the brandy too, which was all that mattered. He felt the liquid burn its way pleasurably down to his stomach. Idly he looked at the faces of the other customers reflected in the mirror that ran the length of the bar. Two elderly women sipping sherry, one in an old-fashioned cloche hat of pale green taffeta. Two stout, ruddy-faced men, probably farmers up for the day, downing Guinness with gusto. They both had froth on their upper lips. A young man with an attractive young girl who sipped Babycham and held her little finger at an acute angle, glowing in the adoring gaze of her escort. A thin man in a raincoat, alone, holding half a pint of lager but making no attempt to drink it. Their eyes met for an instant in the mirror. Immediately the man looked away, looked down at the bar, and moved an ashtray closer. For some reason that Robert could not fathom he looked familiar. He found himself studying the man. Nondescript suited him best. About forty. Clean-shaven. Straight, close-cropped, dark-brown hair. No visible distinguishing features, as they put it. Again their eyes met. Again the man flicked away his gaze. This time he drank some lager. He made a face as if the taste displeased him. He put the glass on the bar, and walked swiftly from the room. Robert turned on his stool and watched him leave. Just outside the bar he hesitated, then signalled someone with his finger, hooking it towards him. A porter came, and the man gave something which the porter concealed in a clenched fist. He looked pleased. The man said a few words, and the porter nodded. Then the man left the hotel, buttoning his raincoat as he left.

TEN

The next morning Robert got up early. He hadn't slept all that well. The room was too hot and although he'd tried he hadn't managed to adjust the central heating. He went down to the dining-room, catching the staff on the hop, but they greeted him cheerfully enough. He ordered a real breakfast: eggs and bacon, sausage and tomato. That was something you couldn't get in New York. Well, you could get it, but they made such a song and dance about it, muttering about cholesterol, that it wasn't worth the bother. That finished, he leaned back, ready to enjoy just one more cup of coffee. He had it poured and was adding sugar when the man he'd seen in the bar the night before came in. He looked out of breath, his face red, small beads of perspiration on his forehead. He came directly to Robert's table. 'Mr Larski?'

'You know I am.'

'Yes. Yes. Ah, well.' He took a deep breath, and smiled. 'I thought you might have finished and gone out before I got here.'

'How did you know I'd started?' Involuntarily the man glanced over his shoulder.

'Ah,' Robert said. 'The porter.'

'The porter,' the man agreed. 'May I?'

'Make yourself at home.'

The man sat down. He lifted the coffee-pot and shook it gently. 'Another cup, my dear,' he called to the waitress. 'You don't mind?' he asked Robert, screwing his face into an impish pucker.

Robert shook his head. 'Help yourself.'

The waitress brought the cup, and the man helped himself. 'Had to dash out, you see,' he explained. 'Terrible thing for a man to start the day with nothing on his stomach except last night's drink.'

'Terrible.'

The man drank three mouthfuls of coffee, slurping, and refilled his cup. 'You'll be wondering who I am, I suppose.'

'You could say that.'

'I'm a messenger. A Mercury, you might say. Without the wings, alas.'

Robert was forced to smile.

'That's better. Always worries the hell out of me when a man doesn't smile at a bit of a joke. I'll give you something else to smile at. The name's Rupert. What in the name of God my parents were up to when they picked that one I'll never know.'

Robert smiled wider and shook his head. 'It suits you,' he said.

'Does it hell! It is a bit classy though, don't you think? Not like your Tom, Dick or Harry. Anyway, it's Mr Clancy that sent me.'

Robert felt the smile drop from his lips.

'Thinks it might be better if you met somewhere in town rather than traipsing all the way out to his house.' Rupert leaned forward confidentially. 'Between you and me and the wall, he's having a little bit of wife trouble,' he confided and winked in the manner of a man who expected his information to be understood. 'So he asked me to pick you up and take you along to Bewley's. Grand place, Bewley's. As a coffee-drinking man you'll think you're in heaven.'

'Fine by me.'

'Oh it will be. It will be. Finest coffee this side of Brazil, and that's no word of a lie.'

'Why were you following me last night?'

Rupert puckered his face again. 'Made a mess of that, didn't I? A terrible mess. I'm not really cut out for that sort of thing, you know. Too gregarious, I must be. Never a one to hide my bushel in the shadows, as it were. I suppose it would be too much to ask that you keep it to yourself? You spotting me, I mean. Mr Clancy has this bit of a temper, you see, and he wouldn't take kindly to it if he knew I'd made a balls of trailing you.'

'I won't say anything,' Robert promised. 'Not a word.'

Rupert looked genuinely relieved. 'I do appreciate that,' he said with such sincerity Robert believed he had made a friend for life.

'You still haven't told me *why* you were following me.'

'Mr Clancy's idea. He's what you might call a very cagey man, Mr Larski. Very suspicious. Even though you come from a highly respected source, so to speak, Mr Clancy wanted to satisfy himself you weren't meeting any . . . any undesirables before you contacted him. Just a precautionary exercise.' Rupert's eyes pleaded for forgiveness and understanding. 'It's nothing personal, you see. He'd do the same to anyone.' He leaned forward again. 'He even had me followed once when I was following someone else,' he added as though that was truly significant and explained fully Mr Clancy's cagey disposition.

Robert couldn't resist it. 'Not last night, I hope.'

Rupert thought that was funny. 'I tell you what, I certainly hope not! No, I know I wasn't being checked up on last night. Got wise to it now,' he said, tapping the side of his nose. 'Can even smell it coming.' He stopped and frowned. 'That doesn't make much sense, does it? What I meant was I get this feeling now when Mr Clancy's up to one of his tricks.'

'The tricky Mr Clancy,' Robert said under his breath, but Rupert must have heard for now he was agreeing with him.

'That's just what he is all right. Tricky. Couldn't have put it better myself. Tricky. Perfect. And I'll tell you something, Mr Larski, since you're going to keep my little blunder of last night under your hat: you mind and keep your wits about you when you're dealing with Mr Clancy. A very plausible man, he is, but like you said, tricky. You can be a hundred per cent certain that if he seems to be doing you a favour he isn't. There's bound to be something in it for him. Always is. Usually something more than he's giving away too.'

'I'll remember that. Thanks for the warning.'

Rupert took to looking about him as though making sure the coast was clear, and Robert wondered what secret he was about to reveal. 'You wouldn't, I suppose,' Rupert said finally, 'be leaving that bit of toast behind you, would you?'

Robert laughed, and pushed the toast rack across the table, watching as Rupert smothered it in butter and marmalade, and ate it in two mouthfuls.

'God, that was grand,' he said, wiping his fingers on the overfall of the tablecloth. 'My belly was just starting to think my throat'd been slit,' he added, beaming. 'I'm ready for anything now.'

'I'll just get my coat and then we can go.'

'I'll be waiting out on the steps.'

'Fine.'

'Are you fit for a bit of a walk or will you be wanting a taxi?' Rupert asked as Robert left the hotel.

Robert looked up at the sky. The sun was trying very hard to come out. It seemed a shame not to encourage it. 'The walk would do us good.'

'I was afraid you'd say that.'

Together they ambled towards Grafton Street, and to make conversation Robert asked, 'Always lived in Dublin?'

'Always. Never set foot outside the place. No, that's a lie. I did once. Went to Cork. To a funeral. It's a wonder I didn't die there myself, Mr Larski. Oh, avoid Cork if you can possibly manage it. It's like visiting another planet. Can't understand a word they're saying to begin with. And yourself, a London man are you?'

'Lived there for years. Up to three years ago. I live in New York now. Born in Buckinghamshire, though.'

'God, you get around. New York. I think I've a cousin in New York, but then, what Irishman hasn't?'

They arrived at Bewley's café. The smell of freshly

roasted coffee carried out on to the pavement. Everyone who passed sniffed the aroma.

'I'll just come with you to the mezzanine and point Mr Clancy out,' Rupert said. 'Great name that, isn't it? Mezzanine. Mr Clancy always goes there. Likes to be served. Can't stand those self-service places they've introduced. Very fussy about that, he is. Says he'll be damned if he'll do the café's work for them.'

Robert held out his hand. 'Thanks for your help.'

'And thank you for my breakfast.'

They climbed the short flight of stairs. At the entrance to the mezzanine Rupert stopped and peered about. Then he gripped Robert's arm. 'That's him over there. The little fat geezer in the corner. See him?'

'Yep. Thanks.'

'Watch yourself now. Remember what I told you.'

'I will.'

''Bye then.'

For no good reason Robert had imagined Mr Clancy would be elderly, overweight, and short. Yet he was surprised to see that Mr Clancy was, indeed, elderly, overweight, and short. He was, in fact, almost exactly how Robert had visualized him, down to the groomed grey hair and tiny hands and feet. He was busy with a crossword as Robert came to the table. He didn't look up. He did, however, say, 'Sit, sit,' and then, as Robert sat, 'What on earth is small and dainty in five letters beginning with D and ending with Y?'

'I've no idea.'

Mr Clancy cast aside his newspaper irritably. 'I don't know whether it's me getting old and stupid, or these crosswords getting more difficult. There was a time when I could do them before they brought me my first cup of coffee. But now . . . now . . . So you're Robert Larski?'

'That's me.'

'A terrible thing about your brother,' Mr Clancy said, yet somehow he managed to convey that he considered it terrible only because he had had nothing to do with it. For Mr Clancy was not beyond conceiving great brutality if not actually ever inflicting it personally. His allegiances were variable. For years he had tenuous links with all the warring factions in the North, but in the last five years he had concentrated on consolidating his business arrangements with the Provos. Money donated (although he was aware that this was certainly a euphemistic word) was sent to him by Declan Finch, the IRA fund-raiser (this, too, being a euphemistic word). It came, quite literally, by the suitcaseful, and it was Mr Clancy's duty to filter it nicely into legitimate holdings. He took his duty seriously, and was successful. Currently slot machines were doing well. These he imported and leased out to the various Fun Palaces throughout the country. He leased them at exorbitant rates, and took a slice of the profits to boot. It irked him that he had as yet not found a system whereby he could gauge accurately what the exact profits were. He suspected many of his clients were still outwitting him, despite the fact that he had dealt severely with those he had caught at it. So severely had he punished his defaulters, indeed, that it was now said by the wags that any man between twenty-five and forty in Ireland who limped had either been born that way or had brought upon himself Mr Clancy's displeasure. There was very little Mr Clancy wouldn't do to make more of his already considerable fortune. It broke his heart that he had been unable to persuade his Northern associates to invest in the lucrative drugs market. Mr Clancy knew Declan Finch would have been willing had it been up to him, but to Finch's superiors drugs were anathema. Still, Mr Clancy did manage to run a stylish little racket on his own, although nothing worse than cocaine. And he kept very quiet about it, keeping his hands clean, for Mr Clancy was every bit as scared of Finch's superiors as Finch was himself. 'A terrible thing,' he said again.

An elderly waitress came and stood by the table. She didn't inquire what they wanted, just stood there with a little pad in her hand.

'Coffee?' Mr Clancy asked.

'Thank you. Black.'

'One black coffee,' Mr Clancy told the waitress. 'And a glass of Jersey milk for myself.' He pushed his newspaper to one side, and folded his arms on the table. He blinked intermittently, like an owl. 'Our friend Douglas tells me you need a contact in Belfast,' he said in a matter-of-fact tone.

'Yes.'

'And which denomination would that be?'

'I'm sorry?'

'You – are you Catholic or Protestant?'

'Catholic – what difference –?'

'I thought as much. Polish, isn't it – Larski? Ah yes. A good Catholic country. We have a great affection for the Poles even if you did beat us to the papacy.' His eyes twinkled for a second, and then went opaque again. 'Difference? Oh, it makes a great difference. Indeed yes. My Catholic friends up there wouldn't be at all amused if I sent them a Protestant visitor. Not at all amused. Nor vice versa, come to that. It's a question of territory, mind. Where to house you.'

'I was going to stay in an hotel,' Robert said.

Mr Clancy sucked in his breath. 'Oh dear me no,' he said, frowning and shaking his head. He was still shaking his head when the waitress returned. When she had placed the coffee and milk on the table, pushed the bill underneath the sugar bowl and left, Mr Clancy continued. 'Far too risky,' he explained, taking the bill, glancing at it and stowing it away in his top pocket. 'For my friends, I mean. Makes for a lack of what they call security. Very security-conscious, they are. Very. Oh no. A small and comfortable bed-and-breakfast. That's what you need, and, would you believe, I have just the place in mind.' He beamed.

'I guessed you might have,' Robert answered, answering the smile also with a weak one of his own.

'Run by an excellent lady. A Mrs Doherty. A widow, poor thing – but then so many of them are up there.' He looked rueful. 'Cooks like a dream. Nothing very fancy. Good plain food and plenty of it,' he said, his voice now sounding rueful also as though good plain food were something he longed for but didn't get. Not plenty of it at any rate. 'Twenty-nine Agnes Street. That's where you go. She'll be expecting you. Give her my love, won't you, please?'

'I'll do that. Twenty-nine Agnes Street?'

'That's it. I'll arrange for my friend to get in touch with you there.'

'Thanks.'

'It might be a day or two before he calls, so don't start fretting.'

'I'll try not to.'

'Good. Good. Things can't be hurried north of the border, you know. Everything takes time. Everything worth doing anyway.'

Robert nodded.

'Well, I think that's that. Nothing more we can do for you?'

'No. I don't think so. Thank you. I'm obliged.'

Mr Clancy gave a cunning smile, his little eyes glinting. 'Obliged,' he repeated. Then, 'Obliged?' he seemed to ask, but answered it himself immediately. 'Dear me, no. You're not obliged. You may be grateful, which is, of course, gratifying, but not obliged. Our friend across the pond, our Mr Parr – now he *is* obliged.'

'Oh. Yes. Well, I'm grateful then.'

'And I'm gratified.'

Mr Clancy held out a tiny pudgy hand. It was soft and damp in Robert's grasp. It was the sort of hand on which one would expect to find mittens in winter. 'Have a nice time,' he said, and anyone not knowing him would have believed he meant it.

Robert appreciated the irony. 'Ha!' he snorted mildly, and left the table.

He was almost at the exit when he turned and came back. Mr Clancy eyed him warily. 'By the way,' Robert said. 'You might try dinky.' Now Mr Clancy looked baffled. 'Dinky?'

'Small and dainty in five letters, beginning with D and ending with a Y. Dinky.'

Mr Clancy peered at his crossword. Then he pencilled in the word, spelling it out to himself as he wrote: D-I-N-K-Y. He looked up at Robert. 'You know, I do believe you're right? My dear Mr Larski, I really could become very fond of you.'

'I'm legitimized then, am I?'

'Legitimized? I don't –'

'It's the in FBI word. I thought you'd like it. It means –' Suddenly Robert laughed. 'I don't know what the hell it means,' he confessed. 'They use it about people who are cleared to go about their business.'

'Do they indeed? Legitimized. I *do* like it. And I'll remember it. Legitimized.' Mr Clancy mouthed the word carefully. 'Well, you're certainly legitimized, Mr Larski. You're a friend of the family now, so to speak.'

'Which family would that be?'

Mr Clancy was on the point of answering Robert's question seriously, but then he spotted Robert's eyes and knew he was being mocked. He didn't like that much. 'Droll, Mr Larski. Very droll,' he replied coldly.

Robert could feel the little eyes boring into his back as he left the café. As a small act of defiance he straightened his shoulders. Anyway, he was feeling pleased with himself. Things were going well. It struck him that perhaps they were going just a bit too well, too many people were being that much too obliging, too keen to help and advise him. He guessed he was probably being manipulated, but that was all right, wasn't it, as long as he was aware he was being manipulated?

As he walked down Grafton Street, a church bell tolled. It was the sheer incongruousness of the sound that made him stop. He turned into Clarendon Street and, on an impulse, went into the church. Mass was about to start. The priest looked out at his congregation as he descended the altar steps. He was probably disappointed. There were only about a dozen people in the church, mostly old women who thumbed their rosaries incessantly, or gazed with watery eyes at the tabernacle wherein Christ was safely tucked away. A tramp, nursing a monumental hangover, dozed in a side pew, snoring gently. Two pretty little girls, one kneeling either side of their mother, played silent games, making faces at each other behind her back. A young man of about nineteen, pale and pimply, wearing thick-lensed spectacles, read laboriously from a missal, a terrible fervour stamped on his ailing face as though he were determined above all else to impress God with his sincerity. Robert knelt at the back, his face resting in his hands. It had, unaccountably, shaken him when Mr Clancy had asked if he was Catholic or Protestant; shaken him because he had felt a curious guilt when admitting his allegiance to Rome. He had been baptized a Catholic certainly, and gone through the formalities which that demanded – First Communion, Confirmation – but by the time he was seventeen he had ceased to practise his faith. It hadn't been a brutal, conscious decision. He had just fallen away, as people said. Just stopped. And while as a general rule this had bothered him not one whit, from time to time he had felt something approaching remorse. When they had buried Peter and his father, for example. He had prayed for them, sincerely, but something told him God wouldn't be listening, not to *his* prayers anyway. He was prepared to admit, if only to himself, that there was, indeed, something hypocritical in expecting God to heed his pleas, to grant his wishes just as if there had been no breach between them.

Little silvery bells tinkled in the sanctuary. The Host was raised and the old women bowed their heads, the girls stopped playing, the young man buried his head in his hands, the tramp snored on. Only Robert kept his head up. Brazenly he stared at the upraised body of Christ. The weirdness of the miracle frightened him, and he felt a strange loneliness, as though he were being purposely excluded from the lucid familiarity of something he had sought and received comfort from in another time. Looking about him, wondering at those genuinely adoring faces, he could appreciate the emotions, the ceremony, and the wonder of transubstantiation induced in others, yet he himself was stirred only, it seemed, to a reminiscence of sadness.

Quietly, on tiptoe, he left the church.

Mr Clancy was talking on the telephone to Douglas Parr. He had just said, 'Many thanks.'

'You got it then?'

'Indeed yes. You are no longer obliged.'

'I'm sorry?'

'Nothing. Never mind. Just something our travelling friend said.' He glanced at the grandfather clock that thumped away in one corner of the hall. 'He should have left by now.'

'You recommended lodgings?'

'Of course.'

'We'll be in touch.'

'No doubt.'

Douglas Parr replaced the receiver. So far so good. He had now just about fulfilled his side of the bargain; it was up to Chief Inspector Harwood to do the same now. He felt positively light-hearted as he went upstairs to take a bath.

Major John Temple strode down the corridor, heading for the Brigadier's office. In one hand he carried a folded sheet of paper. He flicked it against his thigh as hc walked. 'Come,' the Brigadier called as the Major knocked on his door. 'Ah, John. Come in.'

'This just came in, sir.'

The Brigadier took the message and, still standing, read it carefully. Any good humour that might have shown in his face drained away. 'Damn him,' he said.

A small smile of pleasurable wickedness flicked across Major Temple's lips. 'Sir?'

'Larski.'

'Yes, sir.'

'Damn the man,' the Brigadier said again.

'Yes, sir.'

The Brigadier read the message a second time, taking it with him as he moved to behind his desk and sat down. He threw the paper on to the desk, casting it from him almost as if it were aflame.

'We knew he would go to Belfast, sir,' Major Temple

pointed out. 'It was inevitable. He clearly isn't the sort of man to stop looking for explanations until he's completely satisfied.'

The Brigadier drummed his fingers on the blotter before him. It didn't help matters that he suspected Temple was, for some unknown reason, gloating. 'Have you no suggestions?' the Brigadier demanded.

'As to what, sir?'

'As to what we should do about . . . about him,' the Brigadier said, flicking the edge of the message.

Major Temple made a grimace as if thinking deeply. He was surprised at how much he was enjoying the Brigadier's discomfort, surprised too that he felt a strange admiration for Larski. 'I did suggest you call him in and tell him everything, sir.'

'I mean intelligent suggestions, Temple,' the Brigadier snapped.

'I still think it would have been the thing to do. In my opinion he's going to find out anyway. He'll certainly try and talk to those who were with his brother on the . . . on the supposed patrol.'

Incredibly, the Brigadier brightened. 'Well, that's one thing he won't be able to do,' he said, and Temple was appalled at the smugness of the reply.

'No,' he agreed. 'No, he won't be able to do that, sir, since there was no patrol. But it won't stop him trying, and when he finds he can't – presumably because we won't let him – he's going to get more suspicious than ever.'

'Has Larski's CO been briefed?'

'He's been told only not to co-operate.'

'That should be enough.'

'I think not, sir. Not to stop –'

'So how do we stop him?'

'I don't think we can, sir.'

'Goddamn it, Temple, we've got to.'

Major Temple said nothing. He wanted more than anything at that moment to tell the Brigadier to get stuffed.

'You better get me – what's his name – Larski's CO?'

'Colonel Cairns, sir.'

'Cairns. Yes. Better get him on the phone for me.'
'Very good, sir.'

Brian Delaney told the Commander of the Provisional IRA that Robert Larski had arrived in Belfast. 'Interesting where he's staying,' he added.

The Commander raised his eyebrows and waited for a share of this interesting information.

'At Kitty Doherty's.'

'Indeed? Clearly our Mr Larski is a man of some ingeniousness. I wonder how he got that address.'

'Beyond me,' Brian Delaney confessed. 'Got off the train, into a taxi and went directly there. He knew where he was going before he arrived, that's for sure.'

'You haven't spoken to Kitty?' the Commander asked.

'No. No, not yet.'

'Well, don't. Not for the time being, anyway. Just let's see what develops.'

'Right.'

'Have the house watched, though.'

'I'm having that done already,' Delaney said, clearly pleased to have anticipated the Commander's wishes.

'Very good, Brian. By rights he should never have known about Kitty's. But someone must have told him about it. I'd like to know who.'

'Right.'

'I'd like to know who without that person knowing I know, Brian.'

'I'll see to it.'

'I'd like you to see to it also that Chief Inspector Harwood is informed. Just that Larski is in Belfast. Not where he's staying, mind. Just that he's here.'

'Right. What's he to be told if he asks? Can't tell him we don't know where he's staying.'

The Commander thought for a moment. 'Tell him we have Larski under our wing. He'll like that.'

'Under our wing. Right.'

'And Brian – this information about Larski's whereabouts, that stays between us. You and me. Understand?'

'Sure.'

'Strictly between you and me, Brian.'

'I understand.'

Alone, the Commander allowed the concern he felt to creep into his eyes. There was no possible way that Larski should have known Kitty Doherty's address, not unless someone who shouldn't have told him *had* told him. And the Commander wanted to know who that person was.

Kitty Doherty waited until her guest had gone into the bathroom. She listened for the sound of the shower. Only when she heard it, and the tones of muted singing, did she pick up the phone and dial. When her call was answered she said simply, 'He's here.'

A voice answered, 'Yes. I know. Thanks.' And the line went dead.

ELEVEN

Detective Inspector Frank Fraser pulled up the hood of his anorak and tied it under his chin. He walked backwards along the beach, keeping the bitter wind out of his face. 'This wasn't one of your better ideas, boss,' he said.

'Good fresh air,' the Chief Inspector countered, grinning bravely, he also walking backwards, his hair flapping in strands over his eyes.

They had driven to Craigavad, and despite the cold had decided to take to the beach. It was a decision not without danger, but they had both felt the need to get out of Belfast for a while, away from the prying eyes and ever-listening ears. They had told no one else they were coming, had in fact let it be known they were simply going for an early lunch, and took as much care as was possible to ensure they were not followed. Now they came to a small, sheltered cove and sat on some rocks. The wind whipped past them, sending litter scudding along the sand. 'That's better,' Harwood said.

'You and your fresh air.'

'Enough is enough.'

'That's for sure.'

Harwood reached down and grabbed a handful of pebbles. He started tossing them at a Coca-Cola can, missing. 'Got a message last night that Robert Larski's in Belfast.'

'He's not wasting time, is he?'

'No.'

'Tell me, boss, have you thought what you'll do if Larski does find out something?'

'Never crossed my mind,' the Chief Inspector said with amused sarcasm. 'I've been thinking of hardly anything else. If Captain Larski was killed by the military, as is hinted, then it's nothing to do with us, is it?'

'And if it was the RUC?'

'I know what I'd *like* to do – what Stalker wasn't allowed to do – blow the whole thing wide open. It creeps into everything, doesn't it – this shoot to kill. We hit upon it no matter where we turn. Jesus, if I'd honestly known what an effing cesspit this place was I'd never have agreed to come here in the first place.'

'We can ignore it,' Fraser told him. 'It's nothing to do with why we're here. All we've got to do is establish whether or not the RUC has been passing hit lists to the paramilitaries, and then we can piss off.'

'I wish it was that simple.'

'We can make it that simple.'

'We can't, you know. You know as well as I do that we're not just here to find out about the passing of hit lists. God Almighty, everyone knows that such lists have been passed. What we're here for – you mark my words, Frank – what we're here for is to give the whole seedy episode a nice gloss of respectability. We'll be allowed to say, yes, lists were passed to the paramilitaries, and, no, it was not a real conspiracy, just some over-zealous RUC nitwits doing what they thought was the right thing. We'll be handed a couple of unfortunate thickos as scapegoats and then be told to pack our bags and come back home.'

'We could always play along with it. Easier on us in the long run. No hassle. Cushy number for you when you get back, promotion for me. I quite like the sound of that.'

'You're a liar, too, Frank. If you thought I was about to knuckle under, you'd walk out on me quicker than I care to think.'

Fraser grinned.

'No – you know, I *really* want to know about Larski: what he was up to, why he was shot, who shot him, who gave the orders, every goddamn thing.'

'Talk about putting your head in a noose!'

'So be it. Anyway, we'd better get back.'

'Yep. No point in sitting here and making ourselves targets for the old IRA boys.'

Chief Inspector Harwood gave a small snort. 'It's not the IRA I'm worried about, Frank.'

'Lovely,' Fraser said.

Kitty Doherty busied herself in her kitchen. She believed people should have their main meal in the middle of the day, not at night so it would sit on the stomach while they slept and not be given a chance to turn itself into nutrition. She cooked well. She knew that. Everyone told her she cooked well. She was very proud of the fact. Nothing gave her greater satisfaction than to see the smile that lit up the faces of well-fed guests. Mr Clancy was her favourite, always so kind and appreciative. It was a pity he only made the journey north four or five times a year. Still, he did send his friends, which was nice. It quenched the loneliness, and Kitty Doherty was prone to loneliness. It was a special kind of loneliness, a widow's loneliness. A *Belfast* widow's loneliness, which was unique: on the one hand it gave her a curious if morbid standing in the community, on the other people tended to avoid her, to avert their eyes when they happened to meet her, as if her widowhood could be somehow contagious. One minute she was a wife, going about her daily chores, raising her daughter as best she could, tending her husband and loving him dearly, and the next she was bereft and in mourning. It happened so ridiculously quickly: Jerry had stepped out of the house to get, of all things, half a dozen eggs – something *she* should have bought but forgot. Thirty seconds later he was dead, his body almost severed in two by the ferocity of the bullets that ripped through it with such force that they carried particles of his flesh with them as they embedded themselves in the front door. And every night now, still, after seven years, in bed and alone, she witnessed again the harrowing scene . . . For what had seemed a very long time (certainly until well after the assassins had driven off at high speed) the street had remained deserted. Mrs O'Neill's old black and white cat, in the process of cleaning a paw, froze; sparrows that had been foraging for fat spring grubs flew on to the rooftops and gibbered brazenly. A dog barked; encouraged, another down the street joined in. Only then, very slowly, like timid nocturnal animals uneasy in the daylight, did people appear in doorways, stiff and wide-eyed, yet with the dullness of inevitability stamped on their faces. Remarkably, Kitty Doherty was one of the last to venture on to the street. Even now that puzzled her, and it puzzled her too how aloof she had felt. She did not rush to her husband's side screaming her anguish as might have been expected: she walked very calmly towards him, holding her thin dressing-gown across her breasts, her eyes vacant. Those who saw her were mesmerized by this stark, precise, emotionless approach, and in some inexplicable way it made the killing seem that much more appalling. It was only after she had been standing over the body for several minutes, wondering at the look of mild surprise on Jerry's face, and amazed at how lifelessness had made him shrink and look so small and vulnerable, that she collapsed on top of it . . .

Kitty Doherty prodded the potatoes with a fork to see if they were cooked. They needed another couple of minutes. She turned down the gas under the carrots. She opened the oven and turned the parsnips which roasted nicely around the leg of pork. The crackling, she decided, would be just perfect. Everything would be ready at the same time. She lit the gas under the small saucepan of apple sauce, and sprinkled a little nutmeg into it . . .

What she'd have done without the help she got she just didn't know. That nice Mr Fox had come and explained that Jerry had been very shrewd with his money, which was news to her. But it must have been true: the mortgage was paid, and she was given a small monthly sum to tide her over, the payments made with great regularity by Declan Finch. She couldn't quite remember who had actually made the suggestion that she take in guests. Maybe Mr Fox. Maybe Declan. Maybe she'd even thought of it herself, but she didn't think so. Anyway, that's what she had done, and miraculously guests had started to arrive. Like Mr Clancy. Like Mr Larski, who was very pleasant and courteous. And must be important: why else had Declan asked her to phone him immediately he arrived and stressed that it was only he that should be told? Well, she had done that, just as she did everything she was told, unquestioningly. She was well aware of what people said about Declan Finch, aware of his reputation and connections, but that, she decided, was no concern of hers. He had proven himself to be a friend, and that was all that counted.

She heard Robert Larski coming down the stairs, and went to the kitchen door. 'Ten minutes, Mr Larski, and I'll have your lunch on the table,' she said. 'You just make yourself comfy in the front room. There's sherry on the little table. Help yourself.'

'Thank you, Mrs Doherty. No messages?'

'Not yet, Mr Larski. But if you're expecting some, I'm sure they'll come,' Mrs Doherty said, and there was a confidence in her voice that made Robert feel she knew what she was talking about.

It was a good thing that Brigadier Carlisle had been in touch with Colonel Cairns, a good thing too that the Colonel had few scruples, a tenuous concept of morality, and that his ambitions were wholly military. Still, what the Brigadier had told him had given him a sleepless night. The call, of course, had been scrambled, but the Brigadier's instructions had been clear enough, and he had been sufficiently wily to flatter the Colonel lavishly. 'It's a good job it's *you* we have to deal with, Timothy, and not some flibberty chinless wonder,' he had begun, using the Colonel's Christian name to give his message an intimacy that would make refusal that much harder. 'You're just the man to deal with this small problem,' he went on.

'Anything I can do to help, sir,' the Colonel replied.

'Excellent.' There was a pause as the Brigadier summoned his wits to take the plunge. 'It's the Larski business again, I'm afraid,' he said finally, purposely making his voice casual, almost apologetic, as if he regretted having to take up the Colonel's time with something so trivial. 'Oh,' the Colonel said, and the Brigadier might have been perturbed had he seen his expression. From a look of glowing pride at the flattery, the Colonel's face clouded visibly. He had believed the Larski incident was over and done with. Behind him. One of those unfortunate episodes that cropped up in the intricate manœuvrings within the province. Indeed, he had succeeded in convincing himself that Larski's murder had been vital to the security and the success of the military in this monstrous effrontery perpetrated by the terrorists; so much so that he had all but managed to forget it had ever taken place. Over and done with, and best forgotten. Yet here it was back again, in what guise he did not yet know, and his face twitched as he waited to hear the Brigadier explain.

'Yes, I'm afraid so,' the Brigadier said. 'Still, nothing you can't cope with, I'm sure.'

Colonel Cairns said nothing.

'Colonel . . . Colonel?'

'Yes, sir. I'm here.'

'Ah, I thought we'd been cut off. Good. Well, the situation is this – I need hardly stress, need I, Timothy, that this is highly confidential? Highly confidential.'

'I understand,' the Colonel said.

'Well, Captain Larski's brother – a reporter, I'm afraid . . . an *American* reporter, I understand – has been making rather a nuisance of himself.'

'Asking questions, you mean, sir?'

'Exactly. Unfortunate, but there you are. Anyway, he's in Belfast now.'

'Here?' The Colonel sounded surprised and anxious.

'Yes. In Belfast,' the Brigadier reiterated, clearly uneasy at the Colonel's tone. 'It seems most likely that he will try and contact you. So I'm told, anyway. Probably to try and talk to those who were supposed to be on patrol with the Captain.'

'Yes,' the Colonel agreed.

'It might be better if you dealt with him directly yourself. What I mean is *only* you. You understand?'

'Yes. Yes, I understand, sir, but what if he insists on speaking to someone else from the alleged patrol?'

'You'll just have to see to it that he doesn't,' the Brigadier said quickly, then relenting and adding, 'I have complete faith that you can do that, Timothy.'

'Can you suggest an excuse I can give him, sir?'

'Well, not offhand, but I'm sure you'll think of something. Throw the usual things at him, I suppose. You know – security, civilian interference, any damn thing just as long as you keep him at arm's length.'

'And if he insists?'

The Brigadier was not pleased at the way the Colonel was reacting. He had expected to be able to shift everything neatly on to his shoulders. That wasn't quite happening. 'You'll think of something,' the Brigadier said, and then added, 'The Minister and I were talking about you only the other evening and we both agreed that your initiative was admirable. Most admirable.'

The Colonel allowed himself a wry smile. 'Thank you, sir.'

'Oh no. Timothy, we thank you . . . So, I can leave everything in your capable hands, can I?'

'I'll do my best, sir.'

'That's all we ask, Timothy. And we know your best will be good enough.'

And so the Colonel had spent a sleepless night, trying to knock some sort of strategy into shape as he tossed. An impression of openness and willingness to please was what was required. A manner of frankness and an air of nothing whatever to hide were required. And the Colonel tried to inculcate all these things into his voice as he said, 'But, of course, Mr Larski. I'd be delighted to meet you. Your brother is remembered with great affection and anything I can do – well, you have only to ask.' And then, 'Tomorrow? Just let me check,' and he had cupped his hand over the receiver and given the impression of checking his schedule, before saying, 'How would two o'clock suit?' It would suit fine. 'Good. Two o'clock then. I look forward to meeting you.'

Colonel Cairns replaced the receiver. Well, that had gone all right. Larski didn't seem to be the aggressive type indicated by the Brigadier. Sounded quite docile, in fact. Colonel Cairns was quite pleased with himself. He foresaw no great problem. Typical of the top brass to panic. Out of touch, they were. Not used to dealing with civilians. Scared for their pensions, the Colonel decided superciliously. In truth, he quite looked forward to tomorrow's meeting. He pressed a button on the intercom. 'Find Captain Legg for me, will you, and ask him to report to me.' No good being complacent, however. Always keep something up your sleeve. An ace, as they said. Not that Captain Legg was exactly an ace, but he'd have to do in the circumstances. He did what he was told without question, which was something. A great deal, in fact. At least, he always *had* done what he was told without question, and the Colonel sincerely hoped he would continue this admirable habit. 'Yes?' he called in answer to the knock on the door. He smiled affably as Captain Legg entered. 'Ah, Legg. Come in. Come in. Grab a chair.'

Captain Legg was surprised. He'd known the Colonel for some years now and this was the first time he'd known him to be so agreeable. Nevertheless, he did as he was bid, pulling a chair closer to the desk and sitting down.

'You don't smoke, do you?' the Colonel asked, and gave himself a little mental pat on the back when Legg shook his head and showed by a small softening of the eyes that he was impressed by this personal knowledge of his habits. The Colonel lit a cigarette for himself. 'I wish I didn't,' he observed. 'Tried to stop several times. Did once for about three months. But . . .' He spread his hands in an expression of weakness. 'Everything all right?'

'Thank you, sir.'

'Good. I know it can't have been pleasant for you –'

'If you mean Captain Larski, sir, no it wasn't,' Legg interrupted.

The Colonel flinched. 'You do know that it had to be done?'

'That's what you told me, sir.'

'And I'll tell you again. It *had* to be done.'

'That's why I agreed to do it, sir.'

'Quite. He *had* been having dealings with terrorists.'

'Yes. You said that, sir.'

'He could have caused a serious breach of security . . . caused the deaths of many of our men.'

'You explained that, sir.'

'Can't understand what got into the man.'

'No, sir.'

The Colonel was getting uncomfortable. He was straying from his plan, not coming to the point, allowing the Captain to force him into making explanations. He stubbed out the cigarette, deciding it was time to take the bull by the horns. 'Captain Larski's brother has come to Belfast.'

'Yes, sir?'

'He has already telephoned me and says he wishes to call and talk about his brother. I think – I'm certain he means about his brother's death.'

'I see, sir.'

'I might have to call on you, Legg, to . . . to substantiate what I tell him.'

'You mean back you up, sir?'

'Precisely.'

'Yes, sir.'

'It might, you realize, not come to that. But should it, I will expect you to back what I tell him.'

'May I ask what you will tell him, sir?'

'Exactly what we said in the official report. That he was on patrol. Got separated, and was found dead. Nothing more or less than that.'

'Very good, sir.'

Colonel Cairns was pleased again. 'You're a good young officer, Captain,' he said.

'Thank you, sir. Will that be all, sir?'

'Yes. Yes, that's all. Thank you, Captain.'

Captain Legg put the chair back in the precise spot from where he had taken it and walked to the door. When he got there, he turned. 'Sir?'

'Yes?'

'What happens if he finds out we're all lying?'

The Colonel felt a small shiver run down his spine. He

didn't much like being made aware that he was a liar; he didn't much like, either, being reminded of the possibility that it could come to him being publicly branded as such. 'He won't,' he said adamantly.

'He might, sir.'

'Then we'll have to deal with that eventuality should it arise.'

The Captain nodded. 'Yes, sir.' He made again as if to leave, and again he hesitated. The Colonel spotted this and immediately asked, 'Something else, Captain?'

'Just . . . well, sir . . . you won't be calling on Bayliss to –'

'Why?'

'It's just that he . . . he's taken it badly, sir. Keeps harping on about it. How it was wrong for us to do that to one of our own.'

The Colonel was suddenly alarmed. 'To whom?' he demanded. 'To whom does he go on about it?'

'Oh, only to me, sir. He'd never say anything to anyone else. I know that for a fact. Just to me, when we're on our own.'

'You make sure it stays that way, Captain. Make damn sure he says nothing to anyone else.'

'He won't, sir.'

'And no, no I won't be calling on him to see Mr Larski.'

The Captain gave several short affirmative nods of his head. 'That's good, sir.'

'Anything else?'

'No, sir. That's all. Thank you, sir.'

Alone, the Colonel lit another cigarette. Something worried him. It wasn't, curiously enough, Corporal Bayliss, although he could, indeed, become a problem. No, it was something about the Captain, something about his manner, his total acquiescence. It was as though he were willing to agree to anything the Colonel had suggested because *he* had an ace up his sleeve, and the Colonel was none too happy to have those odds against him.

'That was the best meal I've ever had,' Robert told Kitty Doherty.

Kitty beamed. 'I'm sure it's not, Mr Larski, but it's kind of you to say so none the less.'

'I mean it.'

'Just good plain food. That's all I cook. I think people are fed up with all the fancy stuff they give you in restaurants nowadays.'

'You're perfectly right.'

'Excuse me a moment,' Kitty said as the telephone in the hall rang.

She had the smile of a cat on her face when she came back. 'That was a message for you, Mr Larski,' she said, delighted to be able to give him the news. 'The gentleman you're expecting will drop in and see you this evening. He couldn't give a time. He just said this evening.'

'Thank you, Mrs Doherty.'

'Call me Kitty, Mr Larski. Everyone does.'

Robert smiled. 'Thank you, Kitty.'

'You're welcome.'

And he said, 'Thank you, Kitty,' and she replied, 'You're welcome,' again later that evening when Declan Finch came and she showed him into the front room where Robert was waiting, although this time she added, 'I'll see to it that you're not disturbed.'

Declan Finch moved to the window and looked out through the imitation-lace curtains. He gave the impression of being uneasy; not frightened particularly, but on edge. Soon, however, he left the window and sat down, crossing his legs. He was in his early thirties, and dapper. The clothes he wore could have been designer models. His hair was blond and curly. His eyes were very green and they never smiled no matter what act his lips put on. His hands were extraordinary: very square, with short stubby, thick fingers and bitten nails. He was aware that his hands were ugly, and usually kept them in his pockets, or, as now, out of sight by folding his arms over them. Someone had told him once that he had a murderer's thumbs, whatever they were, and Declan had fretted about this for a while. Then someone else told him that Alexander the Great had murderer's thumbs, and that cheered him up. He was ambitious, and greedy, and dangerous. When he spoke, his voice had a strange timbre to it: unusually high-pitched for a man; he kept trying to lower it, giving it a quavering falsity that made him sound oddly camp, butch camp, but camp none the less. Behind his back those jealous or afraid of him flicked their wrists and minced, but only when they were certain they could do so unobserved. He lived alone in Ballymurphy in the house he had shared with his widowed mother until she died. He rarely had visitors, and was known as a man who liked to keep himself to himself and others at a distance. No one opposed these preferences.

'Clancy must have taken a shine to you,' he said.

'We got on OK,' Robert told him.

'Must have done or you wouldn't be here.'

'Like I said, we got on OK.'

Declan Finch nodded. 'Must have done,' he said again, his eyes unblinking. 'What is it you're after exactly?'

'I want to find out what happened to my brother – exactly.'

'He was killed.'

Robert was angered by the tone of Finch's voice, and by the small shrug he gave. 'I *know* that.'

'A lot of people get killed here.'

'I know that too.'

'So?'

Robert knew he was being goaded, for what reason he wasn't sure. 'I want to find out who killed him and why.'

'Everyone says it was the IRA.'

'They haven't said it was them – admitted it, I mean.'

'Maybe they forgot.'

Robert let that flippancy pass. He was not going to allow himself to get unduly riled. He said nothing, waiting for Finch to speak again.

'Do *you* think it was the IRA?' Finch asked.

'No. No, I don't.'

'Who do you think did it then?'

'The RUC or the army.'

Finch shook his head. 'You can forget the RUC,' he said.

'Oh, why?'

'Because of where the body was found. There were no RUC in the area that night.'

'Who says?'

'I do. And some of my colleagues. If the RUC had been anywhere near the place, we'd have known. They weren't.'

'The army?'

Finch shrugged again. 'Always army about. Can't move but you bump into them.'

'That night – were there patrols out?'

Finch nodded.

'You're with the IRA, aren't you?' Robert asked out of the blue.

Declan Finch said nothing. He made no move, gave no sign whatever of being caught unawares. 'What is it you want with me?' he asked instead.

'Mr Clancy said you were the one man who could help me.'

'Clancy exaggerates.'

'Can you help me?'

'Maybe. Depends what it is you want.'

'Look. We were told – my mother and me – that Peter was killed while on patrol. That was the official line, but –'

'But you don't believe it?'

'No. It doesn't matter why I don't believe it, I just don't. If the army is some way involved in my brother's death, and if I can find out a name, can you help me get to that person?'

Declan Finch stood up and went back to the window. He put his hands in his pockets and swayed on the balls of his feet. 'Everything is possible,' he said quietly.

'Will you help me get to that person?'

Declan turned. 'You find the name first and then we'll see. All right for you? Find out who it is you want to . . . to talk to, and *then* I'll let you know if I can help.'

'Thanks.'

'Don't thank me, sunshine. Thank Clancy. Now I've got to go.'

'How will I reach you?'

'I'll get in touch with you.'

'When?'

'Soon enough. I'll know when you're ready.' He went to the door and opened it. 'It's something you might bear in mind. I know just about everything that goes on.'

'But not who killed my brother.'

'I said just about everything. Not every damn thing.' And with that he was gone.

Robert heard the front door slam and walked to the window. He saw Declan Finch get into a car. He didn't drive. He sat beside the driver. The car sped away from the curb almost before he had closed the door. Further down the road, on the opposite side, another car pulled out and went in the same direction. It didn't hurry.

Just as he was getting ready to go upstairs to bed the Commander of the Provisional IRA received a telephone call. 'No one so far,' Brian Delaney told him.

'No one?' The Commander sounded disappointed.

'Nobody been near the house. Only Declan gone to pay Kitty.'

'Declan was there?'

'Yeah. He goes every last Friday to pay Kitty. You know that.'

'How long did he stay?'

'Dunno. Twenty minutes.'

'A long time to pay Kitty.'

'Maybe had a cup of tea. You know Kitty. Great one for the talk.'

'Yes. Yes, she is that. Thank you, Brian.'

'I've left someone there of course, just in case.'

'Good.' The Commander ran a hand over his eyes. 'Tell me – Declan. Where did he go afterwards, do you know?'

'Home. Peadar drove him. Followed him myself.'

'Straight home?'

'Straight home. You don't think Declan is –'

'I'm not sure what to think yet, Brian. When I do, you'll be the first to know. Goodnight.'

TWELVE

Robert Larski didn't take to Colonel Cairns much. He had gone to TAC HQ, he felt, with an open mind, prepared to take the Colonel at face value. He genuinely hoped that here at least would be someone who would be honest and open with him. But the value the Colonel put on his face was disconcerting. He was too suave, too willing to oblige, too keen to impress on Robert what a thoroughly good chap he was. His welcome had been effusive. He had gripped Robert's hand in both of his. He had guided him to a chair by the elbow. And now, his buttocks resting on the edge of his desk, he smiled down at Robert, his facc, he hoped, the epitome of interested concern.

'Thank you for seeing me, Colonel,' Robert said.

'My dear Mr Larski, it's a pleasure to meet Peter's brother. As I think I told you, Peter was greatly admired and respected. His death was a terrible shock to us all. You know that you have our deepest sympathy.'

'Thank you.'

The Colonel heaved himself erect and walked round behind his desk. He sat down and straightened some papers. He folded his hands and placed them on the desk in the attitude of a solicitous bank-manager. 'Now, how can I help?' he asked.

By telling me the truth for once, Robert wanted to say. I won't cause a ruckus, he wanted to assure him. Just tell me the truth, tell me what really happened, tell me what Peter was really up to, and I'll fold my tent and go away and leave you all to get on with your dirty little games, he wanted to promise. And, curiously, he realized that he would now be quite prepared to do just that: go away and forget. At some point the desire for revenge must have left him. So what if he exposed some skulduggery? It would solve nothing, change nothing. There had been many scandals exposed already, and what had happened? Sweet nothing. He gave a small disarming smile. 'I'm not quite sure,' he confessed. 'It's just . . . it's just some of the things we've been told just don't add up.'

The Colonel nodded encouragingly. It was a gesture he was partial to, particularly when dealing with civilians. He believed it conveyed an appropriate message: that he fully appreciated the difficulties civilians had in understanding the intricate workings of the military. And it usually worked. He smiled. 'Let me try and help you with your addition,' he said pleasantly. 'Ask me anything you wish, and if I *can* answer, I will.'

Robert took a deep breath. 'Well, Peter was on patrol when he was shot, right?'

The Colonel didn't answer immediately. He reached across his desk for a folder. He opened it and, using a pencil as a pointer, ran his eye down what looked like a report. His attitude changed slightly too. He was being serious now, treating the question seriously, indicating it was a serious business. Finally he nodded. 'Yes,' he said. That was all he said. He looked up and waited patiently for Robert to continue.

'And he got . . . separated from his patrol?'

The Colonel inclined his head. 'That happens. Regrettably, but it happens.'

'And his body was found . . . when?'

The Colonel consulted his report again. 'The next morning.'

'Is that normal? I mean is it usual for a patrol to return without searching for –'

'Not usual, I wouldn't say,' the Colonel interrupted. 'It depends, Mr Larski. Here in Belfast few things are usual. The officer in charge decided he would be risking other soldiers' lives if an instant search was made in this particular instance.

There could quite conceivably have been an ambush. The terrorists could have been using your brother as bait.'

'Peter wasn't the officer in charge then?'

The Colonel turned a page of the report and read in silence for a while. 'No.'

'Can you tell me who was?'

The Colonel gave Robert a chiding look. 'I think you know quite well that that's impossible.'

'Security?'

'Quite. I can tell you that he is an officer of the highest integrity. If it had been possible for an immediate search to be conducted, he would have ordered it.'

'And Peter was found within yards of where the patrol had been?'

'Some distance from where the patrol had been,' the Colonel corrected.

'And nobody heard anything?'

'No.'

'Why was Peter in civilian clothes, Colonel?'

If Robert had hoped to surprise the Colonel, he was disappointed. Beyond a slight raising of his eyebrows the Colonel remained impassive. He returned to the report. 'There is no mention of civilian clothes here, Mr Larski. Whatever gave you the idea that he was?'

'Something I heard.'

'Well, your source was certainly mistaken.'

'Perhaps.'

'Not perhaps, Mr Larski. Certainly. Under absolutely no circumstances would any member of the forces go on patrol in civilian clothes. It's unthinkable.'

Robert felt himself believing the Colonel. Perhaps Gemma had been misinformed. Perhaps he just *wanted* to believe something untoward had befallen his brother. Perhaps – oh, shit. 'Colonel, I know I'm asking a lot and I'll understand if you have to refuse, but could I just talk to someone who was on that patrol? I don't want to know his name, or his rank, and you can be there when I talk to him. It's just – I don't know – I'd like to talk to one of the last people to see Peter alive.'

'That would be highly irregular.'

'I know.'

Still, the Colonel seemed to be giving the request consideration. He gazed unblinkingly at Robert.'Quite apart from the irregularity, the men who were with your brother are still very upset about the incident. We feel these incidents very deeply. We encourage our men to put them out of their minds as quickly as possible.'

'I understand that.'

The Colonel continued to stare. He felt he had all but convinced Larski that all was above board and that his suspicions were misplaced. All but, but not totally. His instinct told him to let Larski talk to Captain Legg. It would, would it not, be further proof that there was nothing to hide. Yet . . . He made up his mind. 'Five minutes only.'

'Fine.'

The Colonel got up and left the room, leaving the door ajar behind him, but not before he had put the report in a drawer, locking it away and taking the key with him. When he returned, he was accompanied by a soldier of about Robert's age. He was dressed in fatigues which bore no insignia of rank. Robert stood and offered his hand. The soldier shook it. He wore a small gold signet ring. 'You knew my brother, Captain Larski?' Robert asked.

'Yes, sir.'

'You were with him on patrol?'

'Yes, sir.'

'How did he get separated from the patrol?'

'I don't know, sir.'

'What Mr Larski means, I think, is do soldiers often get separated from their patrols?' the Colonel put in.

'Oh. Yes, sir. They do sometimes.'

'Don't you look for them?'

'That depends on the officer in charge, sir.'

The Colonel took to nodding, glancing at Robert, and giving him a look that said something approaching I told you so. Robert nodded back. He was getting nowhere. He wondered what he had hoped to achieve by talking to someone from the patrol. Something more than he was getting, certainly.

'Did you like my brother?'

'The Captain? Yes, sir. All the men liked him, sir. We all had a lot of respect for him, sir. We're all upset about what happened, sir.'

And that was that. Robert could think of nothing more to ask. He thought about asking the soldier about Peter being in civilian clothes, but something told him to let it pass. He wasn't quite sure why, but he wanted the Colonel to believe he had been convinced that he had made a mistake, been misinformed. He offered his hand again. 'Thank you for talking to me.'

'Nothing else you want to ask?' the Colonel inquired obligingly.

'No. Nothing else.'

'Fine,' the Colonel said. He turned to the soldier. 'That will be all then, Captain. Thank you.'

As soon as he said it, the Colonel realized his mistake. His eyes flicked to Robert and back to the soldier again. He moved quickly across the room and closed the door behind the soldier. When he turned, he was pleased to see that Robert's face was bland. Perhaps he hadn't noticed. Christ, he had better be careful.

'Well, thank you, Colonel. I really appreciate your seeing me.'

'Anytime, Mr Larski, although I expect you'll be heading home now. Lucky you. Getting out of this dreadful place. What I wouldn't give to be able to pack up and go back to England.' He opened the door again, and held it for Robert. He was smiling in his most friendly way. Things had gone pretty well.

Robert was out the door, and the Colonel was about to close it behind him, when he turned. 'Colonel, you called him Captain. Isn't that odd – two captains on the one patrol?'

The Colonel's most friendly smile froze to a grimace. 'You must have misheard me, Mr Larski. The soldier you've been talking to is not a captain.'

'Oh. Yes. I must have misheard you, Colonel. Thanks again.'

There was something about Mrs Doherty's manner that made Robert wary. Not that she was unfriendly or cold, she wasn't, but there was a nervousness about her that he hadn't come across before, the sort of nervousness that he'd noticed in people who were hiding something. He'd stopped in the city centre for a coffee. He'd phoned Gemma from the Post Office but had got no reply, which hadn't surprised him – or rather, the damn machine had chatted away, telling him Gemma wasn't there for the moment but that she'd get back to him as soon as poss if he'd leave his name and number. He told the machine he'd call later. He'd phoned Jimmy Fermin too, but without success. He was out, and wasn't expected back until tomorrow, was there a message perhaps? No, there wasn't. The coffee was good, though, and as he drank it, Robert marvelled at how people could carry on with their lives as if nothing were happening about them. It could have been any city in Britain: lights twinkled on Christmas trees, carol music came from the stores, people shopped and laughed and chatted. Mostly, he noted, they laughed. It was incredible. Perhaps, he thought, the season of good will actually meant something here.

Mrs Doherty had come bustling into the hall to meet him. She hadn't said anything, which in itself was unusual; no greeting, no how are you, no and what have you been up to, Mr Larski. Robert was on the point of asking her if anything was wrong, when she forestalled him with a little cackle. 'I've got a surprise for you, Mr Larski,' she said, with a wide-eyed coy look.

'Oh?'

'In here,' Mrs Doherty said, opening the dining-room door.

Whatever he had expected, Robert hadn't expected to see Mr Clancy. But there he was, seated at the table, looking beatific, a cup of tea in his hand, a sandwich on his plate, and the prospect of buttered fruit soda loaf and apricot flan before him. He gave a devotional inclination of his head.

'I didn't expect to see you here' was all that Robert could think of to say.

'Business,' Mr Clancy said. 'No rest for the wicked, isn't that what they say? Quite untrue, of course. The wicked get all the rest they want, it's the good that have to work for a living.'

Robert grinned. 'I'm sure.'

'Join me?'

'Do, Mr Larski,' Mrs Doherty said. 'Sit yourself down and I'll bring you some fresh tea.' She uncosied the teapot and hurried from the room.

'And how have you been getting on?' Mr Clancy asked, but immediately held up a hand to prevent Robert from answering. 'No,' he said. 'Don't tell me. Not my domain. I shouldn't have asked.'

'I've been getting on OK,' Robert told him anyway.

'That's all that matters.'

'I met your Declan Finch last evening.'

Mr Clancy nodded.

'He said he might be able to help.'

Mr Clancy nodded again and helped himself to another sandwich. Then he frowned to himself and clucked, and offered Robert the plate. 'Cucumber?' he said. 'Gives some people indigestion.'

Robert took a sandwich and bit into it. He chewed for a while, and leaned back in his chair as Mrs Doherty returned with the tea and a plate, cup and saucer which she placed in front of him. 'Will I top you up, Mr Clancy?'

'Please, Mrs Doherty.'

Mrs Doherty topped Mr Clancy up. She put the cosy back over the teapot and surveyed the table. 'Have you got everything you want now?' she asked.

'Indeed we have, Mrs Doherty. A feast fit for a king.'

'I'll leave you two with it then,' Mrs Doherty said, and off she went again, carefully closing the door.

'Can I ask you something?' Robert said.

Mr Clancy nodded slowly, but he didn't look happy about it. In his experience when people asked permission to ask a question, the question usually turned out to be awkward, one to which the answer, if he gave one, could land him in hot water.

'Finch – he's something to do with the IRA, isn't he?'

Mr Clancy looked despondent. He looked resigned too, as if his worst fears had been confirmed. He reached for the soda bread. 'Is that something you need to know?'

'It's something I'd *like* to know.'

'Does it matter?'

'No.'

'Then why ask?'

'It's useful to know who you're dealing with, isn't it?'

'You're dealing with Declan Finch. A man who says he might be able to help you. Isn't that enough?'

'It looks as if it's going to have to be.'

Mr Clancy picked a renegade currant from his plate and popped it into his mouth. 'One thing I think you should bear in mind,' he said slowly. 'You're lucky to get any help here in Belfast. Be grateful for that. Take it from wherever it comes. Don't question the sources too closely. Anyone who gives you any information here *wants* you to have it. That will be your real problem – sorting out why they want you to have it, not where it comes from.'

'I'll remember that.'

'Do. Please do. It's how they avoid utter mayhem, you know. A word here, a hint there. One side giving a titbit to the other. No questions. Tit for tat.'

'You're not saying the army and the IRA are in cahoots?'

'No. I'm not saying that, Mr Larski. If I *was* saying that, I'd say it. What I *am* saying is that when it behoves them . . .' He paused and allowed a flicker of a smile to cross his lips at his choice of word. 'When it behoves them,' he said again, 'everyone involved in the . . . the, eh, conflict, is willing to trade what they have to trade, and here that's information.' Mr Clancy cut himself a wedge of apricot flan. He offered to cut one for Robert also, but he declined. 'Anyway, you can always ask Finch himself about his affiliations.'

'I did.'

'And?'

'He didn't answer.'

'That *was* your answer, Mr Larski. That *was* your answer.'

The answer Robert got when he finally contacted Gemma was, 'Yes. I know. I got your message. How are you?'

'Surviving.'

'That's something at least.'

'Listen, Gemma, you know what you told us about Peter . . . about his clothes . . . his civilian clothes?'

'Yes?'

'How reliable was that?'

'I've already told you. Totally.'

'You're sure? It's important.'

'I *know* it's important, Robert.' She sounded angry. 'I'm absolutely sure of its reliability.'

'Can you say where you got it?'

'No. Don't ask me to do that, Robert.'

'I need to know.'

'What I can do is to get the person to contact you direct if he wants to.'

'I don't know when I'll be back in London.'

'He's over there.'

'Here? Here in Belfast?'

'Yes.'

'Jesus, Gemma, get him to contact me, will you, please?'

'I can't *make* him. I'll ask him to, though.'

'Thanks.'

'Clancy,' the Commander said thoughtfully, and repeated the name. 'Clancy.'

'Came in this afternoon,' Brian Delaney said.

'I wonder,' the Commander mused, and Delaney said nothing, allowing the Commander to wonder in peace. He was puzzled as to why the Commander should appear to find anything significant in Clancy's visit. He'd never done so before. And if he was puzzled by that, he was startled when the Commander said, 'Brian, I want a word with Clancy before he leaves. Make sure he doesn't go back south until I've spoken to him.'

'You want me to fetch him now?'

The Commander shook his head. 'No. Leave him be for a while. Let him do what he came to do. When he's about to leave, stop him.'

'Right. You want me to keep an eye on him, I suppose.'

'Very definitely.'

The Chief Constable of the RUC swore quietly to himself. The twenty minutes he had spent at TAC HQ had irritated him. He disliked the feeling that he had been summoned. He hadn't, of course. Colonel Cairns had simply suggested that it would be a good idea if they met, but the Chief Constable was touchy, forever suspecting the army of trying to usurp his power. What had really darkened his mood, however, was the fact that he had been forced to keep quiet when the Colonel told him about Robert Larski, with a crowing glint in his blasted eyes to boot. It would have pleased the Chief Constable no end to have been able to reveal that he had known about Larski for weeks, known about his arrival, known about his suspicions, known about whom he had met in London and Dublin, and knew where he was staying, and knew that he had already been to the Colonel's office. But his instructions had been plain enough: do nothing, and say nothing. Give Larski as much rope as he wanted. Let the military make any moves they wanted against him. Let them take the flak if there was going to be any. Of course he had protested – not from any great feeling of righteousness, however. He had protested because he hated these interferences from the mainland. As if they understood anything! But his protests had been muted, and had halted altogether when it was pointed out that he was, was he not, due for retirement within the next twelve months? And did he really think it was worth running the risk of being dismissed so close to that retirement? And wouldn't it be better, for everyone, if he could retire in grace and with honour? Bloody honour. That was their favourite catch-phrase. Well, let them dirty their hands over here for a while and see how far bloody honour got them. Over his shoulder he said, 'Ever get the feeling that we're being surrounded, Malcolm?'

Malcolm, a man of about forty-five, with a moustache, and dressed in a brown sports jacket of Tyrolean ancestry and a pair of brown cavalry twill trousers, joined the Chief Constable at the window. 'We've been surrounded for years,' he said.

'Not like this. Those ponces on the mainland, the army, the bloody IRA, we can handle them. But now – special investigators investigating *us*, army officers telling *us* what to do, and some bloody civilian wandering about asking questions as free as a bloody bird.' He sighed. 'In the old days we'd have known how to deal with *him*, that's for sure.'

Malcolm sighed in agreement.

'How in the name of God they expect us to wipe out the damn terrorists when all *they* have to do is scream foul and have Whitehall sending over idiots to chastise us, I don't know.' He shook his head wearily.

Probably to console and mollify his superior, Malcolm said, 'I can see their reasoning this time, though.'

The Chief Constable turned and gave him a baleful look. 'You can?'

'Well, yes. For once I think they're right.'

'You do, do you?'

'Yes. I do. This Larski – the dead man's brother – he doesn't matter a shit. It doesn't matter how many questions he asks. The only danger he could become is if he gets other people – people with clout or a political axe to grind – to start asking awkward questions, and if he manages that, it's up to the military to sort things out, not us. They killed the Captain. They put him in to spy on the IRA. The fact that he found out we didn't care how we got rid of the terrorists so long as we *did* get rid of them probably won't even come into it. It'll be the army trying to save their necks and you can bet your life they'll have concocted a good enough story by then that will make Larski sound like a bastard, his brother a fool and themselves the victims of unfounded attack by politicians interested only in the furtherment of their own damn careers.'

'That's quite a speech, Malcolm,' the Chief Constable

said. 'I don't think I've ever heard you say so much in one go in all the years I've known you.' He put a kindly hand on his companion's shoulder. 'It has been a long time, hasn't it?'

'Too bloody long.'

They both laughed.

'And you're probably right,' the Chief Constable said. 'We'll hold our fire. We'll wait and see what develops.'

'Good. Anyway, we've enough to worry about with Harwood. He knows his office is bugged, you know.'

'Of course he knows,' the Chief Constable snapped. 'He's supposed to know. That way he'll understand that we're keeping an eye on him. And between you and me, Malcolm, that's one man we really *don't* have to worry about.'

'No?'

'A very definite no. He's been allowed to make his point with those so-called hit lists. He might even be given a victim or two, but he won't be interfering with us. That I can promise you – *that* I've been promised.'

'I see.'

The Chief Constable was smiling comfortably as he turned away from the window.

'As a reward for what?' Malcolm asked with a mischievous grin.

'Are you here to see Declan Finch?' Robert asked.

Mr Clancy twitched at the question. 'Among other things. He's a business colleague.'

They had just finished supper, and were sitting in Mrs Doherty's front room.

'Good.'

'Why good?' Mr Clancy wanted to know.

'Because I want to see him too, and I don't know where to contact him.'

Mr Clancy smiled thinly. 'No. No, you wouldn't. He's a private man is our Mr Finch. What arrangement did you have with him?'

'That he'd contact me.'

'Well then I'm sure he will. But I'll mention to him that you want a word – if I see him before you do, that is.'

'Thanks.'

But as it happened, they both saw Declan Finch together. He came to the house early the next morning, just as Mrs Doherty was clearing away the plates but leaving the cups and teapot in case her gentlemen wanted another cup. He seemed nonplussed to find Robert and Mr Clancy together, but he quickly regained his composure. He shared a smile between them, a fragile, brittle thing. Mr Clancy seemed to find his discomfort amusing. He leaned towards Robert and said in a whisper, 'You can have him first,' and then looked up at Declan, managing to give the impression that a small conspiracy was afoot. The smile vanished from Declan Finch's face. He became edgy. Indeed, he looked like being on the point of retreating from the room when Robert said, 'Can I speak to you for a minute?'

Finch nodded.

'Alone,' Robert said.

Finch glanced at Mr Clancy, who stared blankly back. Then he turned and walked across the hall to the front room. Robert followed. 'I'm glad you came.'

Finch said, 'Came to see Clancy. Business.'

'Yes. Mr Clancy told me.'

Finch ignored that, although he did scowl for a second. 'What is it you want?'

'A name.'

'You said that the other night.'

'This time I've got a face to go with it.'

'I'm listening.'

'I'm almost certain he's a captain. About my age. A bit taller – maybe six foot one. Blond-reddish hair. Wears a small gold signet ring on his little finger. Left hand.'

'Where did you come across him.'

'TAC HQ.'

Finch raised his eyebrows. 'You get around.'

'Can you get his name?'

'I'll see what I can do.'

'Soon?'

'As soon as I can. Everything takes –'

'Yeah. I know. Everything takes time in Belfast.'

'Just as long as you remember that.'

'I haven't got much time.'

'Then you'll just have to make it, won't you?'

Peadar Mackie was waiting for Declan Finch to leave Kitty Doherty's. As soon as he did, Peadar used his car phone to tell Brian Delaney.

'He's on the move early,' Brian said.

'What's *he* done?'

'What d'you mean – what's he done?'

'Why all the interest in him?'

Brian Delaney was on the point of reprimanding Peadar in no uncertain terms when he thought better of it. No point in arousing his suspicions that Declan might indeed have been up to something. 'Don't be daft,' he said. 'Declan? He's done nothing. The Commander just wants to know *everyone* who goes into and leaves Kitty's. That's all.'

'Oh. Well, he's left.'

'Thanks.'

'By the way – he's not the only early bird. You know who's sitting in his car down the road?'

'Tell me.'

'Sammy Meagher.'

'The photographer?'

'Yep. Been here since about seven this morning.'

'What's he doing?'

'Sitting in his car, pretending to read a paper. I *think* he's watching Kitty's place too.'

'Well, keep an eye on him.'

'Jesus, Brian, how many eyes do you think I have?'

'I'll send a couple of boys down to help you.'

'Make it quick, will you?'

'As soon as you hang up they'll be on their way. You stick to Larski – OK?'

'Right.'

'I'll be down myself about noon.'

'See you then.'

Peadar put the phone back in its cradle, and swivelled in his seat. Through the back window he could just make out Sammy Meagher. He was hunched down in his seat, a morning paper propped on the steering-wheel in front of him.

THIRTEEN

Robert Larski sensed he was being followed. Oddly enough, it didn't worry him. What caused him more concern was that, try as he might, he couldn't spot anyone who looked even remotely as if they were trailing him. As he made his way on foot towards the city centre, he stopped several times to gaze in shop windows, pretending to be fascinated by the wares on display. Once he stood in the bay of the entrance to a small supermarket and peered back the way he had come through the plate glass. There were quite a number of people on the street, most of them women in twos and threes out shopping. Many of them pushed prams, some with children in them, some laden with groceries and provisions. Unless one of these was his pursuer, he was at a loss to know who it could be. An old man with a Jack Russell on the end of a length of twine went past, looking at him and nodding. Robert fell in behind him. The dog turned and snarled and got a throttling for its trouble. Best, Robert told himself, to appear casual. He had set out to buy a newspaper but had passed several newsagents without attempting to enter. Now he slowed his gait, walking aimlessly: that was it, walking aimlessly, and that struck him as appropriate. He found himself eventually outside St Enoch's Church, and on an impulse he went in. Mass had been over for some time, and the church had that drowsy air to it that theatres have after the curtain has come down and the audience have gone. It smelled of stale incense; of unanswered prayers too, he thought. He slid his way along a pew and sat down. A handful of people still lingered in the church, finishing off their supplications, perhaps bribing God with promises to do better. It was indeed curious how Catholicism stuck to you like some irremovable spiritual adhesive. No matter how much one scoffed at the outlandish dogmas, no matter how often one insisted that one had rid oneself of the yoke that was lumped on one's shoulders, one still, or at least he still, thought in terms of sin – those wretched black spots that appeared on the soul like the signal of some oncoming disease and were counted by St Peter to determine whether or not one was acceptable in heaven. What was most curious was that Robert now felt himself wanting to pray, and he was shocked and hurt to discover he had nothing whatever to say. He stared at the faithful praying away, and envied them. He felt himself jump when a voice behind him whispered, 'Robert Larski?'

Robert turned his head slowly. It wasn't God, nor St Peter for that matter. It was a bald head. A long, sad face. A pair of thick-lensed spectacles. A wart with hairs growing from it on the right cheek. Lips with dried saliva sticking to them, or maybe unrinsed toothpaste. A missing front tooth. 'Gemma Larkin said you wanted to see me.'

Robert felt his heart thump. He started to reply and found his throat was dry. He gave a short cough. 'You're the one who said Peter was in civilian clothes when he was killed?'

'Yes,' the man whispered.

'Let's go somewhere and –'

'No. Here's fine.'

The man was clearly scared. Every tiny noise in the church made him twitch. 'OK, OK,' Robert said, trying to soothe him. 'About Peter – are you sure?'

'I'm sure.'

'Everyone denies it.'

'I've got photographs.'

'You've got *what*?'

'Photographs. One photograph. I could only get the one before they stopped me.'

Robert could hardly contain himself. 'Of what?' he asked, and immediately, '*Who* stopped you?'

'Of your brother. Just as they were carting him off. The army stopped me. That's what made me wonder. Usually they like to have photographs taken of IRA victims. Use them to revolt people. This time, though, they weren't allowing any.'

'And the picture? The one you did get?'

'See for yourself.'

The man reached into his inside pocket and pulled out a photograph. He slid it towards Robert. 'Keep it down,' he said.

Robert stared at the picture. It wasn't the best he had ever seen. Well enough in focus but dark. It showed a couple of things clearly enough, though. It showed a body on a stretcher, with a blanket thrown roughly over it. One arm hung down from the stretcher. It was clothed in a tweed sleeve. The feet of the corpse stuck out from under the blanket: they were sockless, the shoes casual slip-ons. The two soldiers carrying the stretcher were unidentifiable, their backs to the camera, but to one side, staring at the body, was the soldier Robert had spoken to in Colonel Cairns's office. 'You're sure that's Peter?'

The man gave a small shrug. 'What do you think?'

'I'm asking you.'

'Of course it is.'

'And him – who's he?' Robert asked.

'No idea. In charge he seemed to be. Gave the orders, anyway. Told me to bugger off.'

'You've no idea what rank he was?'

'Look, I was taking pictures, not looking at rank.'

'Of course. Sorry.' Robert looked again at the body of his brother, and shuddered. 'How come you were the only photographer there?'

'I'm freelance. Get the odd tip now and again. Got a tip they found a body and followed it up like I always do.'

'Why didn't you use this?'

The man grimaced. 'Tried. Thought it should be worth something. I even had it sold but they pulled out. Didn't say they were pulling out or anything. Just didn't print it.'

'Didn't you ask why?'

'Sure I asked why. They said there was no appropriate space. You know what that means? It means they were told not to print.' He gave a small smile. 'They paid me for it, though. Gave them the copyright, you see. Couldn't go anywhere else with it. Even if I had, it wouldn't have done any good.'

'Can I keep this?'

The man shrugged. 'If you want.'

'Can you get me more copies?'

'Sure. I do them myself. At home. How many?'

'Another five.'

'No problem. Get them to you this evening.'

'Great.' Robert put the photograph on the bench beside him, and took some notes from his pocket. He folded two twentys and a ten into a tight little bundle and slipped them to the man.

'Thanks.'

'Thank you . . . eh?'

'Sammy. Sammy Meagher.'

'By the way – were you following me this morning?'

'Yes. Had to try and get you on your own.'

Robert grinned. 'I knew someone was following me but couldn't spot them. You're good.'

The man smiled shyly. 'I saw you looking about. I was in my car. That's why you didn't see me. You weren't looking at cars.'

'Oh.'

'I'd better go and do those copies for you. Wait a bit before you follow me out, will you?'

'Sure. Sammy? Why are you so scared?'

'You're joking, aren't you? Scared? I'm shitting myself. I don't have much of a life but I don't mind hanging on to it as long as I can. If anyone knew I'd passed that to you I'd be dead meat.' He stood up. 'If anyone finds out you've got them, you're dead meat too, so watch it.' He hurried from the church.

Alone, Robert held the photograph in his hands. The elation he had felt at the information faded. He stared at the body of his brother, and quietly he wept.

*

On his way back to Kitty's, Robert bought a newspaper. He also bought five brown envelopes large enough to take the photograph. He hid these under his overcoat.

'Ah, Mr Larski. I was wondering where you'd got to,' Kitty Doherty greeted him.

'I went to church, Kitty.'

'That's nice,' Kitty said. 'I hope God was good to you.'

'He was, Kitty. Very good.'

'Isn't that grand!'

Grand! Well, he would probably have chosen another word, but grand was good enough. All he had to do was wait for the copies, and then . . . He sat in his room and decided what he would do.

'What do you mean you lost them?'

'Jesus, Brian, I can't be in three places at the one time.'

'I told you to stick with Larski, dammit.'

'I know you did. You also told me you'd send someone down to help. Larski left Kitty's before anyone came. And I did stick with him. He knew I was following him, though. Kept stopping and looking back. I had to stay well out of sight.'

'And you lost him?'

'Couldn't help it. Honest.'

'What about Sammy?'

Peadar Mackie shrugged. 'Dunno. He was gone by the time I got back here.' Brian Delaney shook his head in exasperation.

'Anyway, he's back in Kitty's now – Larski.'

'But we don't know where he's been or who he might have met.'

'He had a newspaper when he came back. Maybe that's all he went out for.'

Brian Delaney grasped at that. 'Maybe. I hope for your sake that it was.'

'And Clancy hasn't been out at all,' Peadar said encouragingly.

'You're sure of that?'

'Oh yes. He was there when I left and Tim told me he'd seen him at the window several times.'

'That's something, I suppose. For Christ's sake don't lose Larski again.'

'I won't.'

'You'd better not.'

'I said I wouldn't.'

'And I said you'd better not.'

But the Commander took the news with considerable calm. 'I don't think it matters, Brian. Not in the long run. I don't believe Mr Larski is a devious man. He's just trying to find out what actually happened to his brother. A reasonable quest, I would have thought. If I'm proved wrong we can always . . . well, ask him to come and see us, can we not?'

Delaney smiled at the Commander's question.

'Quite,' the Commander said. 'To tell the truth I'm more concerned about Declan and what *he's* up to for the moment. I suspect that he might be – what's the term? – might be misappropriating – that's it – misappropriating funds.'

'He'd never dare.'

'You think not?'

'I can't see him doing that. He'd never dare.'

The Commander shook his head. 'Greed, Brian, has a strange way of making even the most frightened man do very silly things.'

'But –'

'Oh I've no doubt he will have counted the risk and seen to it that he has a very plausible explanation. He's not a total fool. But he does fancy his chances, you know. He would very much like, you see, to be in control. Of everything.'

'Some chance.'

The Commander chuckled. 'He does actually *have* some chance. You'd be surprised how many people dislike me. Find me too –' The Commander chuckled again but this time there was an edge to it. 'You know what Fox said?

That I was too reasonable. Can you believe that? I wonder what Madam in number ten would think of that!'

Delaney braved a laugh.

'Of course, that's the trouble with so many of our young men. Impatience. They're not prepared to talk.'

'Neither is . . . Madam.'

'No. Well, you can understand her position. She's been saying "no dialogue" for so long that she now thinks it's law. But that doesn't stop *me* talking, does it? One thing I've learned, Brian: if you meet people and talk to them, you'll learn more that way than trying to force them to tell you something.' The Commander stroked the old red setter that had placed its head on his lap. 'Mind you,' he added with a wicked twinkle, 'it doesn't always work. Sometimes, alas, we do have to *encourage* people to talk. As you know.'

'What about Declan, then?'

'I'll speak to him when it's time. Not yet. I want a chat with Clancy first. He's not showing any signs of leaving?'

Delaney shook his head.

'Well then, as ever, it's a question of waiting.'

'For what, though?'

'Well, not for Godot, Brian.' The Commander smiled to himself and took to polishing his reading glasses on the hem of his pullover. 'It's my experience that if you wait long enough everything falls into place eventually. No point in rushing in and scattering the chickens. And here we have quite a flock of chickens, don't we? Chief Inspector Harwood *happens* to know a certain Douglas Parr, who *happens* to know Clancy, who *happens* to do us the odd favour through Declan Finch, who *happens* to be the one who delivers Kitty Doherty's remuneration, who *happens* – quite surprisingly – to be acting as landlady to Robert Larski. Now, you explain to me how such a string of coincidences can happen?'

'I can't.'

'No. Because there isn't an explanation. They aren't coincidences. So the only sensible way to find out what the connection is, is to wait. To speak to each one of those involved separately. Take them, shall we, say, by surprise.

Let *them* betray each other – which they will, believe me, although hopefully without knowing it, of course.'

'I hope you're right.'

'So do I, Brian. So do I.'

And he was certainly right about one thing: Declan Finch's greed, although he might have been surprised if he knew what form that greed took. It wasn't, indeed, power, as he suspected. Nor was it a longing to acquire the trappings of good living. It was simply an overwhelming desire to have money. Not to spend it; simply to have it. He was like someone who had been forced to scavenge during the war, someone who had now gone simple, someone who felt an ineluctable urge to hoard those things which were now freely available. For years he had been filching a little here, a little there, and secreting it. No one suspected him of this since his lifestyle was modest, well within any means he might reasonably be expected to have. And he might have been contented to continue thus had not Mr Clancy dangled the carrot of plenty before his eyes. Drugs: cannabis and cocaine. True, Finch had tried to resist the temptation, but even as he resisted he knew he would eventually give in. And Mr Clancy was persuasive. He had explained how foolproof his plan was. Douglas Parr would get the stuff across to him in Dublin – certainly no problem there – and he, Clancy, would deliver it, if not personally, at least under his expert supervision, to Belfast, where he, Finch, would deal with the distribution. Come now, he was a man of considerable perspicacity, was he not? A man with all the right contacts. And think of the rewards! Yes. True. But think of the risks. Think of what would happen if anyone discovered his trade. My dear chap, did he really think that Mr Clancy was so stupid not to have secured the – how should he put it? – the gratitude of enough police who would smooth things over in such an eventuality? Possibly. But Declan Finch wasn't thinking of the police. He was thinking of his colleagues. He was thinking of the Commander. He was thinking of what had happened to anyone who had been caught dealing in drugs. The idea of spending the rest of his life in a wheelchair did not appeal. Yet . . .

'I'm glad you've decided to be sensible, Declan,' Mr Clancy told him.

Declan Finch opened the buttons of his shirt and shoved the two packets of cocaine close to his skin. He rebuttoned his shirt, and straightened his tie. He looked at Clancy. Suddenly something had changed. He had always treated Clancy with mild contempt. He had regarded him as someone who did what he was told, someone who would not dare not do what he was told. But he hadn't disliked him. But as soon as he had accepted the drugs, Declan knew he hated the little fat man. He knew too that he would have no compunction about killing him if needs be. And Mr Clancy noticed the change. He let his eyelids droop and tightened his mouth. Without saying a word he let Declan Finch know that he, too, would be conscienceless when it came to defending his freedom. For the first time since they'd known each other they didn't shake hands at the conclusion of their business. Declan Finch left Kitty Doherty's without speaking. Mr Clancy went back to his crossword.

That exchange had taken place in the morning, and Mr Clancy had thought about leaving immediately. He had changed his mind, however. There was always the chance that Declan would change his mind also, and return the cocaine. Mr Clancy didn't think he would, but there was always that chance, and Mr Clancy didn't like leaving anything to chance. He decided to wait one more day. And now that day was almost over. He glared at the television. Wogan was talking to someone famous Mr Clancy had never heard of. A woman. An American. The mother of a film star who had been involved in something called *Rambo*. He heard someone come to the front door, and heard Kitty go to answer it. He heard the door close, and heard Kitty go upstairs. He heard her knock on Robert Larski's door. He heard them exchange a few words and Kitty come downstairs again. The woman had finished her stint and a group of pop singers, clouded in artificial smoke, were singing what sounded like '... but nothing ever changes'. Mr Clancy gave a little grunt.

Upstairs Robert Larski sat on his bed, the photographs spread out before him. Somehow the tragedy of Peter seemed greater now that it was multiplied. And the sight of those sockless feet struck him as particularly pathetic; the fact that his brother's head was covered as though he had been decapitated was more horrific. He shook himself into action. He took one of the pictures and wrote on the back:

> Jimmy, enclosed two pictures. Gruesome, I'm afraid. Please keep this one safe. The other – could you see to it that Major Temple – you remember him, no doubt – gets it. Just get it to him as it is. No covering note. Yours, Bob.

Then, on the photograph that was to go to Temple, he took a felt-tipped pen from his pocket and drew a circle round the dangling arm and another round the feet of the corpse. He put both photographs in one of the envelopes he had bought with the newspaper that morning. He addressed it to Jimmy Fermin care of his home. He addressed the third photograph to Gemma. The fourth he thought about for a while. On this he again circled the arm and the feet. He thought about encircling the head of the soldier who was looking at the body but decided against it. That would identify him too clearly as the sender. He wanted Colonel Cairns to get it and *think* he had sent it, but he didn't want him to be certain. Not yet. He addressed an envelope for this photograph too, ready for stamping and posting. The two remaining photographs he hid: one under the carpet in the corner, the other under the lining-paper of a drawer in the chest. And that was that. All he had to do now was wait. Like the Commander, like Mr Clancy, although he didn't know it, wait.

In London Brigadier Carlisle was in a good frame of mind. Things were going swimmingly at last. Or so he said. He said it to Major Temple after he had told him, 'Just spoken to Cairns on the phone. Seems to have handled everything well. Larski went to see him and the Colonel tells me he is confident he persuaded the young man that everything is above board.' That's when he added that he felt everything was going swimmingly.

Major Temple held his tongue. He decided he might as well let the Brigadier have his moment of swimming satisfaction. Besides, he could be wrong in thinking that everyone, including himself, was underestimating Robert Larski. He had seemed to agree with the Brigadier and then popped the embarrassing question about the clothing. He had seemed to agree with Temple himself and then –

'Cheer up, John,' the Brigadier was saying. 'It's supposed to be good news I gave you, you know.'

'I'm sure it is, sir,' Temple answered.

'Well, cheer up then.'

'I'm very cheerful, sir.'

'God, I'd hate to see you when you're depressed.' The Brigadier laughed extravagantly. His body shook with merriment. His face flushed. He looked a little drunk.

'It's just ... just that I don't think we should take Larski's apparent reactions for granted, sir. He has a way of *seeming* to be satisfied, and then ...' Major Temple shrugged and left Larski's possible attitudes in question.

'Colonel Cairns assured me –'

'And I'm sure he means it, sir. But ... I don't know. I just don't know.'

'There you are then: you don't know. You're just guessing. My Lord, Temple, you are a terrible pessimist.'

'You're probably right, sir.'

'Thank you for that, at least. Well, I'm off home. Got the Minister coming for dinner. *He'll* be pleased with my news at any rate.'

'I'm sure he will, sir.'

'See you in the morning, John.'

'Yes, sir.'

'Go out and enjoy yourself. Take that pretty wife of yours out for dinner.'

'I might do that, sir.'

'That's better.'

But Major Temple didn't take his pretty wife out for dinner. He ate beside her from a tray in front of the television. 'He's such a bloody old fool,' he said.

'For heaven's sake don't you dare tell him that,' Mrs Temple warned jokingly.

'I just might.'

'Then you won't have to quit. They'll boot you.' She glanced sideways at her husband. 'Are you still thinking of leaving?'

Major Temple blew air from his mouth. 'Thinking, yes. But that's about all. I keep wondering what the hell I could do if I did leave.'

'Oh John, there's any number of things you could do.'

'Name one.'

'Don't be silly. You know you could easily get another job.'

Major Temple sighed. 'Let's hope it doesn't come to that.'

'Maybe the Brigadier is right. Maybe you are being pessimistic.'

'Maybe. But you haven't met Larski.'

'I wish you'd tell me what it's *all* about. Just saying that there are complications about some soldier's death and that his brother is being a nuisance doesn't tell me much.'

'I can't tell you, love. Maybe I'll be able to one day.'

'Well, when you feel you can, you know I'll be ready to listen.'

'I know that.' He leaned across and kissed her.

Before nightfall Declan Finch had rid himself of the cocaine. It had been remarkably simple: no shortage of buyers, and most of them willing to pay over the odds. He had sold it in two lots, both to dealers in the Protestant areas. They had, of course, paid in cash. He sat alone in his kitchen fondling the money. There was the ghost of a smile on his lips. The radio played a lilting ditty; he knew it and hummed along. Yet there was something edgy about him, as though he were expecting something further of the night. When the phone rang he jumped to his feet and snatched at the receiver. 'Yes?'

'Declan?'

'Yes.'

'Can only be one of two. Legg or Hilliard. Both captains. Legg's the most likely one.'

'Thanks. I owe you.'

He put down the phone and walked slowly back to the kitchen. He wondered now why Clancy was so insistent that helping Larski had to be part of any deal. Clancy must owe someone a favour. A big favour. His supplier? Douglas Parr? Possible, although what the connection between Parr and Larski might be was anyone's guess. As he gathered up his money and stowed it away in a schoolboy's leather satchel, Finch found himself grinning as he wondered what Clancy would say if he knew that Parr had already put out feelers in Belfast, bypassing him. More to the point, what would he say if he knew that he, Declan Finch, had already arranged for an intermediary to contact Parr, and that he had received information that Parr would be interested, most interested, in a meet? Declan's grin widened as he thought about the possibility of cutting out Clancy, and the more he thought about it, the more the idea pleased him. Take the fucking, supercilious smile off his face, it would. Then the grin left *his* face. Parr had intimated that he would phone. But he hadn't. Maybe he would. Maybe he wouldn't. Declan didn't enjoy being left dangling. He carried the satchel up to his bedroom, and slept with it under his pillow.

FOURTEEN

Mr Clancy had ordered a taxi for ten o'clock. He was almost ready when it arrived. Obligingly, Mrs Doherty said she'd tell the driver he'd be down in a minute. Mr Clancy was therefore surprised when he stepped out of the front door to find not a taxi, but Brian Delaney waiting for him. He knew Delaney – not his name, but his face. And this morning there was a cold severity about that face that didn't please him; nor was he thrilled when Delaney told him curtly that he was 'wanted'.

If Mr Clancy was alarmed by the summoning, he didn't show it. He kept his round face impassive, and merely nodded. He had, of course, been 'wanted' before, but it had never been in such a perfunctory manner. He decided to treat it as a nuisance rather than something to be fearful of. He put his bag on the ground and looked at his watch. He tutted. 'I do have a train to catch,' he said.

'You'll catch it,' Brian Delaney told him. 'Or another one,' he added, and put Mr Clancy's bag into the back of the car. He stood back and waited for Mr Clancy to get in. When he did, he shut the door and got in beside the driver.

The journey didn't take long, no more than ten minutes, enough time, though, for Mr Clancy to consider his position. Clearly something was wrong, and for some few, terrible moments Mr Clancy wondered if Declan Finch had been caught with the merchandise; or if, perhaps, he had been devious enough to report the transaction, thereby putting himself in a good light and Mr Clancy in the mire.

That was possible but unlikely. It wasn't Finch's style. He would prefer profit to plaudits. As to his being caught red-handed – that too was a possibility. But Mr Clancy was confident he would have heard of any such action: he had enough contacts in Belfast who would have alerted him if only to ingratiate themselves, would do him a favour so that, at some future date, they could remind him of it and demand a favour in return.

Mr Clancy began to feel a bit better. He was, he knew, in a strong position. He knew a great deal about the various business arrangements of the IRA. He had negotiated many of their deals. It would be difficult for them to punish him too severely. They would need, above all, his silence. It did cross Mr Clancy's mind that there was a way for them to ensure his silence. A very definite way. But he preferred not to dwell on that for the moment. Anyway, he had no more time to think: the car slowed, swung left into a pleasant, tree-lined road, and stopped almost immediately.

The Commander was waiting. He was in the sitting-room of the house on the pleasant, tree-lined road, and the room was pleasant too. The curtains, however, were drawn tight. A single lamp in one corner gave a sobre, amber glow. The Commander, still wearing his overcoat, sat on a fragile-looking approximation of a Chippendale boudoir chair. He didn't look comfortable. He gave the impression that he wanted to get this business over and done with as quickly as possible. Behind him, almost in the shadows, stood two men. Because it was impossible to make out their features, they gave an air of menace to the otherwise cosy scene. Mr Clancy eyed the two men dolefully: Banquo's ghost squared, he thought absurdly.

The Commander came straight to the point. He didn't greet Mr Clancy apart from a brief nod of recognition. His voice was terse and cold, but he couched his questions in such a way that anyone not knowing him would be forgiven for thinking he regarded Mr Clancy highly, needing his help, yet at the same time giving him every chance to explain any inconsistencies of his own accord. 'It is a surprise to see you back in Belfast again so soon,' he said.

Mr Clancy spread his hands apologetically. 'Business,' he said. 'Always business. One takes advantage of situations. Alas, one has no control over when or where those situations will arise.'

'I'm sure. And this business . . . this pressing business?'

Mr Clancy feigned innocence. 'Why, looking after your interests, of course. Hasn't Declan told you? I am surprised.' He became very co-operative. 'The slot-machine business, the one-arm bandits,' he explained with a whimsical smile, 'is, shall we say, saturated. We need to expand. Into England, I thought. The Continent, perhaps.' His voice became dreamy as he extended his horizons. 'I needed Declan's – your – approval before even exploring such a possibility. As it happens, an opportunity has arisen, in Torquay. A quick decision was – is – vital. Hence . . .'

The Commander didn't look impressed. He didn't look unimpressed either, which was something. 'I see,' he said quietly. 'You are not, then, having any – shall we call them private deals? – with Declan?'

Mr Clancy was pleased with the way he managed to counter this slur. He looked shocked. 'Private? With Declan? Behind your back? Good heavens no.'

'You are quite, quite sure?'

'Oh quite sure.'

For several moments the Commander fixed his eyes on Mr Clancy, saying nothing. 'I need hardly tell you,' he said finally, the words unmistakably a threat. 'But since you say you have *not* –'

'I'm sure Declan would have told you if I had even broached the possibility of –'

The Commander stopped whatever there was a possibility of with a thin, dismissive smile. 'We do know about your other activities, Clancy. And you know we know. And you also know how we feel about them.'

For the first time Mr Clancy showed a hint of discomfort. He looked away from the Commander's gaze. In an odd way he felt a sort of remorse about his drug-dealing, but the profits he made soon overrode such qualms. It was, he comforted himself, a question simply of supply and demand: others demanded, he supplied. If he didn't, someone else would. Someone else would make the profits. And that would be a shame. Now he bowed his head as though humbly accepting the implied chastisement. Clearly Declan had not been caught or said anything as he feared. They were just eradicating their manic suspicions. He would soon be on his way. He jumped when the Commander asked, 'Why did you give Robert Larski Mrs Doherty's address?' That was something he hadn't expected. So all this had something to do with Larski. He decided his continued bluffing was the best course. 'Shouldn't I have?'

'It was – could have been – imprudent.'

'Oh dear. I didn't think.'

'Has Larski had any contact with Declan?'

Mr Clancy knew he had to be careful. 'I wouldn't think so. Not to my knowledge anyway.'

Again the Commander took to staring unblinkingly at him. Then, abruptly, he stood up. 'Eamonn, take Mr Clancy to the station,' he said to one of the two men behind him.

'Well, what do you think?' Brian Delaney asked when Mr Clancy was gone.

The Commander stood by the fireplace, his hands clasped behind his back. 'What do I think?' he repeated thoughtfully. 'I *think* he *wanted* Larski to stay at Kitty's, and I think Declan is part of the reason. I also *think* he is having some private dealings with Declan. But thinking isn't good enough, is it?'

'You want Declan in?'

'Should I?'

'Let me ferret about for a bit. See what turns up.'

The Commander nodded vaguely. 'What I can't understand is why Declan would be so stupid as to –' The Commander shook his head as if he weren't sure what he meant exactly.

'Let's see what I can come up with,' Brian Delaney said.

Almost as if he didn't hear him, the Commander went on, 'To tell the truth, Brian, I'm not too worried if Declan *is* up to something with Clancy – we can soon deal with that. I really want to know what the tie-in between Declan and Larski is. And there is a tie-in. I can feel it. And I can't fathom why Declan wants to keep that so secret.'

'Perhaps helping Larski – if he *is* helping him – is part of a trade-off.'

'For what?'

Brian Delaney shrugged. 'You never know with Declan.'

'Who would want him to help Larski?'

'Clancy?'

The Commander shook his head. 'Why should he? Doesn't make sense.'

'Not unless Clancy arranged it as a favour to someone else.'

'Who else would want Larski helped?'

Brian Delaney screwed his face into an attitude of concentration; it was falling into the lines of surrender when he suddenly brightened. 'Hey, what about – didn't you say Harwood was working on something else before he was sent over here. A drugs ring. That would tie in with Clancy.'

The Commander nodded slowly. 'Parr. That was the name he gave me. Douglas Parr.' His face clouded and he shook his head again. 'But why would this Parr want Larski helped?'

'Maybe *he* doesn't. Maybe he only agreed to do what he could to keep Harwood off his back.'

'And Harwood *would* want Larski given every assistance . . . Yes. Yes, that *could* be the connection. He did say that Parr had given Larski the name of a contact. That could have been Clancy.'

'It surely could.'

'I wonder. I wonder.' The Commander came to a decision. 'Brian, see if you can arrange another meeting with the Chief Inspector. Let him know it's urgent.'

'Right.'

'And do some serious digging on Declan.'

'I'll get Brophy on to that.'

The Commander was making his way to the door. 'And we're going to have to talk to Larski soon. Very soon.'

'Yes. Just tell me when and I'll get him in.'

'Not *just* yet. Harwood first. Then Declan, I think.'

'What do we do if Declan is up to something?'

The Commander gave him a baleful look, blinked once, and went to his car.

Chief Inspector Anthony Harwood was in England, however. He went back periodically to report on his progress, and to see his family, although this was viewed by his superiors as incidental. More precisely he was in London. He wanted to see Douglas Parr. He wanted information that he could trade. He took his wife with him, using her desire to shop as an excuse for going south.

Parr said, 'We really must stop meeting like this,' smiling broadly at his little joke.

'We shouldn't really be meeting at all.'

'No. It wouldn't be . . . eh, healthy for you if anyone spotted us together . . . socializing, as it were. Still, Brixton isn't the Bahamas exactly, is it? They can hardly say I treated you to any lavish holidays.'

'Funny.'

'I thought so.'

The pub was filled with lunchtime trade. There was the smell of shepherd's pie and lasagne. Pretty office girls picked delicately at salads. A gaggle of workmen in British Telecom uniforms gorged ploughman's lunches. Parr and Harwood stood at the bar, at one end, out of the way. 'I need something I can use. Something with clout,' Harwood said.

Parr remained impassive.

'I mean it. And I know you can give it to me. If you don't, I swear I'll have your guts for garters.'

Parr winced as though he felt himself being disembowelled. But 'Ask and you shall receive,' he said.

'Your contact in Dublin – who is he?'

Parr hesitated.

'Don't fuck me about,' Harwood told him.

'A Mr Clancy.'

'That's better. Now . . . he was to give Robert Larski a name in Belfast, wasn't he?'

Parr nodded.

'His name?'

Again Parr hesitated. He knew it was Declan Finch, but he also knew that he wanted Declan Finch for himself. However, more than that he needed to maintain his freedom to operate. Finch would be useless if he himself was banged up for fifty years or whatever they gave you now – quite apart from seizing all your assets. Douglas Parr thought about his lovely house, his lovely antiques, his lovely wife, his lovely mistress, his lovely boat in Bournemouth, his lovely bank balance in Lloyds. Declan Finch didn't stand a chance. 'I believe it's Finch,' Parr said. 'Declan Finch.'

Harwood pressed home his advantage. 'What do you know about him?'

'He's . . . he's ambitious. Avaricious, too. And dangerous, they tell me. He has . . .' Parr wondered if he was going too far, but took the plunge. 'He has allegiances.'

'To?'

'The IRA, I understand. But he's rather keen on lining his own pockets. Feathering his nest, as it were.'

'Go on.'

'How far does this go?'

'Not far.'

'How far?' Parr insisted.

'Me. Maybe one other.'

'It's the other that bothers me.'

'I'll cover you.'

'Guaranteed?'

'Guaranteed.'

'Well, Declan Finch wants to do business direct with me. He sees himself, I think, as a sort of godfather; Brando has gone to his head. Wants, I believe, to control the drugs market in Belfast.'

The Chief Inspector shook his head. 'You must be wrong. He'd never be into drugs if he's in the IRA. They wouldn't stand for it.'

'They don't, obviously, know.'

'Are you absolutely sure?'

'Absolutely. I'm supposed to phone him and set up – well, if not exactly our first deal, at least to discuss preliminary details.'

'When?'

'When what?'

'When are you supposed to phone?'

Parr smiled. 'Last week actually.'

'But you didn't. Why?'

'I'm not really all that keen. I like to stay healthy. Enjoy my ill-gotten gains, as you'd call them. A contretemps with those boys might not be all that good for my health.'

'And Finch is helping Larski to – what? – repay Clancy?'

Parr sighed. 'Not quite.' He took a deep breath. 'I'm trying to please you. Finch doesn't know about us – at least I hope not. *He* thinks Clancy owes me. So, when Clancy told him to help Larski, he agreed,' Parr explained. 'However,' he went on quickly as Harwood looked about to interrupt, 'it's not really Clancy he's interested in pleasing. It's me. He wants to impress me. Show me what a capable lad he is.'

'But doesn't he wonder what connection you could have with Larski?'

'No doubt he does. But he would never ask. We don't encourage questions.'

'I've noticed.'

'Except from our dear friends,' Parr said with a satanic leer.

'OK. Here's what you do. Phone him. Finch. Phone him and tell him you've decided to deal. Then pump him for anything he's done for Larski. Anything. Get every damn thing you can out of him.'

'Just like that, eh? And me? What do I get in return, *Chief* Inspector? The piper must be paid, must he not?'

'I'll say I investigated you and couldn't find sufficient evidence to prosecute.'

'That's very dishonest, you know.'

'This happens to be a lot more important than you. To me, anyway. And don't worry. I won't paint you lily-white. I'll make damn sure everyone knows I think you're a bastard. They'll put someone else on to you for sure.'

'Thank you so much,' Parr said. A small respite was better than none. 'Very well. I'll do what I can. Just for you, mind,' he agreed with an endearingly false look.

'Can you do it now? Today?'

'Tonight. We like to do our business at night.' Parr chuckled. 'You know why? It's tradition. The Mafia, good Catholic boys each and every one, liked doing their trade under cover of darkness so their Catholic God wouldn't notice.' He chuckled again. 'I'll call Finch tonight.'

'And let me know?'

'But instantly, Chief Inspector.'

'I'll be at home.'

'As will I.'

'And don't bugger me about.'

'Would I do such a thing?'

'Yes. Yes, you bloody well would if you thought you could get away with it.'

'But I wouldn't, would I? Get away with it?'

'You can bank on that.'

It was just on eight o'clock when the telephone rang in Declan Finch's house. 'Yes?'

'Mr Finch, please.'

'Speaking.'

'Douglas Parr.'

Declan felt his muscles tighten. He controlled himself. 'Yes.'

'I'm sorry not to have called you sooner. I was away.'

'That's all right.'

'I also had to do a little checking.'

'On me?' Declan tried to make his voice sound amused.

'Yes.'

'And?'

'You seem to be – how shall I put it? – suitable.'

Declan realized he had been holding his breath. He let it drift slowly from his lungs now. He clenched his fist when he heard Parr say, 'I think we should meet.'

'Ye-es.'

'You sound doubtful.'

'It could be tricky.'

'Life is tricky, Mr Finch. What's the problem?'

'Getting away just now. Me. It could be difficult.'

'It doesn't have to be just now. I *have* managed without you up until now. No doubt I can manage a little longer.' Douglas Parr paused, his eyes sparkling. 'You can let Mr Clancy know when you're ready,' he said mischievously.

'No! No. No, I don't think that's a good idea.'

'Why ever not?'

'The fewer people who know about this the better.'

'Ah, yes. Yes, of course you're right. Very wise.'

Declan relaxed. 'Is there any way I can contact you direct?' Douglas Parr ignored the question. 'Supposing I phone you again in – when? A week? Ten days? A month? When do you think your difficulty will be resolved?'

'Ten days. Ten days will be fine.'

'Good. In ten days then. Now tell me, have you been able to help my friend Mr Larski?'

'I think I have.' Declan sounded delighted.

'Excellent.' Douglas Parr sounded delighted too. 'In what way?'

'He thinks he's found one of the people responsible for – you know – for . . .'

'Yes. I know.'

'I think I was able to put a name on that person for him.'

'That really *is* excellent, Mr Finch,' Parr told him effusively. 'I *am* pleased.' And without altering his tone he asked, 'And the name?'

'Legg. He's a captain.'

'Legg. I see. Have you told Robert – Larski?'

'Not yet. Haven't had a chance.'

'But you will, of course?'

'If you want me to.'

'Indeed I do, Mr Finch. Indeed I do. And as soon as possible.'

'I'll tell him first thing in the morning.'

'That would be kind. I really am most pleasantly surprised with your abilities, Mr Finch. Most pleasantly surprised.'

Declan glowed. 'It was nothing.'

'It was a great deal,' Parr corrected. 'It means a lot to me to be able to help friends in need. You'll find that out, Mr Finch. If we can't help our friends, who can we help?'

'Yes,' Declan agreed.

'Well, I'll get back to you in about ten days – all things being equal, that is.'

'Fine. Thank you.'

'I thank you, Mr Finch.'

For a few minutes Douglas Parr hesitated before calling the Chief Inspector. Intuitively he was wondering if he could barter the name of Legg to better effect. For the moment he could not think of any such way. In any case, he could always use the information again, later, if the occasion arose. It crossed his mind that undoubtedly Declan Finch's superiors would be interested, but that would mean – he gave a small shudder as the prospect of having to deal with those thugs in their ridiculous hoods and paramilitary gear loomed into his mind. Perhaps it wasn't such a good idea. Not unless things got desperate. And things could get desperate. To stop himself feeling desperate at that moment he dialled the Chief Inspector's number.

'Hello sweetheart,' he said when he heard Harwood's voice, and grinned at the growl that met his greeting.

'Oh, hello,' Harwood said curtly.

'That's not very friendly.'

'I choose my friends carefully.'

'Oh, touchy, are we?'

Harwood relented. 'Not really. Tired.'

'Well, here's something to send the sandman packing. A name. The one you wanted, I think. Captain Legg. Got that?'

'Captain Legg,' Harwood repeated.

'Seems he's the one Larski suspects of being involved. Any use?'

'Great.'

'I'm so pleased. When do you go back to the badlands?'

'Tomorrow.'

'That's a relief. I'll get some peace then.'

'All the peace you want. Thanks.'

'Anytime – no, I take that back. When you've something to offer in return.'

'You've a big heart, Parr.'

'Just be glad I've got one at all.'

Declan Finch changed his mind. He was so elated with Douglas Parr's phone call that he couldn't relax. He decided to go immediately to Kitty Doherty's and tell Robert Larski of the name he had secured. He knew he was taking a chance. With Clancy gone he had no real excuse for being there. But such was his excitement at the prospect of collaborating with Douglas Parr that he foolishly threw caution to the wind. He did, however, take the precaution of parking his car some way from the house and finishing the trip on foot. Kitty Doherty opened the door. 'Mr Finch,' she said. 'This is a surprise.'

'Is Larski in?'

'Why, yes. Up in his room. Will I get him?'

'Please.'

Kitty made her way to the stairs. Then she came back. 'Mr Finch. I don't know if it means anything, but you know Mr Delaney?'

'Yes.'

'Well, he's been watching this house. Him and some other men.'

Declan Finch felt suddenly cold. 'You're sure?'

'Oh yes. And they took Mr Clancy away.'

'What do you mean – away?'

'They were waiting for him just as he was about to get a taxi for the station. They took him away.'

Declan needed time to think. He mustn't panic. Maybe it was nothing.

'Get Larski for me, will you.'

Waiting, he paced up and down the hall. Shit! Just when everything was falling into place for him, just when he was on the point of –

'You wanted me?'

'–? Oh, yes. That soldier you described. His name is probably Legg. Captain Legg.'

'I see . . . Legg.'

'Yeah. I thought you'd better know.'

'Thanks. It really means a lot.'

'Good,' Declan said, but he didn't sound enthusiastic. Then a thought struck him. 'Don't forget, you owe me,' he said.

'OK.' Robert looked surprised, not at the statement so much, but at the way it was put, as though Declan Finch fully expected to call on him for payment. 'OK,' he said again.

Declan nodded.

'Just let me know.'

'I'll do that.'

On his way back upstairs Robert wondered at Finch's attitude. Then he dismissed it with a shrug. He went into his room and shut the door. He retrieved the photograph from under the lining of the drawer. He drew an arrow on it, complete with feathers, pointing to Captain Legg. He shoved it in an envelope and addressed it to the Captain. It struck him as particularly opportune that the Colonel should get his photograph tomorrow, and Legg get his the day after.

FIFTEEN

Colonel Cairns did receive his copy of the photograph the next morning. It was waiting on his desk when he got to his office along with the rest of his mail. The Colonel was meticulous about his letters, preferring to open them all himself rather than have them sorted and only those that were considered important delivered for his attention. Normally he opened his letters in order, as they came to hand, starting at the top and working his way down through the pile, but there was something about the thick printing in felt-tip that Robert had used which caught the Colonel's eye. Besides, he had two weeks' leave due to him when this tour of duty was over, and he was expecting a brochure telling him of the delights of Morocco, where he planned to spend some of that leave with his wife. He would have preferred, say, Crete or Rhodes, but Mrs Cairns had set her heart on North Africa, and he had bowed to her choice. The rain pelted down against the window of his office, and he drew the envelope towards him, thinking that perhaps the sight of some sunny Moroccan scenes would cheer him up. He slit open the envelope with a small Toledo dagger, and took out the photograph. He froze. He felt his stomach heave. He stared at the two circles and small beads of perspiration oozed on to his forehead as he became aware of the significance of the limbs within them. Only after some moments did he recognize Captain Legg, and his hands started to shake. He put the photograph on his desk, an elbow either side, and propped his face in his hands, staring at it, mesmerized. Slowly, he began to wonder who had sent it. He grabbed the envelope and studied the postmark, turned it over and gazed at the back for some clue. Getting none, he tossed it aside, and returned to the photograph. It must be Larski who sent it. It must! And yet . . . wouldn't Larski have encircled the Captain also? Surely that was of equal significance to the corpse's limbs? And how would Larski get such a photograph? He shook his head in bewilderment. But if it wasn't Larski – who then? He thought about summoning Captain Legg, but decided against it. What would be the point? Probably frighten the wits out of him and make him panic, and the last thing the Colonel wanted just now was anyone to panic. Yet only Legg might know who had taken the photograph, and if the Colonel knew who *that* was, perhaps . . . perhaps it would lead to – unless the photographer himself sent it? But why? Or someone more sinister – someone into whose hands the photograph had fallen? The terrorists? That prospect was too appalling for him to even consider at the moment. He reached for his intercom and ordered that Captain Legg be told to report immediately.

The Colonel went to the window and stared out, down and about him. The Brigadier would have to be told, and that was something the Colonel didn't relish. And the RUC – the Chief Constable, should he be made aware of what had happened? The Colonel didn't relish that either, but it was probably inevitable. However, what he said to Captain Legg was more pressing. He could hear footsteps approaching on the linoleum of the hall. He'd better decide. He would not mention the photograph. He would – he didn't know what he would say. 'Come,' he said in answer to the knock on his door, moving quickly back to his desk and sliding the envelope and the photograph into a drawer. 'Ah, Captain. Come in,' he said, relieved by how calm and unfussed he sounded. 'Relax, relax,' he added, managing a small smile. 'It's nothing important. Just something I wanted to ask.' The Captain relaxed.

'Everything all right?' the Colonel inquired.

'Thank you, sir.'

'Good. I'll wager you'll be glad when this tour is over. As, indeed, will I.'

'Yes, sir.'

'Of course. Not too long now, eh?'

'No, sir.'

'No . . .'

The Colonel was aware he was beating about the bush, aware too that a nervousness was again creeping into the Captain's eyes. He decided he'd better get on with it. 'What I wanted to ask – you remember when your patrol went to collect Captain Larski's body?' He asked the question almost brutally, wanting to make it sound matter-of-fact.

The Captain nodded. 'Sir?'

'Eh . . . can you recall if a proper record was kept of that recovery?'

'Record, sir?'

'Yes. You know the sort of thing. What we normally have in such circumstances. Photographs – that sort of thing.'

'I don't think so, sir.'

'Oh. Pity.' Colonel Cairns sounded sincere.

'No – wait, sir. There was a photographer.'

'Oh?'

'I don't think he got anything, though, sir. I remember there was a bit of an argument. He wanted to take pictures but the RUC wouldn't let him.'

'The RUC. I see.' He sighed. 'They do like to interfere, don't they? Always afraid we're out to usurp their power. Forgetting, of course, if they'd done their job correctly in the first place we wouldn't be here.'

'Yes, sir.'

'Well, thank you, Legg. That's all.'

Alone, the Colonel felt pleased with the way he had handled things. If everything else went as smoothly . . . The Brigadier's florid face loomed into his consciousness. The Chief Constable's, also. He decided to deal with what he considered the small fry first. 'Get hold of the Chief Constable for me,' he said into his intercom. 'Tell him I'd like to drop over and see him. No – tell him I *am* coming over to see him.'

Colonel Cairns took the photograph from the drawer

and looked at it again, but briefly. It did his blood pressure no good whatever to dwell on it. He folded it and shoved it into his inside pocket. The phone on his desk rang. 'Yes?'

'The Chief Constable's expecting you, sir.'

'Right. I'm leaving now.'

The Chief Constable was waiting. He had chosen to see the Colonel in the spacious room where he presided over internal meetings of import. He had seated himself at one end of the large, boardroom-style mahogany table. Only one other chair was actually at the table, and that was at the far end; the other chairs were pushed back against the wall. It was as though the Chief Constable figured that by keeping the Colonel at a reasonable physical distance he could keep him at an intellectual remove also.

Colonel Cairns eyed the long expanse between the two chairs. He walked directly to the Chief Constable and placed the photograph on the table in front of him before making for his chair and sitting down. He smiled inwardly at the Chief Constable's obvious discomfort – he certainly wouldn't want to be shouting any questions about that! He remained silent and impassive, waiting for the Chief Constable to speak first. He watched him carefully as he studied the picture. He saw the jaws tighten, the jowls go a deeper purple. He saw him open his mouth to speak. Watched him close it again. And he got untold pleasure as the Chief Constable rose and grabbed the chair by its back rail and dragged it behind him the length of the table, setting it upright close to the Colonel and sitting down.

'When did you get this?' he asked.

'This morning.'

'Any message?'

The Colonel shook his head. 'That's just how it came.'

'The sender?'

The Colonel gave a small, derisive snort. 'Possibly Larski.'

'*He* couldn't have taken it, though.'

'No. Some photographer *before* your men managed to stop him.'

'My men?'

'That's what I'm told.'

'Can you leave me to deal with this?' the Chief Constable asked, and hated himself for asking, hating himself for being in a position where he considered it necessary.

'I'll have to inform . . . inform . . . my superiors.'

'I need twenty-four hours.'

Colonel Cairns considered this. Perhaps he could delay telling the Brigadier for one day: that certainly *appealed* to him. And, of course, if that slimy bastard sitting beside him *did* come up with something, did, even, get his hands on some information that would pacify the Brigadier and stop him being a bloody nuisance – well, that appealed even more.

'Very well.'

'Good.' The Chief Constable sounded brisk and efficient of a sudden, like a man who already had a plan and was confident he could execute it without fuss or fear of failure.

'Twenty-four hours only, mind.'

'That's what I asked for.'

'That's all you'll get.' Colonel Cairns narrowed his eyes. He tried a shot in the dark. 'You know who that photographer was, don't you?'

The Chief Constable shrugged.

'You think you can make him tell you who he gave that to, don't you?' The Colonel indicated the picture in the Chief Constable's hands.

The Chief Constable pushed the photograph across the table, and allowed himself a tiny smirk.

'I'll need any information you get,' said the Colonel.

'Of course.'

'All of it.'

'We always co-operate.'

'Yes,' the Colonel said dubiously. 'And not later than this time tomorrow.'

The Chief Constable nodded.

'And let's not do anything that might have . . . repercussions?'

*

Two hours later the Chief Constable stood alone in his office, staring out of the window. He had been busy since his meeting with Colonel Cairns, and he now waited to hear if his efforts had borne fruit. He swung round as someone tapped on his door. 'Ah, Malcolm.'

'Sorry to have been so long. It took some organizing.'

The Chief Constable appeared to be waiting for something more.

'Anyway, I managed to get hold of the men we wanted.'

The muscles in the Chief Constable's face relaxed.

'It wasn't easy, I can tell you. Not at such short notice.'

'But you succeeded?'

'Oh yes. They'll be here' – he glanced at his watch – 'inside an hour.'

'You made it clear –'

'Yes. I made it clear,' Malcolm interrupted. 'No cock-ups, and if there are they're on their own. Nothing to do with us.'

'They understood that, I hope.'

'Very clearly.'

'All we need is for someone to get wind of this and we're rightly up the proverbial creek.'

'No one will know. Ever.'

'I sincerely hope not.'

At a quarter to seven, when there was a lull in the traffic between those returning home from the city after work and those on their way into it for entertainment, two unmarked cars left Castlereagh police station. One, a Sierra, was maroon; the other, a Vauxhall, was dark brown but looked black in the artificial light of the street lamps and neon signs. There were four men in each. They wore casual, almost sporty clothes. They all looked relaxed. In the Sierra someone might have cracked a joke since all the men were smiling, one, indeed, laughing, his head thrown back. In the Vauxhall, although more serious, the men chatted amiably. They looked as if they might very well be out for entertainment.

The two cars kept close together for about a mile, the

Sierra leading. Then, at the roundabout, the driver of the Vauxhall flashed his lights once, took the first exit, and gathered speed as the car headed off.

Sammy Meagher was working late. He had covered a wedding that afternoon. He didn't care much for weddings, but they paid well, paid most of the bills, and with a wife and three kids to support that was something to be grateful for with things the way they were. He examined the reels of negatives hanging in front of him, trying to find one that didn't show the bride looking as if she were frozen.

Sammy's darkroom was behind the house, separated from it by the length of the small garden. It had been the garage before he converted it. It suited him nicely. An alley ran along the boundary of the garden and he could nip in and out of the darkroom through the small wooden gate without disturbing the household. Sometimes he would get so involved in his work it would be daylight before he emerged. But not this evening. This evening he had promised to take his wife out for a drink and maybe something to eat. His mother was going to babysit. She was already there on duty. He had seen her car parked in front of the house as he came home. He hadn't gone into the house on his return, but went straight to the darkroom. He wanted to get the wedding photographs developed before going out, and there would possibly have been an argument had his wife been aware he was home. She would surely have complained, as she always did, that he loved his work more than he did her. But now he had done all that he had wanted to do and could face her with equanimity, perhaps even lying that he had prints to make but would leave them until the morning.

He switched out the light and left the darkroom, locking the door behind him. The rain had stopped. It was a cold, bright, clear night. Christmassy weather, he thought. He sniffed the air. He lit a cigarette. That was something else his wife disapproved of, so he smoked surreptitiously. He thought he heard a noise in the alley and cocked his head. Nothing. A dog, probably. The number of strays seemed to be on the increase. They came out at night, like their wild ancestors, to scavenge. And this was before Christmas, before the discarded four-pawed presents had been tossed out into the streets. Ah well. He decided to check the gate, to make sure he had bolted it. Then he opened it to take a peep outside. As soon as he had, he was grabbed. His arms were wrenched behind his back, a hand clamped over his mouth. Before he knew what was happening, he was being frog-marched back up the alley. Somebody was searching him. His keys were taken. He was thrown into the back of a car. For a moment it struck him that it could be his own car. It was certainly a Sierra. Then a cloth sack was put over his head and he was pushed to the floor.

When the car had driven off, the two men who had manhandled him into the car walked quietly back down the alley. They went into the garden and paused, staring at the windows of the house for a while. Then one opened the darkroom door and both slipped in.

'He's always the same,' Mrs Meagher complained. 'He's the most unpunctual man I've ever known.'

'Never could keep time, our Sammy,' Sammy's mother agreed.

At about the same time a dark brown Vauxhall that looked black in the artificial light of the street lamps moved up Agnes Street. It slowed outside Kitty Doherty's house, looked as if it were about to stop, but then drove on again, turned right and disappeared. From his car, parked on the opposite side of the road, Brian Delaney watched it. 'See that?' he asked Peadar Mackie.

'Yep.'

'Recognize it?'

'Uh-huh.' Mackie shook his head.

Behind them the Vauxhall turned into Agnes Street again. The headlights had been dimmed. Only the sidelights glowed yellowish. Peadar spotted it in the mirror. 'Here it comes again.'

'Get ready,' Brian told him.

'I'm ready.'

The Vauxhall drew level with Kitty Doherty's house. It pulled into the kerb and stopped, its engine ticking over. Both back doors opened and two men stepped out. They were burly men, each wearing a zip-up windcheater. One of them had unzipped his to halfway. He had a hand inside it. 'Go!' Brian Delaney hissed.

Instantly Peadar Mackie switched on his headlights fully and started the engine, gunning it fiercely. He shoved the car into gear, swung from the kerb and then braked immediately. The two men hesitated, and then, as if in response to an order, dived back into the Vauxhall. Before they had closed the doors, they were being driven away, the car lurching and swaying, its tyres screaming as it turned off Agnes Street.

Peadar Mackie gave a hoarse, sinister chuckle, and reversed the car back into the parking space. 'That frightened the shit out of someone,' he said, and switched off the engine.

'Yeah,' Brian Delaney agreed. 'But who the hell were they?'

Peadar switched off the headlights.

'And what the fuck did they want at Kitty's?'

At half past nine Mrs Meagher came out of the house and walked down the garden to her husband's darkroom, swearing to herself that she'd throttle him if she found him working there. The light was on and shone out into the garden through the open door. That struck her as odd, but she was so annoyed with Sammy she didn't give it much thought. When she came to the door and looked inside her hands shot to her face in dismay. The room had been ransacked. The workbench was overturned, bottles smashed, the white plastic trays Sammy used strewn everywhere. The filing cabinet where he kept his files and negatives lay on its side, the drawers, all empty, stacked haphazardly beside it. She gave a tiny scream and hurried back to the house. 'Something's happened to Sammy,' she cried. Sammy's mother gaped at her uncomprehendingly.

'Someone's turned his darkroom upside down.'

Still Sammy's mother stared.

'Well, *say* something,' Mrs Meagher shouted unreasonably. When there was still no answer she went to phone the RUC.

Just after midnight a maroon Sierra moved swiftly through the city. There were only two men in it: the driver and someone beside him. They didn't speak. When they came to the outskirts, the driver looked at his companion and raised his eyebrows questioningly. He got a nodded, silent reply. He stopped the car. The two men got out and went round to the boot. The passenger opened it. Between them they lifted Sammy Meagher's body from it and dumped it into a ditch. They rubbed their hands together as if removing dust from their fingers. Then they got back into the car and drove off.

The car didn't return to Castlereagh. It went directly to Andersonstown. It stopped outside a neat, two-storey semi-detached house that had lace curtains and a door-knocker in the shape of a lucky horseshoe. A little further up the road, on the opposite side, a brown Vauxhall that looked black in the artificial light was parked. The two men got out of the Sierra and glanced at it. They looked relieved to see it there. They nodded to each other, and then shook hands. One of them went up the path into the house with lace curtains and horseshoe knocker. The other turned up the collar of his anorak, shoved his hands in his pockets, and walked away.

Colonel Cairns did not hear the seven a.m. news. He was up and the radio was on, but he was shaving and the whirr of his electric razor obliterated the newscaster's words.

The Chief Constable of the RUC did hear it. He made sure he did. The voice intoned: 'The security forces found the body of a man on the outskirts of Belfast in the early hours of this morning. He had been shot. His identity has not yet been released. A spokeman for the RUC said it was not believed to be a sectarian killing.'

The Chief Constable looked satisfied. Short and to the

point. No frills. Open and shut. Just the way he liked things.

By eight a.m. there was a little more information: 'The man found shot dead in the early hours of this morning has been identified as Samuel Meagher, a freelance photographer. A spokesman for the RUC revealed that earlier yesterday evening his home had been broken into and a quantity of valuables stolen. Mr Meagher's death is being treated as murder with robbery as the motive.'

The matter was never mentioned again. At no time was it disclosed that Sammy's lungs were filled with urine, nor that the fingers on one hand had been broken.

When Jimmy Fermin opened the large brown envelope and took out the photographs, it didn't register immediately what they meant. Then he read Robert's message on the back. He leaned back in his chair and put his feet up on his desk, staring at one of the pictures, holding it a little way from him as though by so doing he would get a wider view. Slowly he blew through his lips in a thin whistle. '*Jee*-sus Christ,' he swore. 'Jesus *Christ*!'

After he had breakfast the Chief Constable was driven to TAC HQ. There was a lightness to his step as he entered Colonel Cairns's office. He would enjoy telling the Colonel that the twenty-four hours he had requested had been quite ample. In the end he didn't bother to mention it. 'You were right, Colonel. It was Larski who got the copies. It must therefore have been him who sent one to you.'

Grudgingly, the Colonel was impressed. 'How did you find that out?'

'The photographer was questioned.'

'So you *did* know who he was.'

'That's my job.'

'And Larski? Have you questioned him?'

For a second the Chief Constable looked uneasy. 'No,' he admitted finally.

'Why not? I would have thought –'

'It wasn't possible.'

'Oh?'

The Chief Constable tried to ride out the silence that followed, but something in the Colonel's attitude made it clear he was prepared to wait all day if necessary. 'We did . . . did attempt to bring him in for questioning but . . .' Perhaps that would be enough? No. Still the Colonel remained silent, staring stonily. 'But he was being guarded.'

That brought the Colonel to life. 'Guarded?' he asked, amazed. 'By whom for heaven's sake?'

'We're not sure.'

'Didn't you challenge them?'

'Well, no. You see . . . Colonel, the men who we asked to help us in this matter were not – it wouldn't have – a confrontation would not have been appropriate.'

'You didn't use your own men?' The Colonel was clearly getting to like this less.

'No. Not exactly. There are times when it is more . . . more efficient to use outside agencies. This was one of those times.' And having gone that far the Chief Constable felt he might as well go further. 'When the time is right we will question him of course.'

Colonel Cairns felt that things were slipping dangerously out of his control. In an effort to redress this, he said, 'The photographer. I want to question him myself.'

The Chief Constable hadn't expected that. He remained calm and impassive, however. He pursed his lips, and then said, 'I'm afraid that won't be possible, Colonel.'

'And why not?

'He's dead.'

'He's . . .' the Colonel began and then his jaw sagged.

'Nothing to do with us,' the Chief Constable put in quickly. 'A burglary at his home. He must have resisted. He was found shot,' he explained.

'A coincidence, I suppose?' the Colonel said sarcastically.

'Exactly. An unfortunate coincidence.'

Surprisingly, the Colonel looked as if he were about to accept what the Chief Constable had said as the truth, but suddenly he frowned. 'Negatives,' he said to himself. Then to the Chief Constable, 'Negatives. There must have been negatives.'

'Yes.'

'Where are they? Do you know?'

'Yes. He – the photographer – gave them to us before we released him.'

The Colonel's body slumped with relief. 'Good,' he said, 'That's a relief anyway. You'll let me have them?'

The Chief Constable shook his head. 'We destroyed them. We thought that better. Once destroyed they can *never* turn up again in *anyone's* hands,' he said.

Colonel Cairns nodded. There wasn't, it struck him, much else he could do under the circumstances. And there was precious little he could do, either, to calm Captain Legg.

The Chief Constable had only just left when the Captain had come unannounced into the Colonel's office and placed his copy of the photograph on the desk, all the while babbling. The Colonel couldn't understand what he was saying. He stormed across the office and slammed the door shut. 'Pull yourself together, man,' he said as loudly as he dared. 'Pull yourself together. Where did you get that?'

'It came in the post this morning, sir,' the Captain moaned, but trying hard to pull himself together.

'You brought it straight here? To me? You showed no one?'

'Yes, sir. No, sir.'

The Colonel exploded. 'What do you mean, Captain – yes, sir, no, sir?'

'I mean I brought it straight to you, sir, and didn't show it to anyone.'

The Colonel returned to his desk.

'What does it mean, sir?' Captain Legg pleaded.

'Nothing, Captain. That's what it means: nothing. I already knew about this picture. It means nothing.'

The Captain looked bewildered. 'Nothing, sir?'

'Nothing for you to bother your head about. I have everything under control. You can forget you ever got this.'

Perhaps because this was what he wanted to hear, or perhaps because he was so numbed by the terror of what he had let himself in for, Captain Legg meekly agreed. He said, 'Yes, sir. Thank you, sir,' and left the room.

When he was certain the Captain was out of earshot, Colonel Cairns slammed his fist on to the photograph on his desk. It was bad enough having to tell the Brigadier that he himself had got one, but if he had to say that Legg got one also – but perhaps he wouldn't have to mention that. What was the need? But he would certainly have to tell the Brigadier about his own copy, and the sooner the better. A finger reached towards the intercom. No. He'd wait a while. A couple of hours. Give the Brigadier time to settle into the day. Then he'd tell him. *How* he'd tell him he didn't yet know, but he'd think of some way of easing him into it.

He needn't have bothered. Brigadier Carlisle already knew. He was, at that very moment, staring aghast at the print that Major Temple had handed him. For once he was at a loss for something to say. Watching him, Temple recalled having once described his mother-in-law's expression as being like that of a goldfish when she heard she was to be a grandmother: her mouth rounded and remained open but with a curious sucking motion to the lips, while her eyes bulged. And that, to Major Temple, was how the Brigadier looked now: like a goldfish, although, in his case, a carp.

When he finally got over the shock, however, the Brigadier remained remarkably calm under the circumstances. 'You can guess who sent you this, can't you?'

'Yes. Robert Larski.'

The Brigadier nodded. 'I'm afraid I underestimated him. You said I did, didn't you, John?'

Major Temple didn't reply. He couldn't for the life of him understand why, but he was feeling almost sorry for his superior. But not for long.

'Well, it seems you were right,' the Brigadier continued. He rose, and handed the photograph back to the Major, appearing glad to be rid of it. He walked the length of the large office and back again. 'John, I want you to do something. I'll clear it. I want you to go to Belfast and talk to Colonel Cairns. See if something can't be done about Larski.' He paused and flicked something from the side of his nose with his little finger.

'See if we can't reason with him,' he continued.

'It's a bit late for that, isn't it, sir? We should have done that when he –'

'Yes, yes, yes. I *know* you said we should do that too, Major,' he said with some of his old belligerence. 'But that was when he was *here*. Over there' – he waved a hand vaguely – 'over *there* it is different. Over there if he remains obstinate . . .' The Brigadier paused again, taking time to study the Major's face to ascertain some reaction. There wasn't any, none that was decipherable, anyway. And then, meaning only to think it, or perhaps forgetting for the moment that he was not alone, the Brigadier said under his breath, 'Over there something can be done about it.'

At the sound of his own voice, however, he winced. He was pleased to see that the Major, apparently, had not overheard his remark. 'Will you do that, John? I won't order you to. I'm asking.'

Brigadier Carlisle felt a great weight lifted from him when he heard the Major answer, 'Yes, sir. Yes, I'll do that.' He was so relieved that he failed to notice the tone in which the answer was made, failed to notice the curious look of hatred that came to the Major's eyes. 'Good,' he said brusquely. 'As soon as is possible, eh?'

'I've made up my mind,' Major Temple told his wife quietly.

'You're going to quit, aren't you?'

The Major nodded. 'I've got to go away for a day. Two at most. When I get back I'll resign.'

His wife smiled, and put her arms about his neck. 'Good,' she said. 'It'll be so nice to have you to myself again.' She was hurt and saddened to see her husband was crying.

*

And at about the same time as Major Temple was telling his wife of his decision to resign, Brian Delaney was just completing his account of what had happened outside Kitty Doherty's the night before.

'And you're quite sure they weren't security forces?' the Commander asked.

'Quite sure. I've sent an extra man down to watch the front, and put two more round the back.'

The Commander shook his head. 'No, Brian. Not good enough, I think. We'll have to move Mr Larski.'

'He mightn't want to move.'

'I mean to move him whether he wants to or not. Clearly he's done something. Or said something. Or found out something. Something that has made someone panic.'

'I keep thinking it's got something to do with Sammy Meagher,' Brian said. 'I mean, Peadar saw Sammy hanging about outside Kitty's and now he turns up dead in a ditch.'

The Commander was suddenly alert. 'Go on.'

'Well, that business about his house being broken into is all bullshit. It wasn't. His darkroom was broken into and looked like a cyclone had hit it. Someone was after something specific. There wasn't a print or a negative left in the place. Nothing else was taken.'

The Commander spoke slowly. 'So, what could Sammy have had that would, a, be of interest to Larski, and, b, be of such importance that he had to be killed?'

'A photograph?' Brian suggested.

The Commander made a small sound of annoyance. 'Of course a photograph, Brian. But of what?'

Brian Delaney shrugged his ignorance. 'Christ knows.'

The Commander took the time to fill his pipe and light it. 'Is Harwood back in Belfast yet?' he asked out of the blue.

'I . . . I'll find out.'

The Commander nodded. 'Do that, Brian. Do it now, would you?'

'Right away. What about Larski? Do we move him?'

'Can you assure me he's safe?'

'Should be. For a while.'

'I'd prefer to leave him where he is – just to see if anything else happens. But I *need* him, Brian. I don't want anything untoward to befall him.'

'Why don't you have him in and talk to him?'

'I've thought about that.'

Brian Delaney waited.

'I'm not sure the timing is right, that's all. I don't want him to know we're interested just yet,' the Commander explained. Then, 'What do you think?' he asked.

'I'd have him in now. I think we're running out of time.'

The Commander puffed on his pipe. He respected Brian Delaney's opinions. If Brian felt time was, indeed, running out, his instinct had to bc considered.

'I wanted a word with Harwood first.'

'He'll wait,' Brian said. 'He *can* wait. I'm not so sure Larski can.'

The Commander made up his mind. 'Very well.' Then, surprisingly, something amusing seemed to strike him. 'What,' he asked, 'what if we got Declan Finch to bring Larski in?'

'Oh shit,' Brian said, grinning. Then the grin vanished. 'No. You need to get Larski before Declan's had a chance to say anything to him. Warn him in any way.'

'You think Larski knows who Declan is?'

'Wouldn't be surprised. Put two and two together and he'd get Declan, wouldn't he?'

The Commander smiled.

'Besides, I don't think it matters a damn to Larski who or what anyone is as long as he finds out what he wants to know.'

'And he appears to be doing just that,' the Commander observed.

'He surely does.'

'All right, Brian. First find out if Harwood is back. Try and arrange a meeting for tonight. I'll see Larski this afternoon. In Ballymurphy. And talk to Kitty. Frighten her if you have to. I want to know what Declan has been up to in that house. Let me know *that* before I see Larski, please.'

'Right. And Declan?'

'Ah, Declan. Yes. When we know everything, we'll deal with Declan.'

'Right.'

The Commander waited until Brian was at the door. 'Brian – I think some insurance is advisable. Just in case. Larski. That woman who's been helping him. In London. Perhaps you would arrange that she's visited at the time we speak to Larski.'

SIXTEEN

Robert Larski was beginning to wonder if *anything* was going to happen. He knew nothing about the incident of the night before, nothing of Sammy Meagher's murder. Declan Finch hadn't contacted him again. He wondered what he would do if nothing *did* happen. It crossed his mind that perhaps neither Colonel Cairns nor Captain Legg associated him with the photographs. Perhaps he had been just a bit too smart. He took the one remaining copy of the photograph from under the carpet and looked at it again. He traced a finger along his brother's body. Then he folded the picture and put it in the inside pocket of his jacket. Then he threw himself on his bed. It was three o'clock. He felt tired. Kitty Doherty's cooking brought a sense of laziness as well as of nourishment. He would stay there until five. Then, if nothing had happened, he would have to have a rethink.

It was just after three when Brian Delaney arrived outside Kitty's house. He had parked his car up the street and walked down to the Volvo in which Peadar Mackie and Brendan Quirk were parked. Brendan rolled down the window, and Brian leaned in and spoke to them. Both men nodded. Brendan Quirk got out of the car and accompanied Brian to the house. Peadar moved the Volvo from its parking place to outside Kitty's. He kept the engine running and switched on his hazard lights. He leaned across to make certain the back door nearest the house was unlocked. He saw Brian and Brendan go into the house. The front door was left ajar. He gripped the steering-wheel and waited. About five minutes later the front door opened wide. Brian Delaney came out first. Then Robert Larski. Finally Brendan Quirk. Peadar was surprised at how calm Larski seemed. Indeed, he appeared quite willing to accompany his companions. When Brian opened the back door of the Volvo, Robert Larski got in without fuss. He even nodded and gave a small smile to Peadar. Taken unawares, Peadar smiled back. Brendan Quirk got in beside Larski and shut the car door. Brian Delaney walked round the car. He whispered something to Peadar and tapped the roof of the car as a signal for it to be driven off. Then he went back into the house to have a talk to Kitty as the Commander had instructed.

Colonel Cairns had been taken somewhat unawares also, by the attitude of the Brigadier, who had telephoned him. When he heard the Brigadier say, 'Something has come up. A new development,' he had wondered what new catastrophe had befallen him.

'You know Temple, don't you?' the Brigadier continued. 'Major Temple? Spoken to him on the phone, anyway. I'm sending him over to have a chat with you. He'll explain everything. I'm afraid you'll have to liaise with the RUC on this one.' He stopped dead there.

Colonel Cairns decided this was as good a time as any to drop his bombshell. 'There's been a new development here, too, sir.'

'Oh?'

'I received a photograph –'

'You too? Oh dear.'

'I'm sorry? What do you mean, sir, me too?'

'Temple got one.'

'So did Captain Legg,' the Colonel admitted, deciding he might as well tell everything.

The Brigadier was silent for a moment. 'That's *not* so good.'

'He brought it directly to me. Hasn't mentioned it to anyone else.'

'I certainly hope not.'

'I'm sure of it.'

'We are sure it was that Larski man who sent them.'

'Yes. That's what I thought.'

'Something will have to be done.'

'Yes.'

'Major Temple might not be the man to discuss details with.'

'I see.'

'A good enough man, but squeamish. Plagued with a conscience, I fear.'

'I see,' the Colonel said again.

'I suggested you might – between you – be able to arrange to have Larski brought in.'

'To what end?'

'See if he's reasonable.'

'Reasonable?'

'Willing to listen to reason then.'

'And if not?'

'That's why I suggest you liaise with the RUC.'

'That would compromise me rather.'

The Brigadier's breath whistled down the line. 'It's a choice we don't really have, Colonel. A small compromise or a full-scale exposure – which do you prefer?'

The Colonel made no reply.

'I thought so,' Brigadier Carlisle said. 'Anyway, have a chat with Temple and see what you come up with. He'll let you know when he's arriving. Perhaps you'd be good enough to arrange that he's met?'

'Of course.'

'Excellent.'

Chief Inspector Harwood came quickly into the office the RUC had supplied for his use. 'Afternoon, Frank,' he said to Detective Inspector Fraser without stopping, going straight to his desk and scribbling something on a pad. He passed it to Fraser. THEY WANT ANOTHER MEET, it said.

'Good trip then?' Frank Fraser asked. 'Expected you back this morning,' he added, putting a match to the note and placing it in the ashtray to burn out.

'I wanted to be back this morning. Got held up. You know what it's like, Frank. Trip? Not bad. Bloody weather, though,' Harwood replied, turning the pad to see what Fraser had written. WHEN?

'Bet Ellen was glad to see you?'

'Glad to get her hands on my money anyway. Took her to London. That was a mistake, I can tell you.' THIS EVENING.

'Can't stand London myself,' Fraser said. He tore off that sheet and burned it also. 'Can never find my way about.'

'I know what you mean. Ellen amazes me. She's got a nose for the place. She finds her way into every damn nook and cranny – and out again. She's got one hell of a talent for spending money.' CAN YOU ARRANGE A CAR?

'Glad to be back in peaceful, quiet Belfast then?' SURE. WHAT TIME?

'Bloody seems to be peaceful compared to London.' EIGHT. 'By the way, the Secretary has asked me to call on him this evening.'

'Oh? Did he say why?'

'No. Well, an informal chat is what he said.'

'That'll be nice.'

'Care to take my place?' HAS ASKED ME FOR SEVEN. GO FROM THERE.

'Oh, yeah. He'd like that, I'm sure.'

'So, what's been happening here?'

'Not a lot. Still banging my head against a brick wall.'

'Well, let's see if we can't demolish it.'

Within twenty minutes a transcript of their conversation was put on Malcolm Carter's desk. He decided not to show this one to the Chief Constable. He didn't want to upset him unduly. The Chief Constable, he knew, had not been asked to have an informal chat with the Secretary, and that would certainly upset him.

Gemma Larkin grabbed the phone on her desk. It had rung only once. She was expecting a call from Glasgow. 'Yes?'

'Miss Larkin?'

The voice was heavily accented. Had she thought about it she would have recognized it as Northern Irish. As it was she automatically presumed it was Scottish. She glanced at a memorandum on her desk on which she had written the name of the man she was expecting to call. 'Mr Austin?'

'No.' The voice sounded mildly taken aback. 'My name's Fitzroy. James Fitzroy. A friend of yours asked me to call you up. Robert Larski.'

'I'm sorry ... I was expecting someone else to ring. Robert? He asked you to call? Has something happened? Is he all right?'

'No. Nothing's happened,' the man said, and added a short encouraging laugh. 'And Robert's fine. He has to stay ... away ... for a bit longer, that's all. He asked me to get in touch. I've got something he wants you to keep for him.'

'I see. Can you bring it here?'

Fitzroy hesitated. 'It'd be better not.'

For the first time Gemma felt a bit uneasy. Not exactly suspicious. Wary. But this slipped away when the man said. 'I'm near your flat now. Robert gave me the address. Told me to wait here until you got home if needs be.'

Gemma glanced at her watch. Almost midday. 'Well, I wasn't going to come home until this evening, but I suppose I could nip home at lunchtime. Say in an hour?'

'That'd be grand. I can easily wait until then.'

'There's a pub just down the road. You could wait there,' Gemma suggested.

'I'm fine where I am. I'm by the bench opposite your flat. I've got my paper to read. I'll wait here.'

'I'll see you in about an hour then.'

'Thanks, Miss Larkin.'

Colonel Cairns went himself to meet Major Temple at the airport. He sent his driver in to collect the Major. He himself remained in the car. When the Major got in, the Colonel greeted him with a nod. And now he offered the Major a cigarette, although something told him it would be refused. It was. He took one himself, lit it, and stared out at the grey, rainswept streets as the car whisked them into the city. His face was tense and grey, in total contrast to the Major's, which, although drawn, was relaxed and calm. One would have thought (seeing them both, side by side, each in his own way trying to figure out how to approach the subject that linked them) that it was the Colonel who was the junior of the two.

'I wish I knew what that wretched Larski was up to,' the Colonel said finally.

The Major gave a small chuckle. 'Oh, I think we both know the answer to that, Colonel.'

'But why doesn't he just come straight out and accuse us I mean – damn it – he's a journalist, he must have outlets and connections that would be only to glad to have this ... this ... this ...' The Colonel couldn't find the word he wanted.

'Maybe he will. Maybe he's just biding his time.'

'For what reason?'

'Make us sweat, perhaps.'

'Well, he's certainly doing that.'

'Yes, Colonel. He's doing that.'

'And too damn successfully.' The Colonel added a wry snort. 'He actually came to see me in my office – did you know that? That was before he sent out those photographs, of course. You'd swear butter wouldn't melt in his mouth.'

'We underestimated him too,' the Major said by way of consolation.

'Damn pest,' the Colonel spat.

The Major couldn't resist it. 'You don't like him much, do you?'

'I certainly don't. Don't tell me you do?'

'I think I admire him.'

'Personally, I prefer to keep my admiration for the dead. At least they can't make a fool out of you,' the Colonel said, and there was something about the way he said it, some unaccented innuendo, that made Major Temple shiver. And as if to give that reaction justification, the Colonel added, 'And that's how young Mr Larski is going to find himself if he doesn't watch out.'

'Unless he has us first,' Major Temple observed wryly.

'He won't.'

'Oh, I think he might.'

'He won't.'

'He's succeeded pretty well so far.'

Both men swayed as the car pulled sharply to the left to allow a screaming ambulance to pass. The Colonel straightened himself with a cluck of annoyance. He looked as if he was about to reprimand the driver, but instead he said to the Major, 'He's done all the damage he's going to.'

'I'd be happier if I heard *him* say that.'

'I'm saying it, Major.'

The Colonel reached forward and stubbed out his cigarette in the ashtray. As he was leaning back, he added, 'I must confess I find your attitude a little strange, Major.'

'Why is that, Colonel?'

'It's almost as if you're making fun of the situation. As if you didn't care one way or the other about what an unholy mess we're in.'

'Unholy, indeed, Colonel.'

In truth, ever since he had received the photograph through the post, the Major himself found his attitude changing, and found it a little strange also. But he wasn't making fun of the situation as the Colonel suggested. Far from it. Yet, somehow, in the inexplicable way that such things happen, he had, as if for the first time, become aware of the appalling duplicity in which he had allowed himself, quite willingly, to become involved. It was as though, having made up his mind to resign, he had already stepped outside the confines of the military machine, had been enlightened – although such a word would have made him smile – and was capable of thinking for himself for once. Yet there was more to it than that. It was as though some small part of him *wanted* Robert Larski to succeed, as though some tiny demon was urging him, if not to *help* Larski, at least not to hinder him, as though, in some strange and frightening way, he had become part of Larski or, worse still, part of his brother.

*

Gemma Larkin paid off the taxi at the end of the cul-de-sac in which she lived. She always did that. It was all but impossible to turn, and the taxi-drivers always appreciated her thoughtfulness. As she left the taxi she noticed a man, wearing a trilby (which struck her as quaint) and with a folded newspaper in his hand, standing across the road. She thought how lucky he was to have a taxi all but delivered to him. She could not have said why, but the rolled newspaper looked as if it were about to be raised to hail her now abandoned taxi.

As she approached the entrance to the house, another man, one who had been sitting on the bench opposite, crossed the road and approached her. Somehow, he didn't look like a man who could have owned the voice that had spoken to her on the phone. That voice had been – well, light and youthful; the man was middle-aged and stocky. Yet it was the same voice that now inquired, 'Miss Larkin?'

'Yes. You're Mr Fitzroy?'

The man smiled. 'Yes.'

'You said you had something for me? From Robert?'

'Ah, yes.'

The man put a hand in his raincoat pocket. When it came out, it held a gun. Immediately, as if from nowhere, the man she had assumed was about to hail her taxi appeared beside them. He raised his hat politely in an odd, old-fashioned gesture. 'Inside, if you please, Miss Larkin.'

And inside, in the large front room that had a dining area at one end, his politeness continued. He asked her to sit. He explained that she was perfectly safe, that nothing untoward would befall her, hopefully. That as soon as a phone call came through, one that clarified matters, as he put it, she would be free.

'And if your matters are not clarified?'

'I'm confident they will be, Miss Larkin.'

And the Commander was politely friendly also, when he said, 'You have certainly been causing a *lot* of people a *lot* of anxiety, Mr Larski,' although the smile that accompanied the statement was not the most endearing Robert had ever seen. They were alone in the room. As soon as he had been shown in, Robert had felt it was a rented room. It looked like that. Furnished in the way such rooms are: sparsely and with very little that was personal in it. The bearded man opposite him certainly didn't look at home. He made an effort to appear relaxed, certainly, but a look of distaste persisted on his face as though he could smell a particularly unpleasant odour. 'So,' the man now continued, 'we thought that a little chat might be in order. To clear the air, so to speak?' He turned the statement into a question. Just as earlier he had turned the statement, 'Tell Brian to join us as soon as he gets back from Kitty's,' into an order not to be disobeyed.

And it struck Robert that the man was waiting for this Brian to join them before entering into any serious discussion. He was playing for time, yet using that time to probe gently.

Although he had not bothered to ask the man who he was, Robert was under no illusion. The Commander's status might have surprised him, but he was well aware that he was in the clutches of the IRA. And while he had been scared by the sight of the young men who had stood menacingly about as the Volvo pulled up to the house, and during the twenty minutes he had been kept waiting in the kitchen with a particularly nervous youth, he now felt reasonably calm. Something told him that he was safe as long as the bearded man opposite him was satisfied. And he seemed to be satisfied thus far, content for Robert to remain silent for the moment. His attitude changed, however, when there was a tap on the door and Brian Delaney came in. 'Ah, Brian,' the Commander said. 'You know Mr Larski?' he asked impishly. Then immediately to Robert, 'You will excuse us a moment?'

Alone, Robert stood up and walked to the window. The curtains were drawn. Tentatively he pulled one back an inch. He found himself smiling: wooden shutters had been clamped across the window. He returned to his chair and fingered the photograph of his brother in his inside pocket.

'Well, Peter,' he said to himself, 'at least we've caused a *lot* of people a *lot* of anxiety!'

'Sorry about that,' the Commander said, coming back into the room and sitting himself down in the chair he had left, and in precisely the same position. Brian Delaney followed him and stood behind his chair, his arms folded but looking agreeable enough.

'Now, Mr Larski,' the Commander said. 'I want you to listen to me very carefully. *Very* carefully. You know, or have guessed, who we are?' Accepting Robert's nod, he went on, 'Yes. We are members of the Provisional IRA. That need not frighten you. Despite accusations to the contrary, we are reasonable men. As long as we get the information we require you will be perfectly safe – and that's reasonable, wouldn't you say? Of course we don't expect anything for nothing – one never gets something for nothing, does one? Such is life. And so I am going to tell you something – about your brother – things which I believe you have been trying to uncover for yourself. But, as I say, one gets something only by giving something. I propose to ask you certain questions, Mr Larski. I would expect you to answer them. And for each question answered I will impart some information. That's fair, isn't it?' The Commander waited a moment, and when Robert nodded, he smiled. 'Mind you, I must stress that we expect truthful answers. You won't know whether or not we already know the answers, so I would plead with you that you tell us the truth. It would be a pity if we found you lying to us. A great pity.' The Commander looked very sad. 'It would mean we could no longer protect you.'

Robert Larski raised his eyebrows, and managed to make the gesture slightly mocking.

'You won't know, of course, that we have already possibly saved your life? We couldn't, alas, save your friend Sammy Meagher but –'

'Sammy's dead?' Robert asked, the words out of his mouth before he could stop them.

'I'm afraid so. And on the night he was killed someone – several people – called, or attempted to call, at Kitty Doherty's house, we think to kill you.'

Robert felt a shiver pass through him.

'Oh yes. I assure you that is true. Fortunately we were able to deter them. So you see, you already owe us something.'

'What is it you want to know?'

'Patience, Mr Larski. Patience. There are a few things *you* need to know first. To begin with we did *not* murder your brother, but I suspect you've already discovered that?'

'Yes.'

'Your brother was, in fact, working for us.'

'Peter? Working for you? I don't believe –'

'Oh, it's true, Mr Larski. Perfectly true. But remark, I did not say he had pinned his flag to our mast, as they say. No, he still disapproved of our methods. As you do. As everyone who doesn't understand seems to. No, I can assure you that Peter was an honourable young man. He was ordered by the army to infiltrate our ranks. And . . .' The Commander gave a rueful smile. 'And he succeeded. Duped us completely, didn't he, Brian?' the Commander asked without turning and so seeing Brian Delaney redden. 'For a time, anyway. Until the one thing the army hadn't reckoned with happened. They hadn't reckoned with his sense of decency, you see. That peculiarly British sense of fair play or what have you. They thought, I suppose, they'd eradicated that. But they hadn't.' The Commander relit his pipe. Through the smoke he studied Robert Larski's face. He wasn't yet convinced that he was going about this the right way, telling the young man so much. He was banking on the belief that all Robert Larski wanted was to find out the truth about what happened to his brother. Nothing more. Just the truth about his brother. 'How long have you been in America?' he now asked.

'Three years almost.'

'Three years. I see. You won't then, perhaps, have heard of – you know of the security forces' shoot-to-kill policy?'

'I've heard about it.'

'Your brother *knew* about it. He was – quite by accident – caught up in an incident. In Armagh.' The Commander stopped again, and seemed to be thinking about something else. After a few moments he sighed, and continued. 'Foolishly, he decided to do something about it by himself. We had found out about him by then, of course. And I admit that we were intending to use him to help expose that policy. Before we could plan a strategy, however, your brother took matters into his own hands. What he did precisely we have no way of knowing. We do know he contacted the mainland police who are here to . . .' The Commander gave a short laugh. 'To investigate various other incidents. What else he did, however, is, as I say, unknown. All I can tell you is that he was not on patrol when he was killed, and that it was either the RUC or his own colleagues who murdered him.'

'I know. It was the army.'

'You sound very certain.'

'I *know* it was them.'

'Indeed?'

Robert took the photograph from his pocket. He reached out and handed it to the Commander. 'That's why Sammy Meagher was killed, I think.'

The Commander studied the picture for a long time. The expression on his face did not change. 'I see,' he said finally, and passed the photograph over his shoulder to Brian Delaney. 'Who else knows about that, Robert?' he asked, using the Christian name as a sort of condolence.

Robert gave a little puff. 'Quite a few people.'

'How many?'

'Five that I know of. I sent them copies.'

The Commander sucked in his breath, and Brian Delaney looked up quickly from the photograph. 'I need their names,' the Commander said quietly.

'Two friends in England. They're not involved. I just sent them for safe keeping. One to Colonel Cairns. He's here. I've met him. One to Captain Legg. He's the one in the photo – the one whose face is visible. Standing by the stretcher looking down on it. And one to Major Temple. He's in England. Came to tell us Peter had been killed on patrol and has been lying ever since.'

'Colonel Cairns, Captain Legg and Major Temple ... and two friends,' the Commander repeated.

'Yes.'

'No one else?'

'Whoever they told, I suppose.'

'But you told no one else, or showed this picture to anyone else?'

'No.'

'You're certain?'

'Yes, I'm certain.'

'And since you sent the photographs, you've had no reaction?'

'No. I've been waiting.'

The Commander shook his head in something approaching wonderment. 'I don't think you realize just how fortunate you've been, Robert. Luck has certainly been on your side. This isn't England, you know. Over here ...' He stopped and frowned. 'Tell me something – how do you know the man in the picture is Captain Legg? How did you get that name?'

'I was told.'

'Not, I suspect, by the Colonel.'

Robert was forced to smile. 'No. I've had help.'

The Commander tried a shot in the dark. 'That would be from Declan Finch, I presume?'

Robert nodded. So, he had been right about Finch. 'Yes.'

The Commander blinked once. Brian Delaney stiffened, and then bent down to whisper urgently in the Commander's ear. The Commander listened, bending his head to one side and turning it slightly. But in the end he shook his head and dismissed whatever information had been passed with a small wave of his hand, clearly not considering it as urgent as Brian believed. He turned back to Robert. 'And why should he help you?'

'Don't you know?' Robert asked.

The Commander blinked once again, and waited.

'He is one of yours, isn't he?'

Still the Commander waited. It was a trick he used

often. It usually worked. It did now. Robert felt himself wilting under the steady, cold gaze. 'I suspect he was told to.'

'By whom?'

'A Mr Clancy.'

The Commander leaned back, looking well satisfied. 'Ah,' he sighed. 'Mr Clancy. You *do* get yourself about, don't you?'

'I –'

But the Commander wasn't interested in any reply to his trite little remark. What he wanted to know was, 'And how, precisely, has Declan helped you?'

'I've told you that. He got Legg's name for me.'

'Nothing more?' The Commander sounded sceptical.

'I haven't asked him to do anything else.'

'But you were going to, no?'

'I was going to, yes,' Robert said.

The Commander allowed himself a small inclination of his head to indicate he had noticed, if not appreciated, the wit. 'To do what?'

'I was going to try and get him to . . . I don't know . . . arrange for me to see Legg on his own.'

'And how did you think he could have arranged that?'

Robert Larski began to feel uneasy. Now that he was put to explain it, the vague plan he had concocted in his mind sounded outrageous and farcical.

'Well?' the Commander pressed.

'I thought he might . . . well, kidnap him, I suppose.'

The Commander didn't seem to find that too preposterous, although he did glance up at Brian Delaney. 'And had he succeeded in this . . . this illegal act . . .' – the Commander clearly enjoyed those words and gave a broad grin before continuing – 'what would you have done with Captain Legg, I wonder?'

'Made him tell me the truth.'

'*Made* him tell you the truth? Oh dear.'

'You know what I mean.'

'I know what *I* mean when I say I will *make* someone tell me something I wish to know. I don't believe we mean quite the same thing, however.'

The Commander stood up and stretched, but he pushed his arms downwards rather than up. He gave a little groan as his muscles tightened, and another one as they relaxed. Then he put his hands behind his back and stared down at Robert. 'So, now that you know *why* Peter was killed, what you still want is to find out who killed him – is that what you're saying?'

'That's what I'm saying.'

'And when – if – you find that out?'

Robert shrugged. 'I haven't decided.'

'You might not be able to do anything, you know that, don't you?'

'Yes. I know that.'

'And you would be prepared to –'

'I just want to know – for sure – who murdered him.'

The Commander turned to Brian Delaney and reached out his hand for the photograph. 'I think we'd better keep this,' he said, making it clear that he intended to keep it whether Robert agreed or not, but adding by way of explanation, 'There seem to be enough copies floating about already.' He folded the photograph along the crease Robert had made, and stowed it away in his pocket. 'Supposing . . . supposing we' – he swivelled his body to include Brian Delaney – 'said we could find out who killed Peter, would that satisfy you?'

'You'd have to tell me who it –'

The Commander gave a small gesture of vexation. 'Of course we'd tell you. What I meant was, if we helped you find out, would you accept our evidence?'

'If it convinced me.'

'Oh, if we give you any evidence it will convince you all right, Robert. Have no fear on that score.'

'In that case, yes.'

'And you would not question how or where we got that evidence?'

'No,' Robert said with some reluctance.

'Very well. You can leave it to us then. Brian will see you home. I want you to stay indoors. No nipping out for a drink. No wandering about the streets. No sightseeing.

We will undertake your protection. You'll be perfectly safe.'

'Oh? You're expecting another attack on me?'

'Let's just say we don't want another Larski dying on our hands. No. No, that would never do. We will see to it that you're undisturbed.'

'You were very sure I'd agree, weren't you?'

'Not *that* sure, Robert. One can never be *that* sure.'

'And if I hadn't?'

The Commander gazed at him sadly. Then he nodded to Brian Delaney. Brian went to the phone and dialled, whistling through his lips as he waited for a connection. 'Everything's fine. You can go home now,' he said. 'Put the lady on.' He handed the phone to Robert.

'Hello? Hello?'

'Robert? Is that you?'

'Gemma? Jesus. Are you all right?'

'I'm fine, Robert. They're just leaving.'

'Who's just leaving?'

'The two men.'

'What –' The line went dead. Robert spun round and saw Brian holding the disconnected lead in his hand. He rounded on the Commander. 'You bastard!'

The Commander shrugged. 'I've been called worse. You wanted to know what would have happened if you hadn't agreed. Now you know. We are not playing games, Robert. This is a mad, mad world you've stumbled into. However, the point is, you did agree, so your young lady will be left in peace, and you . . . you . . . well, you will be well protected.'

'You're still a bastard.'

'So be it,' the Commander said pleasantly. And then, as if he were tired of the meeting, as if he felt everything that had to be said had been said, he waved a hand at Brian Delaney, and said simply, 'Brian?'

Brian Delaney moved across to Robert and took him by the arm, steering him towards the door. When they had gone, the Commander slumped into his chair. Any sign of pleasantness had gone from his face. He looked furious. As soon as Brian Delaney returned from handing Robert over to be delivered home, the Commander said through his teeth, 'Get me Declan. Now.'

'Shouldn't –'

'Get him *now*, Brian.'

Whatever Declan Finch was expecting it certainly wasn't the effusively warm greeting he got. The Commander appeared positively jovial. He took Declan by the arm and guided him across the room to a place by the fire. He commented on how dreadful the weather was, and inquired if Declan had any special plans for Christmas. That done, he dismissed Brian Delaney almost peremptorily, saying what he wanted to say to Declan was private.

'Between you and me,' he told Declan when the door had closed and they were alone, smiling all the while, but managing to convey that this meeting was a serious matter of considerable import, 'I've been wanting for us to have this little chat for some time, Declan, but you know how it is: we all seem to have more to do than the time in which to do it.'

Flattered, Declan said, 'Oh, yes.'

'Ah, yes,' the Commander continued. 'I knew you'd understand. All that business you conduct for us must keep you on your toes.'

'Indeed it does.'

'Hmm. I was talking to Mr Clancy the other day, and he told me how busy you both were. Slot machines, I believe, is it?'

'That's right.'

'Dear me. Who would have thought of such a thing? Slot machines.'

'We import them and lease them out.'

'Oh, is that how it's done?' the Commander asked, tiring of playing the fool. 'Now, Declan, I have something very serious I want you to do for me.'

'Anything I can.'

'Thank you. You'll have heard, of course, that we've been having some interference from Peter Larski's brother?'

'Yes, I did hear something.'

The Commander beamed. 'I was sure you would.' He leaned a little closer. 'I'm told that not much happens that you *don't* hear about,' he confided, tapping Declan on the knee with one finger.

Pleased, Declan said, 'I do hear most things. Yes.'

'Anyway, somehow, I don't know how, this Larski man got in touch with Brian, demanding to see me. I *had* to see him, of course. The upshot of our chat is that he wants me to arrange for him to talk to some Captain Legg. *Me*. I can't arrange that sort of thing. Not any more, anyway. One time I could have – when I was younger and more in the know. Like you are now, Declan. Which is why I asked you to come. Do you think *you* could do that for me, like a good lad?'

Declan was taken aback. 'Arrange for Larski to meet with – who did you say?'

Clever, the Commander thought. 'Captain Legg was his name.'

'He's here? In Belfast?'

'As far as I know. But of course, if it's too much –'

'No. No, if he's here I might be able to arrange something. It will be pretty risky, though.'

'I'm sure it will. But we all take risks, don't we? – some more than others,' the Commander pointed out, and was disappointed that Declan didn't even flinch.

'I'll ask around. I have one or two contacts in the army. I'll find out if he's still here, and then I'll see what I can do.'

'I'd be very obliged.'

'I'll do my best.'

'That's all I ask, Declan.' The Commander sighed. 'Could you perhaps make it a priority?'

'Sure.'

'And report directly to me, Declan. I don't want anyone else knowing about this. This is far too important for any of it to leak out. I can trust you, but . . .' The Commander let his voice trail off to include everyone he could think of.

'I understand.'

The Commander rose. 'Thank you, Declan.'

'You're welcome. I'll get back to you just as soon as I can.'

'Thank you.'

'Well, how did it go?'

The Commander's face was glowering again. 'As planned, I think, Brian.'

'Did he believe you?'

'I don't know. He appeared to. He was very cunning, though. Pretended not to have heard of anyone called Legg.'

'Well he would, wouldn't he? He'd have to.'

'Never even flinched,' the Commander commented, as though he regarded that as something akin to sin.

'He's had practice. And you think he *can* get to Legg?'

'He'll certainly do his best. And I think he thinks he can. That's what counts.'

'Supposing he does – have you thought about afterwards?'

'Meaning?'

'Well, I don't fancy him wandering about knowing that –'

'Oh, that. Yes, Brian. I've thought about that.'

'And?'

'Declan has become a problem,' the Commander said quietly, as if that explained everything.

'You don't have to tell me that. But that's our fault.'

'My fault, you mean.'

'Ours. We agreed when you asked us if we should allow him the power to control our finances. Now we need him.'

'We could find someone else.'

'Not that easily. No matter what sort of shit he is, he's good at his job.'

'Nobody's indispensable, Brian. You know that.'

'Declan comes bloody close to being it.'

'I want rid of him,' the Commander said coldly. 'Just as I want Clancy's outside business interests curtailed. I want Clancy under our thumbs. I want him so terrified that he never does anything again that could rebound on us.'

'That's a nice wish.'

'More than a wish, Brian. I think I know how it can be arranged.' The Commander thought for a few moments. 'What time am I meeting Chief Inspector Harwood?'

'Eight.' Brian Delaney looked at his watch. 'In an hour.'

'My God, is it that time already?'

''Fraid so.'

'Get me some coffee, will you, Brian? And something to eat. Anything. A sandwich. Anything.'

'Some soup?'

'Yes. Thank you. Brian? You wouldn't be interested in Declan's –'

'Oh-ho no. Not me thanks.'

The Commander grinned. 'No, I didn't think you would be. You said soup, I think?'

'I'm on my way.'

Colonel Cairns and Major Temple had just finished eating. The Colonel had arranged for something light to be brought to his office. He had produced a bottle of Crozes-Hermitage from a filing cabinet, and they had the remnant of that still in their tumblers. Now the Colonel was swilling his about, staring at it, thinking about what the Major had just asked. 'I thought it best,' he said finally. 'Better to have them out on patrol, doing something, rather than moping about here.' He sipped some wine. 'Legg's all right. Panicked a bit when he got that damn photograph, of course. But he's all right. Bayliss I'm *not* so sure of, but Legg assures me he's coping.'

'Leave?'

'I'm sorry?'

'You didn't think of sending them back to the mainland on leave?'

'I did, actually.' The Colonel sucked in his breath. 'Yes, I thought about it. It didn't strike me as the wisest course. To be frank I thought they – Bayliss in particular – might be tempted to go AWOL. I need hardly tell you what that would have involved. All those questions. Simply couldn't risk it.'

The Major looked puzzled. 'Were only Legg and Bayliss involved? I thought . . . I was sure there was someone else.'

The Colonel coughed. 'I got the impression from the Brigadier that you were coming here to make things better.'

'No, Colonel. I was sent to try and salvage the Brigadier's career,' Major Temple said bitterly.

'And your own.'

'Not my own, Colonel. The Brigadier's, and possibly yours.' The Major finished his wine and placed his empty tumbler carefully on the edge of the Colonel's desk. Clearly Colonel Cairns regarded him as an upstart and certainly didn't like having his power usurped. Well, that was just too bad. Major Temple became abrupt, enjoying the annoyance that showed on the Colonel's face. 'I'll want to see Larski. I presume you can arrange that for me, Colonel?'

'Of course. It may mean involving the RUC but –'

'Personally, I don't care who it involves. I want to see him.'

'Very well.'

'And Captain Legg. I want to see him too. First thing in the morning.'

The Colonel agreed with a curt nod. He found the Major's new abruptness impertinent, but there was little he could do about it: the damn man might just salvage his career. Suddenly he seemed to think of something. A furtive, almost conspiratorial look crept into his eyes. 'You're not by any chance thinking what I think you might be thinking, are you, Major? Legg. Larski. The names have been linked before . . .' The Colonel raised his eyebrows questioningly.

It took a moment for the Colonel's implication to register in Major Temple's mind. When it did he felt a wave of intense anger sweep over him. It dawned on him that he had never before hated anyone quite as much as he hated the Colonel at that moment. 'No, Colonel. I'm certainly not thinking that.'

'Oh,' the Colonel said. He sounded a little disappointed.

*

The first snow of the season was falling as Chief Inspector Harwood and Detective Inspector Fraser were escorted towards the safe house. It wasn't the puffy, designer snow of Christmas cards and movies, but mean, thin, sleety flakes that soaked as efficiently as rain.

'They're on their way,' Brian Delaney told the Commander.

The Commander nodded, and placed his tray on the floor beside him. He wiped his fingers carefully, and wiped his mouth too with a paper napkin, which he then crumpled up and dropped into the empty soup-plate.

'Enough?' Brian asked.

'Quite sufficient, thank you, Brian.'

Brian Delaney took up the tray and made for the door. Dirty plates lying around were a sign of slovenliness, and he wanted the Commander to appear always in the best light.

'Brian . . . I want you in on this.'

'I'll just get rid of this and be right back.'

'We'll use the dining-room,' the Commander said. 'Harwood will want Fraser in too if I've got you. Around the table in the dining-room would be better.'

'I'll have the fire switched on.'

'Thank you.'

When Brian Delaney had gone and closed the door behind him, the Commander stood up and brushed himself down with his hands. He tried to concentrate his mind on the forthcoming meeting, but something else rankled him, and it annoyed him that it upset him so. Short of something to say, no doubt, one of the Catholic bishops had accused the IRA of oppressing the people rather than protecting them as they claimed. The Commander took the accusation personally, and it infuriated him. Still, it would take a bishop of the Holy Roman Catholic Church to know about oppression, wouldn't it? What else had they been doing for years if not oppressing the people? And only a bishop of the Holy Roman Catholic Church could issue such a statement without seeing the irony. Not that the bishop's indictment worried the Commander in any spiritual sense.

It didn't. His relationship with God was pretty tenuous. But he genuinely felt he was doing his best to help people. He was prepared to admit that at times his methods were extreme and abhorrent, but he believed, perhaps naïvely, that they would ultimately force talks to take place, and it was talks he wanted.

'They're here.' Brian stuck his head round the door and made the announcement.

The dining-room was small. It just had room for a four-seater oval table, four chairs and a sideboard. Chief Inspector Harwood was waiting by the fire.

'I've asked Brian here to sit in,' the Commander said after the two men had nodded a greeting to each other.

'In that case I'll want Detective Inspector Fraser to be present also.'

The Commander smiled. 'I said you would. By all means.'

The four men settled themselves round the table. Before sitting, Brian placed an ashtray beside the Commander, and now the Commander laid his pipe and a box of matches beside the ashtray, looking up sharply when Harwood said, 'I hope this is important.'

The Commander felt like giving an angry retort, but controlled himself.

'If I didn't think it was I wouldn't have asked you to come,' he said.

Harwood relented. 'Yes. Of course.'

'We have got to solve this matter once and for all – to the satisfaction of both of us.' The Commander spoke deliberately.

Harwood nodded. 'We'd all agree with that, I think.'

'It will mean an amount of give and take.'

Again Harwood nodded. 'Just as long as it's not one side that has to give and one that takes.'

The Commander gave him a scolding look. 'Quite,' he said tersely. 'We will have to bargain.'

Harwood put his elbows on the table and leaned forward. 'With what, I wonder?' he asked.

'With what we have at our disposal.'

'Like?'

'I want that dealer contact of yours – Parr – immobilized,' the Commander said quietly. He watched Harwood carefully. He saw him stiffen slightly, and frown. To forestall his question the Commander continued, 'He is supplying someone I don't want supplied. Not here. In Dublin.'

'Clancy?' Harwood suggested.

'Yes. Clancy. I would prefer if Clancy was forced to retire from that particular trade.'

'May I know why?'

The Commander smiled. 'You may. It would suit our purposes if he was more reliant on our business for his livelihood. The profits from drugs are, I fear, greater than we can match. It has led Clancy into temptation. We would prefer if that temptation was removed. It would, we feel, help to concentrate his mind on our needs rather than his own.'

Chief Inspector Harwood found himself forced to return the smile. 'You have a delicate way with words,' he pointed out.

The Commander shrugged.

'When you say immobilized –'

'I mean just that,' the Commander interrupted. 'In whatever way you wish,' he added.

'Supposing that could be arranged, what do I get?'

The Commander leaned back in his chair. He balanced it on its back legs, and clasped his hands behind his neck. He stared at the ceiling as he replied. 'Chief Inspector, it may hurt, but both you and I know that your current investigation into alleged collusion between the RUC and certain paramilitary forces is getting nowhere. And we both know also that it will never get anywhere. You will be allowed to get so far and no further. You will be recalled to the mainland after an appropriate time and either promoted or castigated – the former, I hope, for your sake. If I was you I would want to come out of all this with something – something that I could use to protect my position – protect my back, if you wish.' He let the chair fall on to all four feet with a clatter. He fixed his eyes on Brian Delaney, all but daring him to contradict what he was about to say. 'I can give you the man who killed Captain Larski,' he said.

Brian Delaney held his breath. Harwood stared at the Commander for a while, then transferred his gaze to Fraser. Fraser gazed back. The room was so quiet that the bars of the electric fire humming sounded like a small engine.

Chief Inspector Harwood was the first to recover. 'When you say "give" – you mean his name?'

'I mean give, Chief Inspector. Body and soul.'

'You have him?' the Chief Inspector asked. He sounded dumbfounded.

Unflinchingly the Commander continued to stare at Harwood, ignoring the question.

'So he *is* one of yours,' Harwood said.

The Commander shook his head. 'Indeed no. The unfortunate Larski was killed by his colleagues.'

'And you have the soldier who did it?' Harwood asked again.

And again the Commander evaded the question. 'I said I could deliver him,' he replied. 'To do with as you will,' he added significantly.

The Chief Inspector felt his eyes drawn towards Fraser. Imperceptibly Fraser nodded. 'Very well,' Harwood conceded.

The Commander relaxed. He reached for his pipe and stuck the stem in his mouth but made no attempt to light it. Abruptly, like a man who was trying to quit smoking, he removed it again and replaced it on the table. 'There is another matter. In order to tie up all the loose ends it may be necessary for me to call on your connections – your influence with your colleagues in our excellent constabulary.' He grinned like a pike. 'To have someone eliminated,' he explained, the fierce grin dissipating. 'One of our men,' he went on. 'Someone who has overstepped the mark and who could disrupt our arrangements.'

'I would have thought you could manage something like that yourself,' the Chief Inspector remarked caustically.

'Indeed we could. And most efficiently. However, this

would need to be seen very clearly as an RUC operation, the police acting on information received, as it were.'

'The informant being you?'

The Commander baulked at that. 'From someone reliable,' he said. 'But as I say, it only *might* become a necessity. I would need to be sure that you could and would organize it, however, *should* it be required.'

'One of your men, you say?'

The Commander nodded, carefully avoiding Brian Delaney's eyes this time.

'God, you're a lovely lot.'

'It's a question of balance, Chief Inspector. Balancing power demands extraordinary methods. You should know that. Besides, it is sometimes better to have our difficulties removed for us rather than remove them ourselves. It makes for better – how shall I put it? – better relations within the ranks. Yes. Better relations.'

'I'm sure it *could* be arranged,' Harwood said.

'When do we get to meet . . . what's his name?' Detective Inspector Fraser asked.

'Larski's killer?' Brian Delaney put in quickly.

'Thank you, Brian,' the Commander said with a warm smile. 'As soon as we're sure Parr has been made to see the error of his ways.'

'You wouldn't like to immobilize him yourself, would you?' Fraser asked, facetiously.

'We will if you like,' Delaney told him seriously.

'No thank you,' Harwood interposed. 'We'll deal with it.'

'Good,' the Commander said. 'We'll wait to hear from you then.'

The four men stood up. The Chief Inspector put on his overcoat and buttoned it carefully. Fraser zipped up his parka. As they reached the door, Harwood turned. 'One thing to remember,' he said. 'If you bugger us about . . .' He left the threat hanging.

The Commander smiled. 'I was about to say the same thing to you, Chief Inspector.'

*

'Declan better come up with Legg then,' Brian said, and waited for the Commander to get his pipe going. 'It's an awful chance you're taking.'

'One has to take chances, Brian. Anyway, I suspect Declan will deliver. He has to. To consolidate the position he thinks he's attained. The one I *let* him think he's attained.'

'But if he doesn't?'

The Commander shrugged. 'We'll just have to give Harwood someone else. There were others involved.'

'But we don't know who.'

'Robert Larski does.'

'Will he tell us?'

'Oh, he'll tell us, never fear,' the Commander assured him.

'Ve have vays of making zem talk,' Brian said in a grotesque parody of old Nazi war films.

The Commander was not amused. 'We can do without that sort of stupidity, Brian. I don't expect that sort of childishness from you.'

Brian Delaney helped the Commander on with his coat, pulling at the collar with one hand, and tugging his jacket down with the other. 'It's not me you're planning to eliminate, is it?' he asked with a grin, hoping the Commander would appreciate the joke and not find it stupid.

'Not yet, Brian,' the Commander said, giving him a friendly pat on the back. 'Should I?'

Suddenly the humour was gone from it, and Brian Delaney knew that if he ever did step out of line, he would be, indeed, eliminated without a qualm. He chose the Commander's own words as a reply. 'Not yet,' he said.

Later as they drove in the Commander's car, heading for Brian's home to drop him off before the Commander continued to Clones, Brian asked, 'It's definitely Declan, isn't it?'

The Commander nodded.

'He's got a lot of friends,' Brian warned.

'So have I.'

'I know, but his – they're a crappy bunch, you know. Most of them hate you. They could cause problems.'

'They could,' the Commander agreed. 'That's why I want the RUC to rid us of Declan.'

'And who'll take his place?'

'We'll discuss that when he's buried.'

Robert Larski's room had been changed while he was out. He was now on the top floor, the attic, in fact, which had been converted into a bedroom. There were no windows; a double skylight provided light and air. His old room was directly below, and as he had come up the stairs the door had been open. An extra bed had been put in, and two men he had never seen before were in the room, one reading, the other playing chess with himself. As he passed, they both looked up and smiled. One winked at him and raised a thumb encouragingly.

He lay on his bed staring at the skylight. Well, he had wanted something to happen, hadn't he? A helicopter flew overhead. He waited to see if it passed directly over his line of vision. It didn't. It whirred away. He switched off the light. The sound of the helicopter died out. Everything was darkness and silence again. If they thought he was going to stay in his room like some recalcitrant child, they were mistaken.

SEVENTEEN

Declan Finch was on a high. He floated. Everything was going as he hoped. Better, in fact. Clancy had said nothing. Larski had said nothing. He was certain of that. The Commander's attitude proved it. And he was now in the Commander's good books, in his confidence too, by the sound of things. He was one step closer to attaining the power he craved. He bounced about the house waiting for the replies to the phone calls he had placed. He was the great manipulator. The great organizer. The great all-round bloody genius. Who else had his contacts, eh? Who else had so many people willing to help in the hope of a favour returned? Who else could make a simple phone call and get information delivered from within the army, the RUC, the Protestant paramilitaries? God! This was better than anything any of the drugs he supplied could give. True, it had taken him three days to set up, but it had been so incredibly simple. That was the marvellous thing. He quietly congratulated himself on his foresight in choosing carefully to whom he had sold the drugs Clancy had supplied. All he had been required to do was suggest that no more would be forthcoming unless . . . And so everything had gone like clockwork. The most difficult thing had been ensuring that Legg would head the patrol. Usually some dumb corporal was enough if it was routine. So information had to be planted in the right ear that would necessitate a special patrol. That was tricky. It had taken someone to tell someone to tell someone to tell someone. But it had been done, that was the main thing. It had gone down the line and all for the price of one lousy injection or snort or spliff. Christ, no wonder it was easy to get information. But that was how it worked. If you can't get information yourself, have someone in your debt who *can* get it. *That* was power. With the promise of cocaine and cannabis he now knew that Legg *would* lead the patrol and how many other men would be on that patrol. He knew what weapons they would carry, and what vehicles would support them. And they would be heading for the site *he* had chosen. It was like manipulating puppets. All he needed now was two more phone calls: one to tell him that the explosives were in place, the other to tell him his men were ready. And they would be ready. By Jesus they'd be ready or his name wasn't Declan Finch.

He jumped when the telephone rang. He ran to answer it, grabbing the receiver. 'Yes? . . . Yes . . . Great . . . No, you collect them . . . That's it . . . Good lad . . . Cheers.' The men he had counted on were, of course, ready. As were their Armalites. Now the explosives. The explosives. The explosives. He slammed into the kitchen, thought about having a mouthful of beer, decided against that, and returned to the hall. He stood there, staring at the phone, shaking, urging it to ring. When it did, he lunged for it. 'Yes? . . . Right . . . Exactly where I said? . . . Great . . . Got it . . . I'm on my way.' He paused to study himself in the mirror. He was amazed that someone as ordinary looking as he knew himself to be could be so goddamn brilliant. Like clockwork: click, click, click.

Captain Alex Legg led his patrol along the perimeter of the estate. Despite the dangers he was glad to be out with the men again, and away from the confines of the barracks, away, too, from the questions and from the menace those questions had held.

'Ah, Captain. I'm Temple. Major Temple. John Temple.'

'Sir.'

'The Colonel told you why I wanted to see you?'

'Yes, sir.'

'I want you to know – and believe – that I'm truly sorry you've been dragged into all this. We had no right to do it.'

'That's all right, sir.'

'No, it's *not* all right, but there's nothing we can do about it now. You *are* in it, and what I want to do is make sure you come out of it in one piece.'

'Thank you, sir.'

'I'm going to recommend that you're sent home on leave.'

'Thank you, sir.'

'But I must have your word that you won't mess me about, that you won't go AWOL.'

'I wouldn't do that, sir.'

'No, I don't think you would. You have family?'

'My mother, sir.'

'Girlfriend?'

'I think so, sir. Had when I last heard. Sir?'

'Hmm?'

'Corporal Bayliss, sir.'

'What about him?'

'Does he get leave too?'

'I think not.'

'May I know why, sir?'

'Because . . . because Bayliss is a risk. A risk one cannot take.'

'He won't say anything, sir, if that's what you mean.'

'He might, and we simply can't take that chance.'

'He'll have to have leave sometime, sir.'

'Yes. I know. I know. When things have been cleared up.

'Will they be cleared up, sir?'

'Of course they will. Of *course* they will.'

'Couldn't Bayliss have leave with me, sir?'

'No. I said no.'

'He would be staying with me, sir. At my mother's.'

'No. Good God, man, one slip from him – from you either for that matter – and you could find yourself up on a murder charge.'

'That's what we were told to do, sir. Murder. That's what we did.'

'It was necessary. That's been explained to you. It was necessary for security.'

'Yes, sir. It was still murder, though, wasn't it?'

'It was, it was a necessary killing.'

'Yes, sir.'

The estate was quiet. The feverish snow had turned to sleet, and the wind was bitterly cold. Everyone seemed to be indoors, wisely. In any of the rooms where light was in use the curtains were drawn, but the curtains were thin, and the lights glowed through, dull and patterned. Captain Legg signalled the armoured vehicle that had transported them to the estate to pull to the side of the road and cut its engine: without the sound of the motor it was very silent. Not completely. Music and muffled applause could be heard, perhaps from radios, perhaps from television sets. It suggested warm fires and contentment. A couple of weeks' leave suddenly became very attractive. In the house on the corner, in a room at the top of the house, someone was playing Pink Floyd. Legg recognized it. *Dark Side of the Moon.* He smiled at the appropriateness of the words. 'Home, home again/I like to be here when I can/When I come home cold and tired/It's good to warm my bones beside the fire.'

The patrol continued slowly into the estate. Somewhere in there, further in, one of those homely homes was being used to store weapons. That was the information anyway. More were expected to be brought there tonight. That's why the patrol was there. The RUC should be approaching from the other side of the estate. Captain Legg hoped to hell they were. He turned to Corporal Bayliss who tracked him.'OK?'

Bayliss nodded. 'OK.'

Captain Legg winked at him.

Pink Floyd sang, 'You lock the door/And throw away the key/There's someone in my head but it's not me.'

A shadow, crouched low, came round the side of one of the houses and crept up behind the armoured car. It left something under it, and slipped back the way it had come.

In one of the houses a light was switched off.

In another a curtain moved imperceptibly.

Pink Floyd sang, 'And if the cloud bursts, thunder in your ear . . .'

Captain Legg pressed on. To his right an industrial complex sprawled its ugliness, to his left a building site looked as if it had been permanently abandoned. Suddenly, without warning, all hell broke loose. The first explosion lifted the armoured car several feet into the air. It was instantly engulfed in flames. Glass shattered, people screamed, and there was a burst of rapid gunfire. In quick succession there were other explosions, on the edge of the industrial estate, on the building site, on the road behind the patrol, on the road in front of the patrol. And all the while the crackle of gunfire. In the shifting light of the flames Captain Legg could see some soldiers lying motionless by the side of the road. He saw one, alight, running blindly in circles; he saw him lurch suddenly and collapse. Without remembering himself falling he found himself flat on the ground. He shifted his head to find Bayliss. He couldn't see him. Incongruously, 'Larry?' he called in a hoarse whisper. He heard a moan. Bayliss was directly behind him. Captain Legg swivelled himself round. Bayliss was on his back. His chest was oozing blood. Legg thought he was grinning. He wasn't. A bullet had ripped away half his jaw. A bullet zinged off the road. Legg grabbed the Corporal's collar and tried to manœuvre him towards cover. Bayliss screamed. Another bullet ricocheted off the tarmac. Bayliss said, 'What a fucking way to die.' He shuddered and lay still. Captain Legg froze in horror. Then something thundered on to his head, and all was blackness . . . And Pink Floyd sang, 'You shout and no one seems to hear . . .'

'I see you've heard,' Brian Delaney said.

The Commander nodded.

'Well, he did it.'

'He's a maniac,' the Commander said.

Delaney shrugged. 'You told him to get Legg, and he got him,' he pointed out.

'And killed eight men in the process.'

'Brits.'

'Men,' the Commander snapped, but he seemed more worried about something else. 'There's going to be hell to pay. Christ above, Brian, I didn't expect wholesale slaughter.'

Brian Delaney looked perplexed. 'They were only –'

The Commander cut short Delaney's excuse with a dismissive wave of his hand. 'I don't care what they only were. How in the name of God am I going to get Harwood to deal now? Answer me that?'

Brian Delaney felt his face burn. Then he brightened. 'Harwood doesn't know it's Legg. He won't connect this with the deal.'

'And when he finds out? And he *will* find out when we hand Legg over – what then?'

'It'll be too late. Things will have died down. You know the way things happen. A day or two and nobody remembers or cares.'

'I wish I could believe that.'

'And it'll make it easier for Harwood to get the RUC to act.'

The Commander looked at him questioningly.

'To get Declan. Jesus, they'll be falling over themselves to get him if they believe he was responsible for this.'

The Commander wasn't convinced. He shook his head. 'I don't think we can wait that long. We might have to deal with Declan ourselves, Brian. I feel uncomfortable with him running loose.'

'OK, so we deal with him. We can always arrange for the RUC to take the credit. We've done that often enough.'

The Commander seemed somewhat appeased. He stopped frowning anyway, and stopped pacing too. 'Where's Legg now?'

'Declan's stashed him.'

'Where?'

'Corrigan's.'

The Commander approved. He nodded. 'Any . . . any damage?'

'Just a sore head, Declan said. Feeling sorry for himself too, I suppose.'

'And Declan?'

'He's at home. Said he was going to keep his head down. Says he's tired.'

The Commander shook his head in wonderment. 'I tell you, Brian, Declan frightens me to death.'

'Why's that?'

'He's so conscienceless.'

'You haven't been listening to the sermons. We all are. We're doing Satan's work,' Brian told him with a grin.

Colonel Cairns was thinking along those lines also as he faced Major Temple across his desk. He had been up all night. He was unshaven. His eyes were red-rimmed. He looked haggard. Major Temple didn't look much better. They had been sitting there for the best part of five minutes, and neither of them had spoken. They were, of course, appalled and shaken by the wanton killings of eight soldiers, but uppermost in their minds were the disappearance of Captain Legg and the shattering disclosures that promised.

'We can't blame Larski for *this*,' the Colonel said finally in a tone that suggested he was, by absolving Larski, in some strange way absolving himself.

'No,' Major Temple agreed. 'It means, of course, that the terrorists know about Legg.'

'Maybe not,' the Colonel said with timid hopefulness. 'They might have shot him and dumped his body somewhere.' But when Major Temple gave him a baleful look, he added, 'No, I suppose not.'

'You released news of his disappearance?'

The Colonel nodded. 'Had to.' He sighed and grimaced. 'I know. London.' He glanced at the phone. 'I'm waiting for it to ring.'

'He'll want me,' Major Temple said ruefully.

'He'll want my *head*,' the Colonel countered. Then, surprisingly, he gave a little laugh. 'You know, I bet Robert Larski thinks we planned this.'

'Would you blame him if he did?'

'Perhaps not,' the Colonel conceded.

'If I were in his shoes I'd be thinking just that. We'll have to speak to him.'

The Colonel nodded. 'I'll speak to the Chief Constable. We'll have to arrange it through him.'

Major Temple wanted to ask why it had to be arranged through the Chief Constable, but he didn't. He didn't care who it was arranged through. He didn't care if he never heard of or saw Robert Larski again. He had to speak to him, but he wished he didn't. All he wanted was to get away from the entire dirty mess, to get home to his wife and children, to sleep at night.

Brian Delaney was right about one thing: Chief Inspector Harwood did not, for the moment, connect the killings and the disappearance of a Captain Legg with any of the arrangements he had made with the Commander. Indeed, although well aware that the Commander had been ultimately responsible for the outrage, he couldn't bring himself to detest the man who had seemed so reasonable, so detached. In truth, he had grown to quite like the Commander and regarded him as no worse, albeit no better either, than any other leader who organized destruction and death yet remained aloof. And there were plenty of those. Besides, the Chief Inspector had been busy organizing the immobilization (as the Commander had coyly put it) of Douglas Parr, upholding his end of the bargain. That, as he had anticipated, had proved a relatively facile exercise. A word to a couple of his colleagues, a rather less gentle word whispered by them in the ear of Jerry Horton, a visit by him paid to Douglas Parr, a package passed, a sudden invasion by the Drug Squad, and Douglas was safely in the Scrubs awaiting trial. But it had been a tense time too. There was always the risk that Douglas would panic and drop Harwood's name in an effort to wriggle his way to freedom, drop it in the wrong place, that is. But, thus far, he hadn't. And the Chief Inspector found himself oddly humiliated by the dealer's loyalty, and he resolved, in a vague way, to see if he couldn't put in a word for Douglas, some small mitigation, when he came to trial. Indeed, if everything went smoothly, who knew? Perhaps he could arrange for the wretched man to be freed without coming to trial. However, that was some way off. More pressing was Captain Larski's killer, and the intricacies involved in securing him. Through Brian Delaney arrangements were already in hand for Harwood and the killer to meet and, thinking about the instigation of those arrangements, the Chief Inspector still found himself amazed at the IRA intelligence network: five minutes after he himself had been alerted to Douglas Parr's arrest, he had contacted Brian and told him. Brian Delaney's answer had stunned him. 'We know.'

Try though he may have wanted to, the Commander could feel little but pity and sadness for the young Captain, tied hand and foot, on the floor before him. He was, he thought, to use the cliché, a pawn in a game, the rules of which were beyond his comprehension. He had been used by those he had trusted, and he was about to be used again by those he had been told were the enemy. He could probably see little difference between his users. Probably there was little difference between them except in name or acceptability. What upset the Commander most, though, was the sight of the sheer terror that gleamed in the young man's eyes, for although the Commander struck terror regularly into the hearts of many (and, indeed, enjoyed doing so on more than one occasion), it disturbed him to come face to face with it, to see the Captain reduced to what he thought of as something akin to a petrified animal. 'Untie him, and bring him upstairs,' he ordered and left the cellar abruptly.

Corrigan's pub was closed for the afternoon. It wasn't usually, but it was today, and most of the regulars seemed to know about that since none of them turned up. There was a small, high-ceilinged room off the main bar, where a turf fire was blazing. It was called the snug or snuggery, and in it the Commander settled himself. Corrigan, without being asked, placed a bottle of Bushmills and two glasses on the table, and withdrew without a word. The Commander unscrewed the cap on the bottle and poured whisky into both glasses, a little into the one he was himself to use, a larger amount into the other. When Captain Legg was brought in, the Commander indicated that he sit, and pushed the glass across the table towards him. He then nodded to Brian Delaney, and waited for him to withdraw before saying quietly, 'Drink that. It'll do you good.' He waited again until the Captain drank the whisky, waited while he coughed, then poured more whisky into the glass and leaned back, taking his own glass with him, cupping it in both hands as though warming the liquid.

Captain Legg was shaking. He tried to stop but couldn't. He gulped some more whisky, and looked apologetic for his jitters.

'Delayed shock,' the Commander explained. 'You'll be all right in a minute. Once the whisky takes effect. Give it time,' he said, and looked as if he had all the time in the world for his prediction to come true.

And it did come true. Soon the Captain stopped shaking, but one of his legs quivered uncontrollably. He folded his hands and placed them on his knee to stop it. 'Who are you?' he asked hoarsely. He cleared his throat of phlegm, and asked again, 'Who are you?'

The Commander shrugged. 'That doesn't matter. Suffice it to say that you have nothing to fear from me. It is not my intention to harm you.'

The Captain looked disbelieving.

'No, I mean it,' the Commander insisted. 'The fact that you are here is all I wanted.' He sipped his whisky sociably. 'The fact that you killed Captain Larski doesn't concern us,' he added, and watched as the Captain's face drained of blood, and the terror raced back into his eyes. 'No, I mean that. I am well aware that you were ordered to do it, that you would probably . . . probably . . . not have done it with any great pleasure.' The Commander took another sip. 'However . . . unfortunately . . . others, others than ourselves, that is, are anxious to . . . to lay the blame on those who are responsible. I say unfortunately because it is only through you, through your co-operation, that this can be done. You understand?'

Captain Legg didn't look as if he did fully, but he nodded anyway, and followed the Commander's example, and took a drink.

'Soon,' the Commander continued, checking his watch, 'yes, quite soon, someone will come and ask you questions. Not a military man. Not one of us. Not even someone from the Province. My advice to you, young man, would be to tell him everything he wants to know – indeed, *everything* you know whether he asks you about it or not. Only by so doing can you hope to come out of this – not unscathed, but relatively so. I make myself clear, I hope?'

Again Captain Legg nodded.

'Good. Now, let me pour you another drink.'

Corrigan's pub wasn't Corrigan's pub at all. It had been purchased with IRA funds some five years earlier when the previous owner had died, and run since by Barry Corrigan, a Provo of unquestionable loyalty and somewhat obsequious gratitude. It was a small, crumbling, ramshackle affair with a slated roof and a couple of permanent, weed-ridden hanging baskets either side of the entrance, but it was strategically situated, close to the border, and approachable only by a narrow dirt track the length of which was clearly visible from the windows.

It was up this track that Chief Inspector Harwood was now being driven. He was alone in the back. Detective Inspector Fraser had remained in the city. He had been used as a decoy, driving the Chief Inspector into the city, seeking the thickest traffic, slowing to let him out, and then continuing merrily to drive round and round the city while Harwood slipped into a supermarket by one entrance, out by another, and into a waiting car which Brian Delaney had prearranged. He was grateful when the car stopped under a sign with an arrow and the word GENTS painted in white, the arrow pointing, it seemed, to a clump of overgrown shrubbery. The ruts in the track had played havoc with his stomach, havoc with the suspension too. He got out of the car and allowed the driver to lead the way round to the entrance. Corrigan greeted them, nodding, and guiding the Chief Inspector to the snug. For a moment he hesitated, listening at the door. Then he tapped, and let Harwood in, closing the door instantly after him.

Chief Inspector Harwood removed his overcoat and threw it on the small bench set in a niche in the wall. He nodded to the Commander. He nodded to Captain Legg too, then gazed about the room, finding himself under the watchful eyes of young men in sepia photographs that hung on the walls, young men from 1916, he noted, ghostly and ethereal behind the grime on the glass, their names written in Gothic script, half-hidden by the dark-brown wooden frames, as if their identity were sinking away from them. A converted oil-lamp hung from the ceiling but it had not been switched on, and only the blue-gold flames from the fire saved the room from the late afternoon's gloomy darkness.

There was another tap on the door, and Corrigan, apologizing under his breath, came in, carrying a chair and another glass. He placed the chair between the Commander and Captain Legg, the glass on the table, and left, taking a couple of strides backwards before leaving. The Commander raised the bottle. Harwood nodded with a wisp of a smile, waiting until the whisky was poured before sitting down.

The Commander was the first to speak. 'This is the young man you wanted to meet,' he said simply.

'Does he have a name?'

'I believe so.'

Harwood fixed Legg with a steady gaze.

'Legg, sir,' the Captain said. 'Alex Legg.'

'*Captain* Alex Legg,' the Commander put in, and for a moment regretted doing so.

Chief Inspector Harwood furrowed his brow as though the name meant something to him, a name he should remember but couldn't. 'Well, Captain Alex Legg,' he said, said slowly as if the repetition of the name might trigger his recall, 'you've found yourself in a nice little mess, haven't you?'

Legg nodded.

'I've been explaining,' said the Commander, 'that we – *you* and me – we understand the, eh, little mess he's in is not of his own making. Not entirely, anyway. I also told him that his co-operation would entitle him to your special consideration. Was I wrong?'

'No,' Harwood said, but he didn't appear all that happy about it.

'Good,' the Commander said with a smile, a smile that widened and passed itself on to the Captain as well.

'I take it that you admit killing Captain Larski?'

Legg nodded.

'I didn't hear,' Harwood said sharply.

'Yes.'

'That's better. You were ordered to do it?'

'Yes.'

'By whom?'

The Captain hesitated.

Harwood snapped, 'Come on, man. Don't start buggering me about.'

'I would answer,' the Commander interjected.

'My CO.'

'Name?'

'Colonel Cairns.'

Harwood glanced at the Commander. The Commander raised his eyebrows in a fashion that indicated nothing could surprise him. Harwood gave him a damning look before continuing. 'Did you know Larski was a member of the forces when you killed him?'

'Yes.'

'And what reason did the CO give you for this . . . this execution?'

Captain Legg winced at the word. 'He said Larski – the Captain – had joined the IRA and was giving them secrets, had been for over a year. He said that if he wasn't stopped, the IRA would be able to pick us off like target practice any time they wanted.'

The Commander made an exaggerated gesture of burying his face in his hands.

'Didn't you question that?' Harwood demanded.

Legg shook his head mournfully. Then, remembering, said, 'No.'

'Didn't you even question the Colonel's order to kill him?'

'No.'

'Surely to Christ it must have struck even you as . . . as . . . as sheer bloody lunacy?'

'He made it sound right.'

'He made it sound right,' Harwood mimicked. '*That's* going to sound nice when you're facing a life sentence.'

The Commander leaned forward and interposed. 'I did mention that things might not come to that. That . . . perhaps . . . under the circumstances we might be able to assist the Captain.'

'Oh, did you?' Harwood demanded, looking angry.

'Yes. I did,' the Commander answered, all sign of benevolence gone from his tone.

Harwood decided to relent, to pretend to at any rate. 'To the killing itself. How many were involved?'

'Just the three of us.'

'Three? What three?'

'Me, Corporal Bayliss and –'

'Corporal Bayliss?' Harwood interrupted.

'He's dead. He was killed last night.' Captain Legg looked as if he were about to cry.

The Commander felt a bit like crying too. This was a line he didn't want pursued just yet. 'That episode on the estate,' he explained quietly to the Chief Inspector.

'Oh. And who else?'

'The CO, Colonel Cairns.'

Chief Inspector Harwood felt his mouth go dry. He was at a loss for words. He had never heard anything so preposterous in his life. He simply could not bring himself to believe that any commanding officer would be so stupid as to place himself in such a position. Unless . . . unless the stakes were higher than he had ever imagined. He jumped as the Commander touched his arm. 'A word in your ear – outside,' the Commander said.

It was Harwood who spoke first when they left the snug. 'I just don't believe it. It's totally incredible.'

'It's entirely possible,' the Commander said. 'You must understand what would have happened if Captain Larski had lived to tell all he knew about the so frequently denied policy of shoot to kill. It would have caused mayhem here. That would have been bad enough. On the mainland ... well, you'd certainly have been looking for a new prime minister.'

'You believe him?' Harwood asked.

'Absolutely. He's no reason to lie. He's admitted killing the Captain. He's nothing whatsoever to gain by lying.'

'Dear God!'

'You're learning the hard way, Chief Inspector. But what I wanted to say, why I asked you out here was – well, a suggestion –'

'I dread your suggestions.'

'I know. I know, but ... could we not – in return for that young man's confession, of course – could we not allow ourselves to believe ... allow him to say that it was the now dead Corporal who ... well, who administered the actual shot that killed?'

'That's ridiculous –'

'You don't want *him*,' the Commander pointed out with a small jerk of his head towards the snuggery. 'He's nothing. A stupid, frightened nobody. You want the Colonel.'

'Well the Colonel certainly isn't going to –'

'Oh, the Colonel will agree to any proposal you make – provided, of course, you word your proposal correctly. I suggest that succinct line from that excellent film *The Godfather*: make him an offer he cannot refuse. It's not the little men who should shoulder the blame. It's the people with power who cause the damage – the commanding officer in this case. You and I sometimes.'

'You have a ... a *proposal* in mind, don't you?'

The Commander gave an enigmatic smile. 'One had crossed my mind.'

'I bloody thought so. Are you going to tell me?'

'Later. I think later would be better. When we've tidied up with the Captain in there. Decided where to take him.'

The Chief Inspector stiffened. 'What do you mean – decided where to take him?'

'Well, you can't take him with you, can you? He'd be whipped away from you before you came to the first full stop in his statement – through *official* channels, of course. You've no *authority* here, my friend.'

'So what are you suggesting?'

'I'm suggesting you leave him to us. We can get him to England without too much bother. You can get your statement there.'

'Just like that?'

'Not quite *just* like that. It will take some organizing, but we're rather useful at that. Used to it, too.'

The Chief Inspector looked suddenly worried. 'Why, though? Why do all this for me – for him, Legg?'

'For Legg?' The Commander shrugged. 'Would you believe compassion?'

The Chief Inspector gave a derisory snort. 'No.'

The Commander beamed. 'I didn't think you would. Well, then, try this – it would be much more beneficial to me if the commanding officer, Colonel Cairns, was humiliated. Will that do?'

'It's more the sort of thing you would want. OK. And for me?'

'For you? Ah, well. There is that other little part of our bargain. We will, after all, need your help with that. We have decided to eliminate him ourselves . . .' The Colonel paused and gave an irritated frown as Corrigan appeared, a fresh bottle of Bushmills in his hand, holding it aloft and asking whether he should leave it in the snug or not. The Commander waved him away. 'As I said, to eliminate him ourselves, but we'll need you to organize the discovery of his body by the RUC.'

'Has the unfortunate a name?'

'Not that it matters, but yes. Finch. Declan Finch.'

'I'll do what I can.'

'That will do admirably.'

It was only later, as he was being driven back to the city, that the Chief Inspector found himself trembling as it dawned on him how casually he had been discussing Declan Finch's murder as if it were nothing, a whimsy, the tossing of a coin. His finger touched the photograph the Commander had given him, and he felt better.

Declan Finch was devastated. Anger had given way to fear, and fear had multiplied itself into terror. He still held the phone in his hand, and Corrigan's flat, nasal tones still scoured his brain. 'I'm telling you, Declan, it's true. I heard the pair of them talking about it. Eliminate you, that's what they said. Mentioned your name and all. Part of some deal they've got going.'

Declan hurled the receiver away from him. It smashed against the mirror, cracking it down its length, dragging the phone to the floor. Declan kicked it. Fuck them. Fuck the whole fucking lot of them. If they thought he'd just quietly let them eliminate him they had another think coming. He'd bloody show them. He ran upstairs and into his bedroom. He took a small travelling bag from the wardrobe and crammed clothes into it willy-nilly, anything that came to hand. He rolled back the carpet and dragged out his leather satchel. Ten grand in that, anyway. That would keep him going a while. Shit. He left the bedroom and bounded downstairs, the bag in one hand, the satchel hanging from his shoulder. He sat on the bottom step. What if Corrigan had got it wrong? Corrigan wouldn't have got *that* wrong. He might, though, and if he had . . . Car headlights swept across the glass panel of the front door. Declan eased himself to his feet. He slipped into the sitting-room and from behind the television took his gun. His back flat against the wall, he peeped out of the window. His breath left him in one, long, grateful sigh. Nothing. Neighbours coming home. Nevertheless, he checked his gun. Six bullets. Well, six of them would go down with him. What was he saying? He wasn't going to be round long enough for them to get him. They didn't know he knew. They wouldn't expect him to make a run for it. They'd think they had all the time in the world. He drew the curtains. He switched on the light. He switched on the television and turned up the volume. Let them think he was still here. He crossed to the hall again. He picked up the phone and set it back on the table. He took the receiver off and laid it on the table. If they rang to check, they'd believe he was talking to someone. Carefree, that's what they'd think he was. Unsuspecting. He gathered up the travelling bag and moved through into the kitchen. He didn't bother with the light. The light from the hall was ample. He unlocked the back door. Shit – he couldn't take his car. If his car wasn't there, he wasn't there. On foot. On foot to the main road and then a taxi. A taxi to the station. Was there a train to Dublin? Or – well, he couldn't stay here. He slipped out the door, and froze.

'Ah, Declan,' Brian Delaney said. 'Just coming to see you.'

Declan Finch tried to raise his gun. It got entangled in the strap of the satchel. There was a quiet phut from Delaney's silencer, and Declan felt his knees give way. He was dead by the time he hit the ground.

Two hours later Brian Delaney telephoned Mr Clancy in Dublin. Mr Clancy was surprised but managed to hide it.

'Bad news, I'm afraid,' Delaney said.

Mr Clancy lowered himself into the chair by the phone. Only that afternoon he had heard of Douglas Parr's arrest in London: more bad news was not what he wanted. He put on a brave voice. 'What would that be?'

'It's Declan, I'm afraid. He's been shot.'

Mr Clancy managed a convincing gasp. It could have been worse. A lot worse. 'That *is* bad news,' he said.

'Yeah. He must have annoyed someone.'

'Indeed he must.'

'There's a rumour he was dabbling in drugs, but we don't believe that.'

'Declan? Drugs? Oh, I'm sure not.'

'Mind you, he hasn't been found yet.'

'Oh dear,' Mr Clancy commiserated. Then it dawned on him. 'Then how do you know he –'

'Not found only because we haven't told anyone where to find him. Not a good day for you, is it, Clancy? First your old pal Douglas Parr getting done, and now Declan. Not a good day at all, I wouldn't think.'

Mr Clancy said nothing.

'Be warned, Clancy. Be warned,' Delaney said slowly and quietly, and hung up.

Chief Inspector Harwood knew he was entering new territory. He had struck many deals with villains in his career: every officer did, it was the way information was received, convictions achieved. But this was the first time he would attempt a deal with someone within the police force, albeit the RUC. As he waited for the Chief Constable, he said to Fraser, 'Tell me, are we mad?'

'Probably.'

'We're way out of our territory, and I don't mean just this room.'

Fraser looked about the Chief Constable's boardroom. 'Nice, though, isn't it?'

'You're some help.'

They both laughed nervously.

The door opened and the Chief Constable came in, accompanied by Malcolm Carter. 'Gentlemen,' he said by way of greeting, and sat himself down at the head of the table, looking from Harwood to Fraser, an expression of boredom on his face. He was on home ground. He was confident.

And it was that look of smug confidence that decided Harwood to take the photograph of the murdered Captain Larski from his pocket and slide it across the table without a word.

The Chief Constable looked at it. His expression didn't alter one whit. He passed it to Malcolm Carter. Carter looked at it briefly, and passed it back to the Chief Constable. The Chief Constable carefully folded it along the crease and handed it back to Harwood. He adopted an almost impudent little face, but his eyes remained steely. 'Yes?' he inquired.

Harwood tapped the photograph on his thumb. 'You know what it is?'

'The recovery of a body by the military.'

'You've seen it before!' Fraser said suddenly.

'Oh yes,' Malcolm Carter answered.

'In that case you *do* know its significance,' Harwood said.

'Its small significance,' the Chief Constable corrected.

'By itself – yes, it could be considered small. But . . . the soldier looking down at the stretcher – Captain Legg? – with his testimony *and* the photograph . . .' Chief Inspector Harwood let the significance of *that* sink in.

It took a little while. The Chief Constable and Malcolm Carter looked at each other, looked away, then looked at each other again. Then the Chief Constable joined his hands as if in prayer, fitting the tips of his fingers exactly together. 'Are you telling me you know the whereabouts of Captain Legg?'

Harwood nodded.

'And are you telling me he is prepared to make a full statement about the affair?'

'That's exactly what I'm telling you.'

'Naming names?'

'Naming names.'

'And reasons?'

'And reasons.'

'*All* the details?'

'*All* the details.'

'I see. And I take it you're telling me this for a reason?'

Harwood nodded again.

'I'd like to know it.'

'Them,' Harwood said with satisfaction.

'Them,' the Chief Constable amended.

Chief Inspector Harwood was enjoying himself. With black humour he felt himself adopting some of the Commander's mannerisms. Playing his little games. Toying. He wished he had a pipe to stick in his mouth. 'One of the reasons you'll like. The other you won't. Which would you like first?'

'Let us not waste time, Chief Inspector. I'll take them in any order you care to mention them.'

Unperturbed, Harwood folded his hands in the exact manner the Chief Constable had chosen. 'I'll give you the good news first, shall I? Before I leave I will give you the name of the man responsible for that atrocity the other night. I'll tell you where you can find him. He's dead, and the gun that killed him is under his body. When you go to collect him I would like it to be a reasonably large RUC operation. I would like a number of shots to be fired at the scene. And when you return with the body I would like you to issue through your spokesman a statement saying something along the lines of acting on information etc. and after a siege in which shots were exchanged – you know the sort of thing.'

'You want to make it look like we killed this man while trying to arrest him? That's it, isn't it?' Malcolm asked.

'That's about the size of it,' Fraser answered.

'You keep saying *you* would like this, and *you* want that – this isn't anything to do with you, is it? You're arranging it for someone else, aren't you?' the Chief Constable asked.

Chief Inspector Harwood didn't answer.

The Chief Constable went on, 'Yes,' he said in a drifting voice as if things were slowly coming into his mind. 'Of course. That would explain how you have access to Captain Legg.' He frowned. 'A very dangerous game you're playing, Chief Inspector, but I don't suppose you need to be told that. You said there was something else?'

'Oh yes. Indeed there is,' Harwood said, his tone changing, making the Chief Constable eye him with suspicion. 'Let's be frank for once, shall we, Chief Constable?'

The Chief Constable spread his hands in an odd Jewish gesture as if frankness was all he had ever wanted.

'All right. To be frank – ever since I came here you and your colleagues have done everything in your power to block my investigation. Oh, on the surface you were cooperative and bending over backwards to help, but you were determined I would leave here, or be called back from here, with nothing. Well, Detective Inspector Fraser and myself are not accustomed to getting nothing. We don't like it one little bit. You know and I know and all four of us know that hit lists *have* been passed by members of the RUC to Protestant paramilitaries. I *don't* have any names, and I'm not going to get them by any legitimate means. You *do* have the names, Chief Constable. I want those names on my desk by tomorrow morning. That way we can close this investigation, we can go home, and you can get on with whatever you do over here. Simple.'

The Chief Constable eased his chair back from the table, and crossed his legs. He stared out of the window, drumming his fingers on one knee. He seemed to be thinking, but then he turned and fixed his gaze on Chief Inspector Harwood, and it became clear he was waiting to hear what was in all this for him.

Harwood gave a thin smile. 'In return, my report will indicate that at all times I received the fullest co-operation. There will be no mention, for instance, of the fact that the office you so kindly put at our disposal was bugged.' The Chief Inspector paused and looked the Chief Constable squarely in the face. The Chief Constable stared back. He didn't flinch. If anything, there was amusement in his eyes. 'Perhaps more importantly,' Harwood continued, 'Captain Legg will make no reference to you in his statement, and Colonel Cairns will be *persuaded* to do likewise.' He waited in silence for about a minute and then stood up. He started to button his coat, conscious of the Chief Constable's eyes watching him intently. His coat buttoned, he faced the Chief Constable. 'Well?'

'Names on your desk tomorrow morning?'

'Yes.'

The Chief Constable nodded slowly. 'And the name of this man?'

Chief Inspector Harwood reached inside his overcoat and took a slip of paper from the top pocket of his jacket. He passed it over.

The Chief Constable unfolded the paper and read it carefully. His eyes brightened as he spotted Declan Finch's name. He smiled. 'You write so badly, Chief Inspector,' was his comment, making it clear he knew the writing wasn't Harwood's. He passed the note to Malcolm Carter.

'We'll deal with that for you,' he said.

Chief Inspector Harwood gave a small bow. 'Thank you, Chief Constable,' he said, and followed Fraser from the room.

The Chief Constable and Malcolm Carter remained seated. 'How long has he been here?' the Chief Constable asked.

'A month, about.'

'Only a month and he's learned how we do things. Amazing. A good thing for us, Malcolm, when he *does* leave.'

'What about this?' Malcolm asked, tossing the slip of paper on to the table.

'I'll leave you to organize that. You heard what he wants. Give it to him.'

'And the other?'

'Give him that too.'

Malcolm looked uneasy. '*All* the names?'

The Chief Constable gave a small huff. 'Of course not. Give him two. Three. Yes, give him three.' He stood up.

'Which three?'

'*Any* three. It doesn't matter.' He made for the door. 'You can put your own name forward if you like,' he added with a cunning grin.

'What about Cairns?'

'Who?'

'Colonel Cairns.'

'Never heard of him.'

Malcolm was getting peeved. 'You told him you'd deliver Larski to his office.'

'Larski? Larski?' The Chief Constable feigned puzzlement. 'Another name I've never heard, Malcolm.' He left the room. There was a spring in his step as he marched down the corridor, and his shoulders were thrown back and straight as though a great burden had been lifted from them.

EIGHTEEN

By the following day the snow had ceased. It was bright and cold and clear. And something of the brightness must have rubbed off on the Commander since his mood was sprightly. He was waiting for a ten o'clock phone call from Chief Inspector Harwood, and with three minutes to go he passed the time by rereading the article that had made the morning editions. It referred to a successful RUC operation conducted the night before in which, acting on information received, the security forces had shot dead a known terrorist, named as Declan Finch of Ballymurphy. It further transpired that after searching the victim's house evidence had come to light that indicated the same Declan Finch had been involved in a major way in the atrocity in which eight soldiers had been slaughtered.

As he read, the Commander nodded his agreement with the text. He did wonder how, if asked, the RUC would explain what possible sort of evidence would indicate that Declan had been involved in the massacre; but he didn't wonder for long. They wouldn't, of course, be asked. And no one would question the veracity of their statement. People would just think that another damn terrorist had been removed from their midst, thank God, and get on with their lives. Then the phone rang. 'Good morning, Chief Inspector. I see you had a successful chat with the Chief Constable. I trust you got *everything* you wanted.'

'Yes. As a matter of fact I did.' The Chief Inspector sounded as chirpy as the Commander.

'I think we'll have to get you to work for us.'

'Huh. It seems I have been working for you.'

'I meant on a permanent basis.'

'No thanks.'

'A shame,' the Commander said with an exaggerated, good-humoured sigh. A curious noise came down the line. 'Where are you calling from?'

'A phone box.'

'Ah. Good. Well, if you *did* get everything you wanted, I suspect we won't have the pleasure of your company for all that much longer.'

'A week or two.'

'Home in time for Christmas. That will be nice.'

'Lovely.' The Chief Inspector waited for something more to be said. When only silence was forthcoming, he asked, 'What about the other one?'

'The big one?'

'Yes.'

'Oh, I think you can leave him to us. I thought it might be a considerate gesture to let Robert give him the sad tidings – sad for him, that is.'

'Will he?'

'I'm sure he'll be delighted to.'

'You haven't asked him?'

'Not yet. There's someone else I want him to talk to first.'

'Oh?'

'Legg.'

'You want Larski to meet Legg?' Harwood sounded appalled.

'I think they should meet. It would do them both good. For the one it could be absolution, for the other – well, a way to rid himself of his anger.'

'On your head be it.'

'Yes,' the Commander said thoughtfully. 'And then we shall be shipping your goods to the mainland.'

'When is that?'

'Probably tonight. Second class they should be there in a couple of days. They'll be waiting for you when you get back. Properly matured.'

'Right. That's that, then.'

'So it would seem. A happy Christmas to you.'

'And you. Behave yourself.'

'I always do. It's those others . . .'

'It always is.'

They were both laughing quietly as they hung up.

There was nothing bright about Robert Larski's humour, however. For too long he had found himself confined to Kitty Doherty's house, a bloody prisoner to all intents and purposes. He had, of course, made several attempts to go out, but on each occasion he had found himself blocked. Although there were only two of the Commander's men inside the house, they seemed to be everywhere. They were very polite, very friendly and very adamant that he should stay indoors until they had instructions to the contrary.

'Can't you just relax,' one of them had said. 'Watch telly, or read, or something. There's a lot of business going on right now, and you sticking your nose in will cause nothing but trouble.'

It was that which had upset Robert the most: a lot of business going on right now, and he objected to being excluded. Everything was being taken out of his hands. He was being told nothing. He had been used, he believed, and was now shoved into the background and expected to wait uncomplainingly. He had even tried, absurdly, to escape, as he thought of it, through the skylight. Had mounted the chair and eased the panel open. But there, on the roof, like dark avenging angels, sat two more men, who dissuaded him from exiting by wagging their forefingers at him as if he were a naughty boy.

So, it was something of a surprise and a considerable relief when Brian Delaney turned up at the house and told him that they were going for a drive.

'A drive in the country, I suppose,' Robert remarked facetiously.

'Not quite,' Brian replied.

They didn't go near the country. Robert was driven to the Shankill Road and led into a house by the back door.

The Commander was waiting for him in the kitchen. A kettle was about to come to the boil on a gas stove. There was a stack of saucers on the table, and cups piled one within the other. There was the smell of eggs and bacon. A cat cleaned itself on the window-sill, its head bobbing up and down rhythmically like one of those strange toys one sometimes sees in the back windows of cars.

'Robert,' the Commander said welcomingly, and he held out his hand.

Robert ignored the hand. 'What the hell is going on?' he demanded. 'Why have I been kept bloody well locked up?'

'Locked up?' the Commander sounded shocked. 'Oh, I think not. You have been under protection. For your own good. Please sit down.'

'I haven't been allowed leave the house,' Robert said, and remained standing.

'Sit down, Robert,' the Commander repeated. It was a quiet command.

Robert sat.

And the Commander sat.

The cat stopped cleaning itself, yawned, and curled itself into a ball. The kettle boiled, and Brian Delaney switched off the gas. He looked at the Commander. 'Tea?' the Commander asked Robert.

Robert Larski shook his head.

'No, thank you, Brian.'

Brian Delaney put the kettle to one side and left the room, pulling the curtain that acted as a door.

'Robert,' the Commander began quietly, reasonably, 'I know you feel that you have been excluded. And so you have. But you must believe me when I tell you it was – truly – for your own safety.'

'So you keep saying.'

The Commander twitched at the interruption. 'Now, however . . . now that certain matters have been dealt with – successfully, I might add – it is for you to . . . to . . . to make the *coup de grâce*,' he concluded melodramatically.

'Oh really?' Robert asked sarcastically.

'Really,' the Commander confirmed.

'And what does that mean?'

'It means that you are going to tell Colonel Cairns that you know all about the death of your brother. That you know why he was killed, who killed him, and why the cover-up was instigated.'

Robert Larski fixed his stare on the Commander's face. He felt a curious numbness. He clasped and unclasped his hands under the table. 'That's just it, though. I don't know. I don't know who killed Peter or why.'

'I will tell you,' the Commander said, his voice paternal. 'But first, I want you to meet somebody.'

Robert felt his body jerk. 'Who?'

'Somebody who has been a great help to us – and to you, I might add.'

'Who *is* it?' Robert demanded.

The Commander rose from the table. 'Come with me.'

Stubbornly Robert remained seated. He was, he felt, about to be used again.

'Come . . . come . . . come,' the Commander said.

Robert rose and followed the Commander out of the kitchen, through the hall and into a small, untidy sitting-room. The wallpaper was Regency stripe and clashed absurdly with the cheap, modern furniture. A Formica-topped table stood in the middle of the room. There were several, perhaps as many as seven, wooden chairs with seats covered in red plastic. On one of these a young man sat. Robert eyed him. There was something vaguely familiar about him. He was dressed in jeans and a thick pullover. They didn't fit well. The pullover drooped at the neck, and the jeans had exaggerated turn-ups. The man was unshaven and looked tired.

'Robert,' the Commander said. 'This is Alex Legg.'

For some reason the name did not immediately register. Perhaps because of his pathetic civilian clothes Robert did not associate the young man with the army. He nodded.

'Captain Alex Legg,' the Commander said quietly.

Robert froze.

'Alex, this is Robert Larski – Peter Larski's brother.'

For a moment Alex Legg didn't move. Then he jumped

from his chair and started to scream, staring at Robert as if he were a horrific spectre. He crossed his arms over his face, still screaming. Brian Delaney was into the room in a flash, grabbing Legg and shaking him. The terrible screams became a whimper. Brian led him back to the chair and sat him down, staying behind him, one hand resting on his shoulder. 'I'm sorry,' Legg said in a whisper, shaking his head. 'I'm sorry. I'm sorry. I'm sorry,' he said over and over, his voice rising with each apology. Brian Delaney squeezed his shoulder gently. 'I'm sorry,' Legg said again, back to a sorrowful whisper.

Robert Larski felt sick. He had never before witnessed anything that appalled or frightened him so much. He had never before felt so impotent. He wanted to hate the Captain, but he couldn't. He wanted to grab him and bash him relentlessly about the room, but he couldn't. All he could do was stand there rooted to the spot and feel sick. Feel like crying too. And there were tears in his voice when he asked, 'Did you kill my brother, Legg?'

'No . . . no he didn't,' the Commander put in quickly, glad to see that the Captain did not appear to have heard the question and had now buried his face in his hands. 'He was there, but he didn't kill him.'

'Who did?' Robert asked, surprised at the tenderness of his own voice, his eyes still fixed on the trembling Captain.

'A corporal. A Corporal Bayliss. He's dead himself now,' the Commander said.

'You killed him?'

The Commander looked affronted. 'No. There was an explosion. He –'

'Get me out of here,' Robert said.

The Commander nodded, and led the way back to the kitchen. He watched as Robert folded his arms on the table and dropped his head on to them. He waited as he cried.

After a few minutes Robert raised his head. He took a handkerchief from his pocket and wiped his eyes. 'I wanted to kill him,' he said with a timid smile.

'Before or after you met him?' the Commander asked.

Robert gave a deep sigh. 'Before,' he admitted.

'Ah,' the Commander gave a small sigh and seemed gratified. 'All right now?' he asked, sounding genuinely concerned.

Robert put the handkerchief back in his pocket and gave a couple of quick nods. 'Yes, thanks.'

'You know, Legg is as much a victim as your brother.'

'He's alive.'

'That can be worse.'

Robert stood up and went to the stove. He lit the gas and put the kettle back on. He stood there, staring at it until it boiled. He took the teapot from the shelf over the stove. There was a box of tea bags on the drainer by the sink. He took out three and put them in the teapot. He added hot water and carried the teapot back to the table. The Commander set two cups on saucers and Robert filled them with tea. Then he sat down and sipped some tea. The Commander looked askance at the milkless fluid, but drank also.

'What about Cairns?' Robert asked after a few moments.

'You want to talk about him now?'

'Yes,' Robert said firmly.

The Commander put down his cup, gratefully it seemed, if the look on his face meant anything. 'I presume you do want to see him?'

'Yes,' Robert said quietly, leaving no doubt that this was what he wanted.

'You will have to be careful,' the Commander warned.

'I know.'

'I mean in what you say.'

Robert eyed the Commander. 'You're going to tell me what I should say, aren't you?'

'I'm going to *suggest* what you might say.'

'I'm listening.'

It didn't take long for the Commander to suggest what Robert should say. When he was finished, Robert asked, 'And that's all?'

'That's all. It's enough. You'll see.'

'If he sees me.'

'I'm sorry?'

'If Cairns agrees to see me,' Robert said.

The Commander laughed. 'Of course he'll see you, Robert. You're the one person he's longing to see. Why don't you give him a ring and find out for yourself. Got the number?'

'No. No I don't. Not here. It's in –'

'Brian!' the Commander called, adding, when Brian came to the door, 'Get the Colonel's number for Robert, would you?'

'Sure thing,' Brian said with a huge smile.

While they waited the Commander fidgeted as if he had something on his mind. Finally he placed the palms of his hands flat on the table and asked, 'Robert, would you do me a great favour?'

'That depends.'

'A favour to me, and to Legg – and to yourself?'

Brian Delaney came into the kitchen and placed a slip of paper on the table. The Commander clicked his tongue, irked at being interrupted.

'You do it, Brian. Please. Get on to the Colonel and tell him Robert Larski wants to see him urgently. Fix the time. Thank you.' His eyes followed Brian as he left the kitchen. He was still watching the door when Robert asked, 'What's the favour?'

'Would you shake hands with Legg before you leave?'

Robert Larski hadn't expected that. For a moment he was stunned. Then angry. But as he watched the Commander's face, as the significance of the request dawned on him, he relaxed, and managed a thin, wistful smile. 'Yeah,' he said. 'All right. I'll do that.'

The Commander looked remarkably sad for someone who had successfully arranged a favour. He patted Robert on the arm. 'Good,' he said. 'Good.'

'Good,' Colonel Cairns said to Major Temple. 'Larski's asked to see me. Saves me having to thank the Chief Constable.'

'What time is he coming?'

'This afternoon. Three-thirty.'

'Do you mind if I sit in?'

'You're the one who *wanted* to see him.'

'Yes. But he didn't ask to see me,' Major Temple pointed out.

'Does he know you're here?'

'No. At least I don't think so. You never know with him. He has a way of finding things out.'

'Indeed he has,' Colonel Cairns agreed. 'Fortunately for us he hasn't been able to make much use of any information he's gleaned.'

'That we know of,' the Major said.

The Colonel preferred to be optimistic; and it was with optimism that he welcomed Robert as he was shown into his office, adopting a somewhat patronizing tone, the tone of someone prepared to be generous with his time to someone who was doomed to waste it. 'And what can I do for you *this* time, Mr Larski?'

Robert ignored the question for the moment. He was focusing on Major Temple. 'I didn't expect to find you here,' he said.

'Just passing through,' the Major said blandly.

'I'm sure.'

'Of course you know each other,' Colonel Cairns said. 'I'd forgotten.'

'Not very well,' the Major said.

'*Very* well,' Robert contradicted.

'Interesting,' Colonel Cairns observed, more for want of something to say than anything else. 'Now, what can I do for you?'

Robert recalled what the Commander had said, and tried hard not to smile. 'I know just what he'll do,' the Commander had said. 'He'll be very suave, and cool, and superior. He'll try and make you believe he's dying to help you. If I was a betting man I'd lay you reasonable odds on his first question being: what can I do for you? When he does' – the Commander gave an outrageous chortle – 'sock it to him!'

'You can resign,' Robert said to the Colonel.

Although thoroughly annoyed by this impertinence the

Colonel decided to treat it as a jolly joke. 'I'm sure you'd find a lot of people to back you in that request, Mr Larski. Commanding officers are not the most popular species in the world.' He laughed hugely.

Sock it to him.

'I spent all last night talking to Captain Legg,' Robert lied.

The laughter gurgled in the Colonel's throat. He sounded as if he were choking. He coughed. His eyes glazed, and when they cleared his voice was filled with menace. 'You what?'

Sock it to him.

'He's told me everything. I wrote it all down and he signed it. It's on its way to London right now. Should make the headlines tomorrow with a bit of luck.'

Colonel Cairns looked at Major Temple for inspiration, but the Major was busily studying his fingertips, and there was something suspiciously like a smile on his lips.

Sock it to him.

'He told me all about the killing. How *you* issued the orders for Peter to be shot. How *you've* been trying to cover everything up.'

The Colonel began to bluster. He said it was preposterous. It was a tissue of lies. It was slander and libel. He actually said 'publish and be damned', which made the Major snort.

'OK,' Robert said and made as if to leave.

'Nobody will believe it,' the Colonel insisted.

Robert shrugged. 'Maybe not. Won't stop them wondering, though, will it, Colonel? See you –'

'Wait.'

Robert turned and faced the Colonel. He wanted more than anything in the world to kill him. He hated him more than he had hated Captain Legg when he found out who he was. But he managed to remain calm, a cheeky, cocky look on his face. 'Yes?'

'What is it you want, Larski? Money?'

Robert threw back his head and burst out laughing. Major Temple went to the window and stared out, his shoulders bouncing up and down, unable to control himself. 'Christ,' Robert gasped between laughs. 'Christ, you're something else, Colonel. I told you what I want. I want you out of the army as fast as that fat arse of yours can be shifted. That's what I want.' Robert felt his anger rising now. 'I tell you what I'm going to do. One week. That's what you've got. I'll put a hold on Legg's statement for one week. If you haven't resigned by then I'll have it splattered over the front page of every newspaper. And you *know* I can arrange that. You're a grade-A bastard, Cairns. You're a fucking coward. You're . . . you're *shit*.' Robert Larski slammed out of the office and crashed the door closed behind him.

'I'll have a word with him,' Major Temple said hastily, and chased after him.

'Robert! Robert!' he called at Robert's receding figure.

Robert Larski stopped. He didn't turn round. He stood in the middle of the corridor, his hands in his pockets, his head back. But as the Major approached he rounded on him. 'Did you hear him?' he shouted. 'Did you hear? Money! Christ, Jesus, is he mad? Doesn't he have any conception even now of what he's done?'

'He's frightened,' the Major said.

'Frightened? Jesus, I'd really like to frighten him.'

'You did. The reason I came after you – I wanted to tell you that I've already decided to resign myself.'

'You don't –'

'I decided weeks ago.'

'Will he go?'

'I don't know. Did you really speak to Legg?'

'Yes,' Robert said truthfully.

'And the statement?'

'What about it?'

'Will you use it?'

'If I have to. Depends on that creep.'

'If you decide you have to – be careful, Robert.' The Major lowered his voice as if about to give some specific warning. Then he bit his lip, and added, 'Just be careful.'

'Yeah,' Robert said.

'And good luck.'

'Thanks.'

Major Temple watched Robert swing his way down the corridor and out of the door.

'Well?' the Colonel demanded when he came back. He was seated, and was sweating a little. His face was patchy white. He held a handkerchief in one hand and from time to time wiped his brow.

'Well nothing,' the Major told him. 'He's sticking by what he said. Either you go or he prints.'

'You think he would?'

'I'm sure he would.'

'Damn him,' the Colonel said between his teeth.

'We're the damned, Colonel. You and me and the rest of those like us.'

'Oh bullshit,' the Colonel snapped.

The Major picked up his briefcase. 'Well, I may as well start making plans to get back to London. The Brigadier is waiting for my report.'

'What will you –'

'Everything, Colonel. Everything.'

'You couldn't –'

'You're right, Colonel, I couldn't. Whatever it is, I know I couldn't.'

Robert Larski packed his bags as quickly as he could. There was a plane in an hour, and he had a seat on it. He hurried downstairs. One of the men who had been guarding him was waiting at the bottom of the stairs.

'Where's Mrs Doherty,' Robert asked. 'I want to pay my –'

'All taken care of, Mr Larski.'

'Oh. Fine. Right. I'll be off then.'

The man smiled. 'Not that easy to get rid of us, I'm afraid. We've been told to see you safely on to your plane.'

'Make sure I leave, you mean.'

'Whatever.'

The second man appeared at the front door. 'All ready? Good. Car's waiting.'

'Some service.'

'Nothing but the best.'

As the car sped towards the airport Robert found himself thinking again about the Commander. Suddenly he laughed. 'Sock it to them,' he said aloud. The two men looked at him as if he were raving.

NINETEEN

'You look –' Jimmy Fermin mouthed a mild vulgarity.

'That's just how I feel,' Robert admitted.

'I wish you'd warned me you were coming back. I could easily have met you at the airport.'

'It was sort of on the spur of the moment.'

Robert had gone directly from the airport to Jimmy Fermin's office, and they sat in it now, one either side of the desk that was cluttered with papers, an old typewriter, and Jimmy's feet. Although Fermin could barely control his curiosity, he refrained from asking anything yet. He contented himself by staring at his friend, sensing a strange fragility about him, the same tense, acute vulnerability he had noticed once before in a hostage he had interviewed on his release from captivity. That hostage had been suspicious and bewildered and reluctant to speak. It had been as though he could not, for the moment, decide whether the enclosed world he had just left, or the chaotic one into which he found himself dumped, was the true one. He had also, Fermin recalled, spoken very quietly, almost constantly in whispers, as though he had become used to sharing secrets with himself and could not quite forsake this private procedure. And it seemed to Fermin that Robert was experiencing similar impediments. He was relieved when Robert broached the subject, albeit in a way he didn't expect. 'You've still got the photograph I sent you?'

'Sure.'

'Here?'

'Yep.'

'Get it, will you?'

Jimmy Fermin swung his feet off the desk and went to a small safe in the corner of the office. From it he took, still in its envelope, the photograph, and brought it back to the desk. Robert reached out and took it. He slid out the picture and stared at it for a long time. Then he looked about the office for something. He stood up, picked up the metal bin and returned to his chair. 'Got a match?' he asked.

Without speaking, Fermin searched in his pocket and handed over a small, disposable lighter.

Robert touched the flame to one corner of the photograph. When it was ablaze he dropped it into the bin. He watched it as it folded in upon itself. When the flame spluttered and went out, and a thin wisp of smoke rose from the ashes, he closed his eyes. Then, with a little shake, he said, 'That's it.'

Fermin said nothing.

'Let's go and get drunk, Jimmy.'

'Best suggestion I've heard in weeks.' He stood up and buttoned the neck of his shirt. 'You should call Gemma,' he said hesitantly.

'Not tonight, Jimmy. Tonight I just want to get drunk. I'll call her tomorrow.'

'Whatever you say.'

'Yeah. Whatever I say. Well, I say let's you and me get drunk and I'll tell you all about it.' He gave a short, grim laugh. 'I don't think I could tell you while I'm sober.'

'In that case, let's get started.'

And a couple of hours later Brigadier Carlisle was giving a short, grim laugh also. He was holding in his hand Major Temple's letter of resignation, which was bad enough, and on the desk before him lay the report of Colonel Cairns's death. He was thinking that soldiers of today had no stamina, no guts, none of the bulldoggedness that he and his contemporaries had. And although he knew it was useless, although he had no inclination to pursue it, he said, 'I can reject this, of course, and hold you to your service commission.'

'You could, sir.'

The Brigadier put the letter to one side. 'Very well. I'll have it processed. You're throwing away a great career, you know?' he said, but there was little enthusiasm or conviction in his voice.

Major Temple remained silent.

'And this,' the Brigadier went on, stabbing a finger at the report with something like disgust in his voice. 'What do we do about this?'

'There's very little we can do, sir, except allow the report to stand.'

'Oh, I see. Just admit that one of our commanding officers shot himself in the head? I suppose you'd like us to tell everyone *why* he did it too?'

'To tell the truth – yes, I would. But I know you won't.'

'You're damn right we won't, Major,' the Brigadier exploded. Then he narrowed his eyes. 'And you won't either, Major,' he said, and there was no mistaking the threat in his voice.

The Major smiled. 'No. No, I won't, sir. I'd be too ashamed to let anyone know I was mixed up in the whole dirty business.'

'You'd better go, Major,' the Brigadier said coldly. 'You disappoint me more than I can say.'

Alone, the Brigadier read the report for the fourth time, shaking his head as he read. Then he pulled a large pad towards him, and started to write. 'In a strange accident Colonel Michael Cairns,' he wrote. He crossed out the word 'strange', and sucked the end of his pen. Then he ripped the paper from the pad, and started again. 'In a bizarre accident . . .'

'What is going *on*?' the Minister demanded to know.

It took some time for Brigadier Carlisle to tell him, and the Minister was none too pleased. 'How could you let things come to such a pass?' he asked.

The Brigadier could find no answer to that. In truth, he could not understand himself how it had all come to pass. It was absurd that one damn civilian could cause such mayhem. He cursed Larski, he cursed the Minister too, under his breath, for his aptitude in pulling unanswerable questions from the air, just as now he tossed another one at him. 'And where's this Robert Larski now?'

'We don't know, sir.'

The Minister looked amazed. 'You don't know?'

'Back in England, we think.'

'You *think*?' The Minister blew on the tip of his cigar. When it glowed, he asked, 'Hadn't you better find out? We can hardly leave him to –'

'I've been advised, sir, that it would be wise to leave Larski be.'

'What do you mean – leave him be?'

'Just that, Minister. To take no further action against him. It seems he has got all that he wanted. It seems also very likely that he has insured himself against any . . . any untoward eventuality.'

The significance of what the Brigadier was saying didn't seem to strike the Minister immediately. 'I don't see how we can just ignore –'

'It's the advice I've been given,' the Brigadier said pointedly.

'By whom?'

The Brigadier didn't answer, not verbally anyway, but there was a cunning look in his eye which the Minister finally spotted.

'Oh,' the Minister said.

'We will just leave him be . . . for the time being. If, at some future date, we feel he is about to – what? . . . stir up a hornet's nest? – well, then we can reactivate his case.'

The Minister nodded slowly.

Brigadier Carlisle waited.

'Very well,' the Minister said. 'I'll abide by your decision. But it is *your* decision, Brigadier. I want to make that clear.'

'You have, Minister. Actually, I'm rather less worried about Mr Larski than I am about one of our own – Major Temple.'

The Minister, who had been on the point of relaxing, looked agitated again. He flung his half-smoked cigar into the fire, and glared at the Brigadier. 'Explain,' he snapped.

'He wants to resign.'

'That would seem an advantage rather than –'

'He has also developed a conscience,' the Brigadier explained, puckering his lips as if the word made an acid taste in his mouth.

The Minister decided evidently that matters of conscience were beyond him. 'Get advice from your advisers,' he said succinctly.

'I already have.'

'And?' the Minister asked, then changed his mind. 'No. Don't tell me. I don't want to know.' He checked his watch. 'I have to go. Have you decided about Cairns?'

'I've drafted a press release. A bizarre accident, I called it.'

'Bizarre . . . I like that. I like that a great deal,' the Minister said. 'Will they believe it?'

The Brigadier shrugged. 'Probably not. They never believe anything we say.'

The Minister found that amusing. 'They never believe anything *we* say either.'

Major John Temple swung his car on to the motorway, and headed home. It was raining again, and the wipers clicked across the windscreen. He shoved a tape into the machine. Mozart. What he called the 'Elvira Madigan bit'. He had no great pretensions when it came to music. He knew what he liked, and that was the sum of it. The wipers were on slow, and they beat time to the music like a metronome. For the first time in a long while he was feeling good about things, good about himself, which was more important. What he was going to do when he finally quit the army he had no idea. A vague idea about emigrating crossed his mind. Australia. New Zealand. Sunshine. Beaches. Sheep. The thought made him smile.

He turned off the motorway towards Wheatley. He noticed the car behind him, but didn't give it a second thought. Mozart had given way to Roger Waters. 'But oh, the tide is turning . . .' Temple turned right for Waterperry. The headlights of the car behind dazzled him for a moment, and he readjusted his rear-view mirror. He bypassed Waterperry and made for Brill. He knew the road well. The car behind irritated him, staying too close but refusing to pass. The Major accelerated. The moment he turned the bend he saw the lorry straddling the road. He could do nothing to avoid it. He slammed on his brakes and felt his car slide away from him. It crashed into the lorry and jammed itself underneath, its roof whipping away. The two men in the cab of the lorry jumped down. One of them checked the Major and gave a thumbs-up sign. The other man nodded, ran to the car that had been following the Major and jumped in. The car reversed into a gateway. Its wheels spun in the mud. The gears grated. Then it mounted the road again and sped off, back in the direction it had come.

Several hundred miles away, in the small fishing port of Kirkcudbright, a fishing boat tied up, its diesel engines coughing. A white Volkswagen van stood on the quayside. A man leaned against it, smoking a cigarette. As soon as the boat docked, he slid back the door of the van. Two men left the boat and hurried towards the van, jumping into it. The door was slammed shut from the outside, and in moments the van left the quay. It turned left over the bridge. About twenty minutes later it stopped outside the Anwoth Hotel in Gatehouse of Fleet. The driver jumped out, leaving the engine running, and opened the door. The passengers waited until he had given them the all-clear, and then they walked swiftly into the hotel and up the stairs to the bedrooms. The taller of the two led the way down a short corridor and opened one of the doors leading off it. 'In here,' he said. 'You'll be grand here. Just an overnight stop. Someone else will collect you in the morning and take you on down south.'

Captain Legg nodded, and sank on to the bed. The man said, 'Don't worry. You'll be OK now. We've more people here to look after you than we have across the water.'

'Thanks,' Legg said.

'Get some shut-eye,' the man told him, and closed the door behind him.

Obediently Captain Legg eased himself down on to his side, and closed his eyes, trying to block everything from his mind, falling into a fitful sleep.

'You'll be off back to New York now, I suppose?' Jimmy Fermin asked.

'Yes. I suppose.'

They were back in Jimmy Fermin's flat. Their drunken spree had failed spectacularly, and although they had consumed more alcohol than either of them cared to think about, it had had little effect. Possibly it was Robert's narration of all that had taken place that had kept them sober.

'I still think you're wrong,' Jimmy said.

'He's not worth it. Anyway, all you're thinking about is a good story. As long as the bastard resigns, I don't honestly care.'

'If he doesn't you will do something?'

'Don't sound so hopeful, Jimmy. He'll resign. Anyway, enough about that. I'm for bed. You know what pisses me off? We're going to wake up tomorrow with two monumental hangovers without even the luxury of having been drunk.'

Jimmy Fermin laughed. He waited until Robert had reached the bedroom door, and opened it. 'Hey, Robert?'

'Hmm?'

'Good to have you back in one piece.'

'I don't know yet if I *am* in one piece.'

'You'll survive.'

'Lots of people *survive*, Jimmy. That's not what I'm talking about. 'Night.'

''Night.'

It was cold in the bedroom. Jimmy hadn't thought to switch on the heating. Robert undressed quickly and got into bed, snuggling down under the blankets. Outside a fight had started. People shouted at each other. Cursing. Someone shouted, 'I'll fucking kill you'. Robert pulled the blankets over his head, and crashed into sleep.

'Oh dear, that is shocking news,' the Minister said.

'I thought you'd want to know.'

'Yes. Yes, indeed. Shocking. People *do* seem to drive too fast nowadays.'

'Yes,' the Brigadier agreed.

'A proper funeral, I hope.'

'Yes. Full honours.'

'Of course. My goodness. You'll have your hands full, won't you? The Colonel, and now poor Major Temple. Married was he?'

'Yes. I've sent someone to inform his wife.'

'Oh good. No problems with the police?' the Minister asked, his voice sounding overly casual.

'None. Unfortunate accident, they say. Lorry turning when Temple came round the corner. Damn near decapitated the unfortunate chap.'

'Oh dear. Well, thank you for letting me know. Better get back. If we don't win this rubber . . .' The Minister hung up without explaining what would happen if the rubber were lost.

The Brigadier returned to his desk, collecting from the side-table the drink he had poured before telephoning the Minister. He took a sip and set the glass on his desk. He picked up the letter of resignation Major Temple had given him and ripped it into tiny pieces. He crossed to the fire and dropped the pieces in, knocking them down between the logs with the tip of his shoe. He was the only one left now. Apart from Robert Larski – Robert Larski. He gave the logs a prod. The Brigadier decided to dismiss Robert Larski from his mind. For the moment. He returned to his desk and finished his drink in one gulp. All that fuss, he thought. All that fuss. Still, the outcome could have been worse. Much worse. He would have to take care when appointing Temple's successor, though. But he would think about that in the morning. Tomorrow, as they said, was another day. He switched out the lights and went cheerfully off home to bed.

TWENTY

Robert Larski awoke with a start. It took him some moments to remember where he was. When he did, he stretched as luxuriously as a cat and glanced at the travelling clock on the bedside table. Eight-thirty. He got out of bed and, in his underclothes, crept downstairs. It was Saturday, and Jimmy Fermin took Saturdays off. He made for the kitchen. Coffee was what he wanted, and plenty of it. Not that his hangover was as bad as he had expected, but it was bad enough. 'Oh. You're up.'

'Been up for over an hour. Couldn't sleep. There's coffee in the pot.'

'Thanks. How's the head?'

'It's been better.' He eyed Robert. 'You'll catch your death.'

'I was going to make coffee and take it back to bed.' He trotted into the hall and came back wearing his overcoat. 'Better?'

'Decenter,' Jimmy said, and grimaced. 'Decenter – that's a good start to the day.'

Robert carried his mug of coffee to the table and sat down. He held the mug with both hands wrapped round it and sipped noisily.

'No toast?'

'Uh-huh. Just liquid.'

'Sleep all right?'

'Like a log – once those yobbos quietened down.'

'Kids,' Jimmy said. 'Nowhere to go. London's full of them. Poor bastards. Some life they've got staring them in the face.' He had a morning paper on his lap, and he half lifted it, but quickly put it back on his lap again.

'Don't you forget to phone Gemma.'

'I won't.'

'Those blokes frightened her to death.'

'I'll call her. Just as soon as I finish this.'

'See that you do.'

'Dammit, Jimmy, I said I would.'

'All right.'

'What's the matter with you?'

'Nothing. Oh shit. Here, you may as well read this.' Jimmy threw the paper across the table. 'Page two.'

OFFICER KILLED IN BIZARRE ACCIDENT, Robert read. It wasn't a big headline, not one that would immediately catch your eye, but big enough to be considered respectful. According to the report, Colonel Timothy Cairns was killed in a bizarre accident. He was apparently cleaning his service revolver, leaning back in his chair as he did it. The chair toppled backwards, the gun went off, the Colonel was dead. Robert snorted. 'You don't really believe that, do you?'

'It's in the paper – it must be true,' Jimmy replied with false sincerity.

'God, they couldn't even file a report that sounded right. You tell me what sort of Colonel he'd have to be to clean his revolver when it was loaded!'

'Turn to page five.'

Robert turned the pages.

'Bottom left,' Fermin instructed. Robert looked where he was told. 'Can't see anything,' he said, frowning.

'Under ROAD ACCIDENTS ON THE INCREASE.'

Robert ran his eye down the article. Near the end he read, 'In another accident Major John Temple was killed outright when his car collided with a stationary lorry near Waterperry, Oxon.' That was all. 'Poor bastard,' Robert said. 'He was another one they used. Told me he had decided to resign as soon as he got back.'

'Two nasty accidents, eh?'

'Meaning?'

'Meaning you be careful, Bob.' Fermin stood up and poured himself another cup of coffee. 'It strikes me they're cleaning up. It might not be over yet. So you be careful.'

'They won't do anything to me. Not while they think I've got Legg's statement. And if they are cleaning up, as you put it, they're cleaning up their own. Anyway, maybe Temple's *was* an accident.'

'Maybe. Page four.'

'Huh?'

'Page four.'

'Where, for Christ's sake?'

'Here, give it to me.' Jimmy Fermin reached over and took the paper. 'The Chief Constable of the RUC announced last night that following investigations into the passing of "death lists" by members of the RUC to Protestant paramilitaries, three RUC officers had been placed under arrest and would appear in court later this week. A spokesman for Chief Inspector Harwood, who has been carrying out the investigation, stated that there was no evidence that the practice was widespread, and that he was satisfied that the three officers under arrest were the only ones involved. He also stated that his investigation was now concluded and he publicly thanked the Chief Constable and other officers of the RUC for their co-operation.' Jimmy Fermin tossed the paper back on to the table. 'Mean anything to you?'

'Nothing.'

'Oh, just thought it might.'

'No.'

'I just thought that coming so soon after – oh well, if it doesn't mean anything . . .'

'Honestly, Jimmy. It doesn't.'

'OK.'

'I'd better ring Gemma.'

'Yes, you'd better.'

The same morning Douglas Parr was taken from his cell in Wormwood Scrubs and escorted to a small interview room in another block. He was told, politely enough, to sit on one of the two chairs. A prison officer stayed with him while he waited. There was a table between the two chairs, and a window with clouded glass set high in the outer wall.

After some minutes the door opened and a man in civilian clothes came in. He had a quiet word with the prison officer, who nodded seriously and left, closing the door behind him. The back of his head remained visible through a glass panel in the door.

The man tossed a packet of Benson and Hedges on to the table. Then he took the empty chair by the back, spun it around and sat down, straddling it. 'Help yourself,' he said, flicking a flame on to a lighter and holding it for Douglas. When Douglas had lit his cigarette, the man said, 'I'm Detective Inspector Fraser.'

Douglas blew out smoke and stared at him without any reaction.

'The name Harwood mean anything to you?'

'No,' Douglas said in a flat, expressionless voice, his eyes unblinking and blank.

'Anthony Harwood?'

'No.'

'Chief Inspector Anthony Harwood?'

'No.' Douglas used the same flat voice. He sucked hard on his cigarette, swallowing the smoke in gulps. His hands were perfectly steady. He was surprised but still showed no reaction when Fraser broke into a huge grin. He just wondered what the detective was up to, what new scheme they were initiating to make him name names. It frightened him that they had connected the Chief Inspector with him.

'I have a message from him for you,' Fraser said, still keeping the grin on his face.

Douglas just stared and smoked.

'He says to tell you that he hasn't forgotten you, and that you might not even come to trial.'

Still Douglas stared, not even shifting his eyes from the detective's face as he flicked ash into the jam-jar lid that served as an ashtray.

'He says he won't be seeing you again, and that if he *does* succeed in getting you off, you'll be on your own.'

Douglas tried to blow a smoke-ring.

'But there's a warning,' the detective said, and he spoke very slowly when he continued. 'There's to be – no – more – trading – with – Clancy.'

'Who's Clancy?' Douglas asked.

'Did you hear me?' Fraser asked, the grin now gone.

'Sure I heard you. Who's Clancy?'

Fraser ignored the question. He waited for Douglas to stub out his cigarette before saying, 'If you ever again supply Clancy it won't be us you'll have to deal with.'

'Who's Clancy?' Douglas asked again.

'It might interest you to know that a man called Declan Finch is being buried on Monday.'

Douglas Parr's hand hovered over the ashtray as though held there by cramp. Then, for the first time since Fraser had entered the room, Douglas looked away. He ran a hand through his hair. When he looked back, his eyes were steady again.

'You *do* understand?' Fraser asked.

Almost imperceptibly Douglas nodded.

Immediately Fraser was on his feet. 'Good,' he said. 'Just keep your nose clean and we'll do what we can, OK?'

Douglas nodded with his eyes.

'You can keep those,' Fraser said, pushing the cigarettes across the table. He went to the door and banged on it. Just before it opened he turned and said, 'You're not the worst of them, Parr. Not by a long way.'

'I want to go up and see Mum,' Robert said to Jimmy Fermin.

'Ah, yes.'

'Just for the weekend. I'll be back on Monday.'

'Then?'

'Back to New York, I guess.'

'You'll want my car?'

'Can I?'

'Sure. Never use the damn thing. Don't know why I bother to keep it. Give your mother my love.'

'I'll do that.'

'And drive carefully.'

Without meaning to Robert glanced at the paper. 'Yes. I'll do that.'

'See that you do.'

It was unfortunate for Douglas Parr that his pretty mistress decided to visit him that afternoon. It was more unfortunate for him that Jerry Horton chose that Saturday to visit his cousin, who was in the Scrubs for aggravated burglary. What was most unfortunate was that his pretty mistress knew Jerry Horton and chose to vent her frustration on him, calling him a little shit at the top of her voice, and swearing that Douglas was going to have him when he got out.

She didn't see him when visiting time was over, which was just as well. The small, tight smile of satisfaction on his face might have frightened her, frightened her almost as much as she was to become the next day when she learned that Douglas had been found dead, hanging by the neck in the prison shower room.

For Robert Larski the journey to his mother's home seemed to take an intolerably long time. It had nothing to do with the traffic or the distance. He didn't honestly know what it had to do with: the miles just seemed to pass with monotonous slowness. It was lunchtime when he reached Aylesbury. The roundabout by the station was jammed. An ancient Cortina had broken down, and three youngish girls were trying to push it to the side of the road. They seemed to enjoy the chaos they were causing, laughing amongst themselves and flirting with the men drivers who shouted lewd remarks at them. Robert thought about giving them a hand, but they seemed to be managing nicely without him, so he stayed put. For no reason he started looking at the other cars about him. A Jaguar, a Fiat, a Mini, a couple of Orions, a Rover almost identical to the one he was driving except that it was a paler shade of blue. He started looking at the people in them. A woman using the time to fix her hair in the rear-view mirror. A pimply young man picking his nose. An elderly couple who looked as if they hadn't spoken to each other for years and certainly weren't on speaking terms now. Two men staring steadfastly in front of them, possibly with their business on the rocks. A handsome young man wearing spectacles, with his arm about the shoulders of a plain young girl who stared at him, clearly in love. A fat man with a boxer on the seat beside him: they looked remarkably alike. Perhaps there *was* some truth in that saying after all. The traffic started to move. Robert manoeuvred the car expertly. Soon he was approaching Waddesdon. When he got there he noticed that the little antique shop opposite Waddesdon Manor was open. He decided to see if he could get something for his mother. He pulled over and parked. He noticed in the corner of his eye that the pale blue Rover whose two occupants looked like businessmen had pulled in outside Angelo's Italian restaurant. They weren't broke yet then.

He had a stroke of luck in the antique shop. He found a pretty, silver snuffbox. His mother collected snuffboxes. She'd be pleased with this. And it was cheap. He was still smiling to himself at his good fortune when he returned to the car. Checking his mirror before pulling out, he spotted the other Rover about to pull out also. He drove about fifty yards. The other Rover followed, keeping the same speed. Robert braked. The following car stopped. Robert pulled in to the side of the road again. The car behind tried to, but other parked cars prevented it from so doing. It swerved across the road and parked on the opposite side. On an impulse Robert jumped from his car and ran back towards the other. The two men didn't look at him as he approached. They waited for him to bang on the window before turning their heads. One of them lowered the window. But face to face, Robert couldn't think what to say, and when he did speak it sounded ludicrous to his ears.

'Are you following me?' he asked.

The passenger smiled. 'Yes,' he said.

That certainly wasn't what Robert had expected. He could think of no answer. He just stared at the two men, and they let him stew for a while. Then the driver leaned across and said, 'The boss thought we'd better keep an eye on you for a few days. Just till you go back to the States.'

Robert felt a quiver in the pit of his stomach. All he could think of to say was, 'Who's the boss?'

The two men looked at each other, and then faced Robert again, smiling. 'You met him on your recent holiday in Belfast.' Somehow they made the word 'holiday' sound sinister.

'I met a lot of people in Belfast.'

'So we hear.' The two men laughed. 'That's why we're keeping an eye on you. He wouldn't like anything to happen to you.'

'Who the hell is *he*?' Robert demanded.

'Just your friend, Mr Larski. A better friend than you'll ever know. You go on – going to see your mother, aren't you? – you go on and see her. Just forget we're here.'

The window was rolled up, and the two men took to staring ahead of themselves again.

'Robert! Robert, darling. This is a wonderful surprise.'

'Hello, Mum. How are you?'

'I'm fine, dear. How are *you*?'

'All in one piece.'

It was only later as they sat in the sitting-room that his mother confessed, 'I've been so worried about you, Robert.' But she hadn't asked him anything, and Robert knew she wouldn't. It was the way she was, always waiting to be told, yet there was something in her silence that gave the impression she already knew the answers.

'It's OK now, Mum. Everything's OK. Honestly.'

Mrs Larski reached out and took her son's hand. She raised it to her lips and kissed it. It was as though she were absolving him of any lies he might be about to tell.

'Mum – about Peter . . .'

Mrs Larski's fingers tightened on his hand.

Robert gazed into his mother's eyes, and saw the pain, the love. He couldn't bring himself to tell her the truth although he had promised he would. 'About Peter, Mum. I was wrong. He *was* killed on patrol like the army said. The only reason they seemed to be . . . reluctant to tell us everything was because they didn't want us – you – to be hurt any more. It seems they act that way every time a soldier is killed. It was just another senseless killing, that's all.'

'Poor Peter,' Mrs Larski said quietly.

Robert nodded.

'Poor, poor Peter,' Mrs Larski repeated. But now there was something in her words that made Robert understand she knew he was lying. She always knew.

Mrs Larski sighed and kissed his hand again. 'I'm glad you found out,' she said.

'Yes,' Robert said. 'So am I, Mum.'

Suddenly Mrs Larski stood up and walked briskly from the room. She went upstairs and went into what had been Peter's bedroom. For a while there was silence, and then Robert heard her crying. It was the first time he had ever heard her cry, and he didn't know what to do about it.